Lausard suddenly _____ ____wards
the burgomaster. The metallic hiss as the steel left the
sheath echoed around the church.

'Is your daughter's blood on my blade?' he rasped.

Keppler moved backwards.

'Look at it,' Lausard snarled, pushing the three-foot
sword towards the burgomaster. 'Her blood is *not* there
but soon *yours* may be.' He sheathed the weapon as
swiftly as he'd drawn it. 'I would not have hurt her, you
have my word. But then, the value of a man's word is
best measured by the worth of the one he *gives* it to.'

Lausard turned and looked at Milliere.

'Is there anything else, Captain?' he asked.

The officer shook his head. 'You may go,' Milliere
said. 'But be careful. Remember what I said. If you are
attacked, you have my permission to defend yourselves.'

'Let us hope it does not come to that,' Royere added.

'Give me a day and I will find the killer,' said Lausard.
He looked at Keppler. 'That *is* what you want, isn't it?'

The burgomaster nodded almost imperceptibly.

'Where will you look?' Milliere called as Lausard and
his companions headed for the doors of the church.

'Whoever killed Claudia was vermin,' the sergeant
answered. 'I intend to visit the nest.'

Also by Richard Howard

Bonaparte's Sons
Bonaparte's Invaders
Bonaparte's Conquerors
Bonaparte's Warriors
Bonaparte's Horsemen

Bonaparte's Avengers

Richard Howard

timewarner
paperbacks

A *Time Warner* Paperback

First published in Great Britain in 2001
by Little, Brown
This edition published by Time Warner Paperbacks in 2002

A CIP catalogue record for this book
is available from the British Library.

ISBN 0 7515 2950 8

Typeset in Plantin by
Palimpsest Book Production Limited,
Polmont, Stirlingshire
Printed and bound in Great Britain by
Mackays of Chatham plc, Chatham, Kent

Time Warner Paperbacks
An imprint of
Time Warner Books (UK)
Brettenham House
Lancaster Place
London WC2E 7EN

www.TimeWarnerBooks.co.uk

Bonaparte's
Avengers

One

⊶•⊰

Alain Lausard took off his green fatigue cap and ran a hand through his long brown hair. Despite the coldness of the day, the dragoon sergeant was sweating. Two hours of drill, followed by another two of grooming his mount and cleaning his equipment had nullified the effect of the December weather. With those tasks completed, Lausard now knew that his horse must be fed.

There were several sacks of feed at one end of the makeshift stable. Lausard glanced up to see Tabor effortlessly carrying one in each of his huge hands. Other members of the squadron were also in the process of feeding their horses, carrying the grain and hay in buckets to the waiting animals. Charvet, stripped to the waist to reveal his bulging muscles, followed Tabor, holding two buckets of water. From these he emptied a little into the troughs at the end of each stall. Every one was home to a mount and the animals ate and drank contentedly as their riders presented them with their meal.

Lausard nodded his thanks to Tabor as the huge man tore open one of the bags of feed and poured some into the trough before his sergeant's bay. The animal began chewing on the food and Lausard patted its neck.

All the animals were covered by green blankets to protect them from the rigours of the winter. The days were bad enough, thought Lausard, but, once night fell, temperatures would rapidly descend several degrees below freezing. He looked around at his companions as his own horse fed.

Tigana and Karim were engaged in animated conversation at the far end of the stable. Lausard didn't doubt for one moment that the subject was horses. The two men were both experts in their own ways about all matters equine and it amused the sergeant to watch, and sometimes listen to, them discuss the merits or otherwise of selected animals.

Gaston, the young trumpeter, was still brushing the mane of his grey horse. He whispered to the animal as he worked on it.

Joubert dipped his hand into the feed and pulled out a small portion for himself. He chewed on it, rubbing his mountainous belly, oblivious to the taunts coming from Delacor and Rocheteau.

The corporal, in particular, jabbed at Joubert's ample gut with his fingers, recoiling in mock revulsion when he felt the flab around the big man's midsection.

Sonnier sat cross-legged before his horse, watching as the animal ate. As Lausard watched, Rostov, the Russian, joined him, puffing away at a pipe that was giving off a cloud of reeking smoke.

Bonet, the former schoolmaster, was chewing on a biscuit he'd taken from his pocket.

Giresse swigged from a bottle of wine then passed it to Roussard. From horse-thief to forger, Lausard mused.

He looked at them all in turn. At these men with whom he had shared his life for more than ten years. These men whom he had come to call friends. Men he would have gladly fought and died with. Men whose lives he had saved and who, sometimes, had saved him too. They had shared glory and suffering during the past decade. They had enjoyed the respite of peace and endured the fury of war. Charged enemy troops with swords flailing or ridden into the ferocity of cannon and musket fire. He had seen them attain the heights of glory, and he had seen them suffer such depravity it had seemed barely possible a man could retain his sanity. There had been times of plenty and times of hunger, more than he cared to remember. They had fought in blazing sunshine and freezing fog, raging across most of Europe and beyond in the service of the man they called their Emperor, Napoleon Bonaparte. And Lausard had little doubt they would continue to fight should the Corsican decide. But it was not something the sergeant dreaded or feared. For him, combat was to be welcomed. He thrived on the battlefield. Grew strong amidst the savagery of war.

It had not always been so but, for Alain Lausard, some of the memories were becoming hazy now. Unlike his companions, he had been of noble birth. A fact that, during the fanatical blood-letting of the Revolution, would have been enough in itself to condemn him to death beneath the blade of the guillotine. But, unlike his family, he had not perished before a howling mob. He had escaped, or, in his own eyes, he had run. From the splendour of his aristocratic lifestyle to the squalor of the Paris gutters. To a life of thievery and starvation. To eventual imprisonment and the promise only of death in some damp, reeking cell in the Conciergerie or whichever prison the men of the Directory saw fit. The same men he had seen Napoleon dismiss from power in 1799. He and his companions had been present when the old regime was destroyed at the Tuileries and also when the new one took shape outside Notre Dame five years later. He had seen Napoleon himself grow from a humble General to Emperor of France and conqueror of the armies of Austria and Russia.

In his quieter moments, especially at night when, as always, sleep came to him with such difficulty, Lausard had pondered on how amusingly elliptical his life had been during the last ten years. How it mirrored the life of his own Emperor. Bonaparte had risen from lowly Corsican nobility to become the most powerful man in Europe. Lausard himself had fallen from the lofty heights of aristocracy to the sewers, only to be offered a way out by the very man he now called Emperor. Both had been forced to battle, and both had attained what they wanted. Napoleon had supremacy over the French nation and its mighty armed forces, Lausard had fashioned himself a new life among men who would previously have called him an enemy. He had their respect for his fighting prowess and his bravery. It no longer troubled him to realise the feeling was mutual. *They* were the closest thing he had to family now. They had suffered as he had suffered. Imprisoned by their own nation for crimes ranging from forgery, rape and perceived political subversion to stealing horses, religious fanaticism and theft. But, to Lausard, they were not criminals but men. Good men. Good soldiers. Good friends.

His own transition from aristocrat to thief had been seamless and, similarly, his transformation from prisoner to soldier had been completed with effortless ease. For the first time in many years, Sergeant Alain Lausard felt more or less at peace with himself. He knew he would never fully quell the inner turmoil he experienced but he had, at least, learned to control it.

He patted his horse's neck as it continued to feed.

'Perhaps we'll be home before Christmas.'

The voice startled Lausard from his silent contemplations and he turned to see Rocheteau standing beside him.

The corporal was chewing on a piece of salt beef.

'Home,' Lausard mused. 'Where do we call home now?'

'Paris.'

'Whereabouts in Paris did you have in mind? Where would you choose to spend Christmas if we are allowed to return? At the Tuileries with our Emperor?'

The other men laughed.

'With his wife,' Delacor offered.

'You will, I fear, have to join a queue,' Bonet interjected. 'I understand she is a very popular woman and not just with our Emperor.'

More laughter filled the stable.

'I would be happy to spend Christmas in the arms

of a woman,' Giresse added. 'Or, for that matter, several women.'

'Christmas is a time to celebrate the birth of the Son of God, not for some pagan act of debauchery with women,' Moreau said, disdainfully. 'I would pray throughout Christmas Day and thank Him for delivering us safely.'

'Do you celebrate Christmas in your country, Karim?' Tigana asked.

The Circassian smiled. 'Allah, all Praise be to Him, has no need of festivals to realise our devotion to Him,' he grinned.

'I'd just settle for a decent Christmas dinner,' Joubert complained.

'Shut up, fat man,' Delacor hissed. 'There's enough blubber on you to keep half of Paris warm.'

More laughter followed.

'Do we still celebrate Christmas in the new Republic?' Tigana chuckled. 'I wasn't sure what the law was on that matter.'

'We don't have a Republic,' Lausard said, flatly. 'We have a dictatorship. It's just preferable to clothe the dictator in the Imperial purple of Emperor.'

'Republic. Dictatorship. Who cares?' rasped Delacor. 'I just want to go home. How long is the Emperor going to keep us here in Germany? I thought once we had won the war it would just be a matter of time before we returned to France.'

'We won a great victory at Austerlitz,' Bonet intoned, 'but the war is not yet over. No peace treaty has been signed. Certainly not with the Russians.'

'The Austrians have fled. The Russians are still running,' snapped Delacor. 'Back to their miserable hovels in the snow. There's no one *left* to fight.'

'There is always *someone* left to fight,' Lausard murmured.

The town of Fürstenberg was indistinguishable from any of the hundreds of other similar hamlets covering the heavily wooded landscape of Bavaria. A population of less than a thousand drew their livelihoods from the rich arable land that surrounded the town. It stood close to the Paar river, ten or twelve miles south of Ingolstadt. Three times a week, the town square was the scene of an expansive market, where everything from potatoes to flax was bought and sold both by the locals and also by residents of neighbouring towns and villages.

Lausard had been surprised at how well received he and his men had been when they had first arrived in the town. They had been greeted like liberators, and many of the men had been billeted with local families. Officers had been housed with high-ranking town officials, including the burgomaster and his family; Captain Milliere had enjoyed the relative luxury of the Bavarian's home. Lausard wondered if the officer had also enjoyed the not inconsiderable charms of his eighteen-year-old daughter. Lieutenant Royere was billeted with a priest in the house adjacent to the large church that dominated the central square of the town.

Lausard and his companions were housed in what had once been a grain storehouse. Several other warehouses nearby had been transformed into makeshift stables to accommodate their horses. The men had been furnished with comfortable straw pallets on which to sleep. These, they had learned, had been made by several women of the town. In addition to the army rations they received each day, the dragoons were also frequently presented with food by the residents of Fürstenberg. Lausard himself had acquired a taste for the local bratwurst and sauerkraut. He wondered if burgomaster Von Keppler was aware that his daughter was also a frequent visitor to the dragoon's quarters, ostensibly to bring them food but, Lausard suspected, she enjoyed the attention of so many men. He also wondered if her visits would have been less frequent had she realised that at least one of them had once been a rapist and that most of the others had not enjoyed the company of a woman for more than a year. Himself included. There were many in the squadron who craved more than the food she brought them.

As he made his way back towards the billet he saw Gaston and Carbonne hurling a bundle of rags back and forth through the air, laughing as a large black dog hurtled frantically between them, eager to seize the object.

'That stinking mongrel has been with us for over a month now and we still have no name for it,' Rocheteau called, pointing at the dog.

'Where the hell *did* it come from?' Lausard mused, watching as the animal continued to chase to and fro wildly, finally catching the bundle of rags. The dog shook them madly until Gaston pulled them away from it, balled them up once again and began throwing them to Carbonne to continue the game.

'It's mad,' Rochcteau said, grinning.

'Then it is in good company here,' Lausard chuckled.

He caught the ball of rags and held it before the dog. It watched him with its wide eyes, waiting for him to throw the sodden bundle.

Lausard launched the rags into the air and the dog hurtled off after them.

'Does it belong to one of the townspeople?' the sergeant wanted to know.

'It just turned up one morning,' Carbonne said. 'I found it sleeping in the hay with my horse. It's been here ever since.'

'Let's hope Joubert doesn't get too hungry,' Lausard grinned. 'He might eat it.'

The other men laughed.

'It needs a name,' Rocheteau persisted. 'What about Claudia?'

'I don't think the burgomaster would be very happy to discover that you had named a dog after his daughter,' said Lausard.

'I wonder what kind of tricks *she* does?' Rocheteau said, licking his lips.

More laughter greeted the remark.

The dog returned to Lausard with the bundle of rags, and the sergeant knelt and patted the animal.

'We could call it Napoleon,' Carbonne suggested.

Lausard shook his head.

'Or Josephine,' Gaston offered, smiling.

The dog was panting, its tongue lolling from one side of its mouth as it watched the sergeant preparing to throw the rag ball once more.

Bonet wandered across to join the men.

'What about you, schoolmaster?' Rocheteau said. 'Any idea what we should name this damned dog?'

'What about Cerberus?' Bonet offered.

'That would be appropriate,' Lausard reasoned. 'He was the dog who guarded the gates of Hades wasn't he?'

Bonet nodded. 'In Greek mythology there was a place *beyond* Hades,' the former schoolmaster continued. 'A place of darkness and despair.'

'We've seen many of those these past ten years,' Lausard observed. 'It would seem fair to give this dog *that* name.'

'The place was called Erebus. Blacker than night. Just like our visitor.' Bonet gestured towards the dog.

Lausard smiled. 'It is a good name,' he concurred.

He hurled the ball of rags and watched as the dog rushed off in pursuit, grabbed the bundle in its jaws and returned clutching its prize.

'He belongs with *us* now,' Rocheteau grinned.

'He *is* one of us. We are nothing more than mongrels with no home either,' Lausard murmured. He grabbed the dog by the head and rubbed its fur vigorously. It responded by licking his face with its long tongue. 'Welcome to the first squadron, Erebus.'

Two

The magnificent gardens of the palace of Schönbrunn were dusted with snow. They looked as if a gigantic but careless hand had covered them with a thin layer of flour. The white flakes had been falling intermittently in Vienna for the past two days, coating the Austrian capital with a white carpet. The sky was filled with swollen grey clouds.

Napoleon Bonaparte gazed out of one of the huge windows overlooking the gardens and watched the snow, his ever alert eyes focussing on one particularly thick flake as it floated gently past the window to the paved area below. Half a dozen grenadiers of the Imperial Guard stood motionless in the snow, their huge bearskins already partially white with the falling flakes. They wore their long blue overcoats as protection against the cold. The metal of their fifteen-inch bayonets gleamed despite the absence of any sunshine.

Napoleon sipped at his wine and moved slowly back towards the roaring log fire burning in the grate. Two members of his household, clad in long, red, gold-trimmed tunics, were feeding more wood into the inferno. The Emperor of the French looked decidedly dour in contrast to his servants. He wore a pair of white breeches, black boots and the green tunic of a chausseur, which was unbuttoned to reveal his white lace shirt.

The Corsican watched the servants finish their duties, dismissing one who offered to pour him some more wine, then he wandered back to the window again, as if seeking something in the gardens beyond. He passed tables heaving with books and maps, some folded, some open. Several small desks had been set up, and at each one there was a pile of writing paper and a quill pen. It was not unknown for the Emperor to dictate four individual letters to four secretaries simultaneously, but for now the desks had been abandoned, the secretaries dismissed.

The other occupant of the room was the first to break the silence.

'Excuse my insolence, sire,' said Charles Maurice de Talleyrand, 'but I assume there is a purpose to your behaviour.'

Napoleon looked at his companion quizzically.

'The Prussian envoy has been waiting here for ten days and yet you still refuse to see him,' Talleyrand continued.

The Corsican smiled. 'I spoke with Monsieur Haugwitz at Brunn at the end of last month,' he said. 'He is well aware of my feelings both for his country and its master. I will see him when I feel it is necessary.'

Talleyrand shrugged. 'I appreciate that, sire, and I do not blame you for taking the opportunity to indulge your spite.' The Foreign Minister smiled.

'It is not spite, Talleyrand. I know too well why King

Frederick William despatched Haugwitz. And so do you. Prussia was ready to commit a quarter of a million men against us until I crushed their would-be allies at Austerlitz. If Haugwitz had arrived at Brunn two weeks earlier he would have been the bearer of a declaration of war, not, as he would have it, an offer of mediation. The Prussian King waited until he thought France was on the point of defeat and then decided to commit his forces to the Third Coalition. A coalition *I* have since obliterated.'

'Monsieur Haugwitz is only too aware of that, sire. Hence his propensity to frequent the corridors and ante rooms of this magnificent building while he waits for you to grant him an audience.'

'Do you think I am wrong to keep him waiting?'

Talleyrand shook his head. 'There is no doubt that Prussia would have joined the war against France in the event of you suffering a defeat at the hands of Austria and Russia, sire,' he observed. 'Haugwitz as good as admitted that to me during our conversations here before you arrived. He believes that peace would now better suit his country.'

'Because he knows they would be forced to stand alone against us. Like jackals deserted by their beasts of prey. Prussia is at our mercy and Haugwitz knows it. So does that spineless Hohenzollern hypocrite who rules there. He is an insult to the memory of Frederick the Great. What would so fine a soldier say if he could see now the kind of man who sits on the throne he once graced? I have the highest regard for the memory of that man. He was a military genius.'

'Responsible for one of France's most ignominious defeats, I hasten to remind you, sire. Frederick the Great masterminded the destruction of the French army at Rossbach forty years ago.'

'I am well aware of that, Talleyrand, and any action taken against Prussia by me would redress the balance somewhat. It would at least avenge that memory. However, how great a victory would it be against so hollow a man as the fool who now occupies the throne of Prussia? He is manipulated by his wife and those who thought they could aid in the destruction of France. Now the prospect of their *own* destruction looms before them, they seek mediation. They seek to court me as if I were a love-sick fool and *they* had all the charms of Aphrodite.' He drained what was left in his glass then refilled it.

'Haugwitz himself favours a policy of neutrality, sire,' noted the Foreign Minister. 'And, if I may offer my own opinion, with one war so recently over, I would impress upon you the need for an extended period of peace. If only to allow the necessary funds to be accrued to finance any future campaigns you may have in mind.'

'I am not the one with war on my mind, Talleyrand. It is the Russians who have yet to sign a peace treaty and I did not threaten Prussia, but I will not allow their duplicity to go unpunished. When they thought they could share in our defeat they were only too willing to take up arms against us. Now that defeat has been turned to victory, they seek the sanctuary of neutrality. When they thought the advantage was with *them* they sought to profit from our failings. Now the advantage is with *us* I intend to push that advantage to its fullest limits. The land of the Black Eagle will pay, I promise you.'

Napoleon walked slowly back and forth in front of the blazing fire, the glass of wine held carefully in his hand.

'So, is Haugwitz to be granted his audience or not?' the Foreign Minister wanted to know.

'He has waited long enough,' Napoleon mused. 'Let him hear what I have to say.'

Talleyrand got to his feet and crossed to one of the ornate doors at the far end of the room. He murmured something to one of the secretaries waiting beyond, and the man scuttled off to complete the Foreign Minister's instructions. Talleyrand himself ambled back towards his seat, close to the warmth of the fire. The cold always exacerbated the pain in his ankle, the legacy of a fall as a child that had left him with a permanent limp. He brushed the sleeve of his black velvet jacket and reached for the glass of water on the desk close by.

'Is your temperance a legacy of your days with the church, my friend?' Napoleon grinned.

'I learned much from the church, sire, but temperance was the slightest of those lessons.'

'You came from nobility too. Your family were aristocrats. An aristocratic priest. How did you ever survive the Revolution?'

'Priest or noble, sire. There is little to choose between them. One must adapt to one's surroundings, to the circumstances of one's life. A tiger fights. A snake slithers to safety then coils around those it knows to be weak. Nature gave me the choice between snake and tiger and I chose to be an anaconda.' He raised his glass in salute.

Both men laughed.

There was a theatrical cough from the far end of the room and both Napoleon and his minister turned their attention to the man who had appeared there.

Count Christian August Heinrich Curt Haugwitz was a tall, thin-faced individual with hooded eyes and greying hair. As he saw Napoleon's gaze turn towards him he bowed low then advanced towards the Emperor, his footsteps echoing on the marble floor of the room. He stopped and bowed once more.

'I thank you for seeing me, your Highness,' the Prussian said. 'It is a pleasure to be in your company once again.' He also nodded a greeting to Talleyrand, who smiled and sipped at his water.

'What is your purpose here?' Napoleon said, sharply. 'What does your king have to say that could possibly interest *me*?'

'Firstly, he offers his congratulations and his compliments on your recent triumph against the armies of Russia and Austria. A magnificent achievement of arms. He salutes you and your army.'

'I feel that those congratulations may have been recently readdressed due to the result of my achievement,' Napoleon smiled. However, there was no warmth in the gesture. 'I suspect that they were originally destined for Emperor Francis of Austria and Tsar Alexander of Russia.'

Haugwitz shifted uncomfortably and attempted a deflective smile, but it appeared more as a leer and he momentarily lowered his gaze from the penetrative stare of the Corsican.

A heavy silence descended, finally broken by Napoleon.

'What does your king send me that I should find so irresistible?' he snapped. 'What errand has he sent you on? What gifts and promises do you carry?'

'My king desires only to aid you.'

'Is that why he considered committing troops to the field to fight me?'

'Prussia has no wish for war.'

'Not now perhaps. But when your king signed the Treaty of Potsdam with Tsar Alexander his wishes were somewhat different, were they not?'

Haugwitz looked stunned.

'Yes, I know of that treaty and all it entailed,' Napoleon told him, defiantly. 'Prussia was to contribute one hundred and eighty thousand men to the Third Coalition. To fight against France. To fight against *me*.' His voice rose slightly in volume. 'You were sent to me with what amounted to an ultimatum. Yet you now purport to bring me congratulations on a victory that has destroyed the Austrian army and sent the Russians running back to their homeland. A victory that has left your own country without allies. All, that is, except the English – my most persistent opponents these past ten years. It is little wonder you are so anxious to secure neutrality. I hear that officers of your king's Royal Guard sharpened their swords on the steps of the French embassy in Berlin. Are these the actions of men desperate for peace? I think not.' He turned towards the fire, showing his back to the Prussian Foreign Minister, who could only stand silently.

Napoleon clasped his hands behind his back, still facing the dancing flames.

'Prussia will pay in land, men and infamy for her intended participation in the war I have just concluded,' the Emperor snapped. 'What did you hope to gain by coming here? My trust? My benevolence?'

'I sought only to bring you the words of my king, your Highness,' Haugwitz said, his voice catching. 'I understand you are in the process of concluding a peace treaty with Austria. My king thought that you would appreciate an offer of mediation in this matter.'

Napoleon turned to face the diplomat.

'I require nothing from your king except his subservience,' he hissed. 'I demand, immediately, an exclusive treaty of alliance between France and Prussia *against* England.'

Haugwitz swallowed. 'Such an alliance will require delicate negotiation,' he began.

'You are not in a position to negotiate, my dear Count,' Napoleon snapped. 'You are in a position to obey. Nothing more. Your king will agree to my terms, I can assure you. Earlier this year, the promise of acquiring possession of Hanover stilled any war-like inclinations he may have pretended to have. He did not act when an entire army corps of mine marched through Ansbach in September. If he would not even rouse himself to protest the invasion of his country, I doubt he will seek war over a proposed alliance with France. If he does he is even more of a fool than I thought.'

Talleyrand sipped at his water, a slight smile hidden by one hand. 'By the terms of the Treaty of Basle in 1795, your country refused to aid Austria in her war against France,' Talleyrand said, clearing his throat.

'Strict neutrality has been observed ever since.'

'So the formation of an alliance with France now is a natural diplomatic progression if war is to be avoided between our two nations,' Napoleon added.

'If I agree to your proposals, Highness . . . ' Haugwitz began.

'I am not offering you a choice,' the Corsican interrupted. 'I am outlining my future plans for your country. Remember, even as we speak, the bulk of my army is camped in Bavaria and on your borders. Your own army is not even mobilised. Were a state of war to break out then the descendants of Frederick the Great would find themselves in dire straits.'

Haugwitz looked first at Talleyrand then back at Napoleon, who sipped his wine slowly.

'What do you propose?' the Prussian said, finally, his voice little more than a hoarse whisper.

'Reparation for the treachery of your country,' Napoleon snapped. 'For your intentions to send an army against me. I am sure you will find my demands infinitely preferable to the ultimate sanction open to me. That of war. Neither of us wants war. It is now encumbent upon Prussia to ensure that peace continues by meeting and enacting my demands. Firstly, the principality of Cleves will be joined to that of Berg. They will be awarded to my brother-in-law, Marshal Murat, as a grand duchy. Ansbach will be given to the ruler of Bavaria. A *loyal* German ally. Neuchâtel is my gift to my own chief of staff, Marshal Berthier. Wesel will be annexed to France.' Napoleon put down his wine glass and began pacing back and forth slowly in front of the fire. 'All existing

Prussian diplomatic alliances are to be declared void. They will be replaced by a unilateral and exclusive treaty with France. Furthermore, Prussia will adopt whatever economic measures against England I feel necessary.' He paused and looked directly at Haugwitz. 'Tell your king, also, I want the dismissal of his Chief Minister, Von Hardenberg. He has less than benevolent views towards France.'

Haugwitz sucked in a deep breath then released it wearily.

'While I appreciate your proposals, your Highness,' he said, 'it seems that my country is to lose far more than it gains.'

'What do you expect?' Napoleon snapped. 'If a man shoots me in the back am I to reward him?' There was a long silence, finally broken by the Emperor himself. 'I will secure from Bavaria, for Prussia, an area containing 20,000 inhabitants for you to add to your province of Bayreuth and, naturally, your king will receive possession of the electorate of Hanover. Something I know he has craved for some time now.'

'There are French troops in Hanover,' Haugwitz offered.

'There are a very small number of my men in the fortress of Hameln. They will be withdrawn in due course.'

'But, Majesty, Hanover belongs to the ruling Royal family of England. Whichever state occupies it will come into conflict with that country.'

'Your king is so anxious to acquire Hanover, that should be a small price to pay.'

'But Prussia will be diplomatically isolated from the rest of Europe.'

'But not from France and, considering the current state of your former allies, my dear Count, I would suggest that an alliance with *my* country was preferable. Would you not?'

Haugwitz said nothing.

'It is a simple choice,' Napoleon continued. 'Either your king approves these measures or there will be war between us. There is no middle ground. I hope he is thankful for my generosity considering his previous subversions. I require you to return to Berlin with these measures as soon as possible. I trust your king will ratify this agreement with all due haste. That is all.' He turned his back on the Prussian envoy and gazed into the flames as they danced before him.

Napoleon remained in that position until he heard Haugwitz's footsteps echo away to the far end of the room. Only when he heard the door close behind him did he turn.

'You have not only isolated Prussia, sire, but humiliated her too,' Talleyrand said, flatly. 'London and Berlin will be irrevocably divided over the matter of Hanover.'

'Exactly,' Napoleon smiled.

'These measures may make war with Prussia inevitable. You said yourself that you wished to *avoid* such an eventuality.'

'I still do. I seek some form of reconciliation with the enemies that still remain before me, not armed conflict. Contrary to most people's thinking, it is not my desire to keep France in a perpetual state of war. You yourself know how difficult it was for me to secure the funds to underwrite the campaign I have just concluded. Back in Paris, my government faces bankruptcy. I must return there soon to attend to matters of a financial nature. But first, Prussia must be cowed. Frederick William and his court will agree to my demands, Talleyrand. They have no choice.'

Three

The town square of Fürstenberg was a hive of activity. Market stalls with coloured awnings were arrayed in almost perfectly straight rows right across the cobbled area. Above the cacophony of conversation, Alain Lausard could hear the shouts of the stall-holders or those who simply sold their wears from the backs of open wagons. Prices were offered, sometimes accepted, sometimes not. He watched as several farmhands hauled huge bags of potatoes and turnips from carts that didn't seem capable of carrying such weight. The horses pulling the carts stood patiently, pawing the stones beneath their huge hooves. The sergeant walked slowly along one of the rows of stalls, stopping to peer at some pieces of pottery arrayed there. Mugs, jugs, bowls and containers were all on show and the woman behind the stall nodded a greeting to him as he inspected her creations. They were all hand-painted too and Lausard marvelled at the intricate patterns etched on the earthenware. Behind him, Giresse was also taking an interest, although his eye was drawn more to the woman then the pottery. He smiled at her and she blushed slightly.

Lausard moved on, enjoying his early morning stroll through the frantic activity of the market. It was like this on every market day. He assumed that Fürstenberg had hosted such a gathering for centuries and would continue to do so until circumstances dictated otherwise. Exactly the same thing was happening in thousands of other towns across Bavaria. Indeed, he mused, it was happening in countless places right across Europe and every corner of the known world – people selling objects they had made or grown, while others were eager to buy them. It was basic economics, supply and demand. The demands of the people of Fürstenberg were simple enough. All they required was enough to eat every day, a roof over their heads and clothes to keep them warm. Food to maintain their livestock, if they had them, and tools to continue their work. Lausard glanced at some of the farmers busily selling produce from their wagons. Grizzled, tough-looking men who would one day be laid to rest in the soil they had tilled and worked all their lives. He wondered how many of them questioned the presence of French troops in this town and so many like it. Did it even bother them? Did they sit over their peat and wood fires late at night in their self-built dwellings pondering on the rights and wrongs of enemy soldiers being in their country? Lausard doubted it.

He stopped at a stall selling vegetables and inspected some of the produce.

Rostov joined him and began picking up the potatoes, testing their weight and firmness. The Russian nodded appreciatively.

Tabor ambled over to partake in the evaluation of the

goods. The potatoes looked like marbles in his huge hands.

Both of the dragoons had been brought up on farms and Tabor inhaled the smell of damp earth and vegetables as if it were some exotic perfume. Rostov did the same and the two men both began laughing.

'How the hell can you two get so excited about a few potatoes?' Rocheteau demanded.

'It reminds me of home,' Tabor said.

'I wouldn't expect you to understand, Rocheteau,' Rostov grinned. 'The smell of a gutter would be more to your liking, wouldn't it?'

Rocheteau shrugged. 'The gutters were my home for long enough,' he conceded. 'I suppose you're right.' He looked at Lausard. 'Isn't that true, Alain? We both have memories of the Paris gutters, don't we?'

Lausard nodded sagely. His recollections of that part of his life were strong but there were other memories too, buried more deeply in his subconscious but just as vivid. Memories he knew he could never share with his companions. Thoughts of the house he had grown up in as a boy, a house where servants toiled inside and out, where a groom prepared horses for him to ride. A place where elegant balls would be held and fine wine and food would be consumed. Somewhere he would share the love of his family, a family now lost to him forever. They were recollections to be savoured in moments of solitude. The memories of an aristocrat. But those days were long gone. So was the youth he saw in those hazy recollections. The youth that had attended the Carabinier school at Chinon and mastered the horse, the sword and the musket – lessons that had been put to excellent and lethal use during the past ten years.

As he walked, his sword bumped against his boot, the scabbard sometimes dragging across the cobbles.

There was a barber's shop across the square and Rocheteau tapped the sergeant on the shoulder and pointed to it.

'Perhaps you should think about visiting him, Alain,' the corporal grinned.

Lausard looked on with amusement.

'Why, may I ask?'

'Your hair,' Rocheteau said. 'It is long. The Emperor has his own hair short now. I understand he wishes all of us to copy him.'

Lausard grinned.

'I heard that he was going to pass a general order that all cavalrymen should have short hair,' Bonet offered. 'He apparently feels that long hair is untidy.'

'I will try to bear that in mind,' Lausard said. 'But excuse me if I do not follow the Emperor's example. At least *you* will have no problem will you, Carbonne?'

The other men laughed as the former executioner lifted his cap to reveal his bald pate. Lausard rubbed it gently, as if he was polishing a cannonball.

Close by, he heard loud barking and looked down to see a familiar black shape.

Erebus was weaving his way amongst the other occupants of the market place, staying close to Gaston but becoming excitable for reasons that soon became apparent. There was a butcher's stall just ahead. The dog scented the meat and Lausard saw dozens of carcasses and joints arrayed on the stall. Pigs, sheep, lambs and

even a wild boar hung from large hooks at the back;
chickens, pheasants and geese were also displayed.
Erebus scampered towards the stall and began licking
at some blood that was dripping from a carcass, splashing across the cobblestones beneath. The owner of the
stall emerged from behind his counter long enough to
take a kick at the black dog but, instead of running, the
animal turned and bared his teeth at the butcher.

'You'd better just leave him,' Rocheteau said.
'Otherwise you'll end up looking like that.' The corporal
pointed to a bloodied joint of beef lying on the counter.

The dog continued to snarl for a moment longer then,
as the butcher retreated, it returned to lapping at the
red fluid on the cobbles.

Charvet inspected the chickens, pressing each with
his fingers, testing for plumpness. He finally selected one
and fumbled in his jacket pocket for some money.

The butcher merely shook his head.

'Take it,' said the man, a meat cleaver gripped in one
fist. 'Enjoy.'

Charvet nodded his thanks.

'This will be better than army rations,' he smiled.

The butcher swung the blade of the cleaver down
with incredible force and hacked the foreleg of a lamb
from a carcass. He threw it towards Erebus who caught
the bone in its mouth.

'Something for that black devil too,' the butcher
grinned.

The dog trotted off carrying its prize, never straying
more than a couple of paces from Gaston.

Lausard also thanked the butcher as they passed.

'The people here are very friendly,' Tabor observed.

'We've given them no reason to be otherwise,' Charvet said.

'We are enemy troops occupying their country,' offered Lausard. 'Our very presence here is a threat to them. Is that not reason enough?'

'But we are not here for war,' Charvet murmured, looking round at his companions. 'I thought we were just waiting for our orders to return to France.'

'And we are *still* waiting,' Lausard intoned. 'The new year is less than a month away. Austria and Russia are defeated. Our Corsican must have a reason for keeping us here.'

'But not war, surely, Alain,' Giresse said, quietly. 'Prussia is our ally, isn't she?'

Bonet nodded in agreement.

'We shall see,' Lausard mused.

'I am tired of war,' Moreau offered.

'Without war we have no purpose. Any of us,' Lausard told him. 'A soldier without a war is as useless as a blunt sword.'

'So, is that to be our fate for the rest of our lives?' Moreau persisted. 'One war after another? One campaign following the next?'

Lausard could only shrug. 'Our fate is in the hands of others,' the sergeant told him. 'It always has been.'

'I will trust my life to God,' Moreau announced.

'As you wish, Moreau. Personally, I will trust my life to *this*,' said Lausard, patting the hilt of his sword.

The dragoons reached the end of one row of stalls and found themselves confronted by the imposing edifice of the church that dominated the main square of Fürstenberg.

'Why not go and visit the house of your God?' Lausard murmured. 'Ask Him what He has in store for us.'

Moreau saw some of the other men grinning but he ignored them and wandered towards the large, ornately decorated main doors of the church. It towered above him, the steeple thrusting towards the banks of grey cloud like an accusatory finger.

'Will anyone join me?' Moreau wanted to know.

Tabor and Gaston also wandered towards the building.

Erebus hurried along to keep pace with the young trumpeter but Lausard whistled loudly and the animal turned and joined *him* instead. He patted its head gently, watching as the trio of dragoons made their way into the church.

'Perhaps we should join them,' the sergeant murmured.

'I thought you didn't believe, Alain,' Rocheteau said.

'In God? I don't. What kind of God would allow some of the things we've seen these past ten years? But perhaps we should look at how He still hypnotises others so easily.'

'I stopped believing when my wife died,' Rocheteau said, softly. 'I felt that God had abandoned me by taking the only woman I ever loved. I decided that if He was going to abandon *me* then I should do the same to *Him*.'

Some of the other men laughed.

'What about you, Alain?' Bonet said. 'Have you *ever* believed?'

Lausard stood gazing at the church, as if considering his answer. He could not speak his mind. He could not tell his companions that, at one time, he had also believed in a supreme power. But, after witnessing the slaughter of his family in the Place de la Revolution, he had not only lost the faith he previously had, he had begun to entertain feelings against God that bordered on hatred. God had allowed his family to be murdered beneath the blade of the guillotine and let *him* live?

'Moreau says we all believe in God in the middle of a battle,' Carbonne offered. 'That we all call upon Him if we're close to death.'

'That may be true,' Lausard murmured, still gazing at the church. 'Why don't we go inside and find out what this God has to offer us?'

'I will wait here with the dog,' Karim volunteered. 'This is the house of *your* God, not mine.'

The Circassian watched as the dragoons walked slowly towards the main doors of the building. When they reached them, Lausard pushed the huge wooden partitions gently and slid through the small crack that opened. He was followed by his companions. They were immediately enveloped by the silence within. The sound of their boots echoed around the inside of the building. Lausard glanced around at the lanterns that lit the church. They were mounted on ornate brackets on the supporting columns of the ceiling, massive stone pillars with carved corbels jutting out, carved into the shape of human or animal faces. As he wandered slowly along the nave he saw that the ends of the wooden pews were also expertly carved. Some of the other dragoons remained at the rear of the church, some gathered around the font. Others were exploring elsewhere. Rocheteau walked a foot or so behind his sergeant, occasionally glancing up at the vaulted ceiling or marvelling at the beautiful colours of the stained-glass windows. The serenity inside the building was overwhelming.

Lausard continued along the nave towards the chancel. He passed more pews, some of which contained civilians. Two women were kneeling in prayer, heads bowed. They barely noticed him as he passed, only the steady clacking of his boot heels on the stone floor breaking the deafening silence.

Moreau was sitting in one of the pews nearest the chancel. Tabor and Gaston were seated across the nave from him. All three were kneeling.

The sergeant approached the chancel, paused momentarily before the three stone steps that led up to the altar then slowly mounted them. Rocheteau joined him somewhat hesitantly. Above the altar was a huge wooden cross. It bore a carved figure of Christ. Lausard looked up into the blank eyes of the statue and held the sightless gaze for a moment before inspecting the rest of the figure — the hands and feet held in place by the three nails, the crown of thorns, the gash in the left side. Lausard took a step closer until he was level with the altar rail, his eyes returning to those of the wooden Christ. Rocheteau also glanced at the figure but his attention was caught by two magnificent golden candlesticks that flanked the statue. They were fully two feet high, white candles burning on each, the yellow flames wavering as small drafts disturbed them. He stepped back slightly, retreating down the steps into the area close to the pulpit. Lausard remained where he was before the figure of Christ, eyes still upturned. It was as if some kind of silent conversation was passing between them. Then he turned away and looked up at the stained-glass windows behind the figure. One depicted Christ carrying his cross to Golgotha, the other showed him nailed there between the two criminals. Lausard barely managed to suppress a smile. Crucified between two criminals. Now it was a criminal who gazed blankly at the tableau. The irony was not lost upon the sergeant, who moved slowly down the stone steps to rejoin Rocheteau. The two men made their way back up the nave to where the remaining dragoons waited.

This time, the two women who had been praying glanced at him. The sergeant nodded a greeting but the women ignored it and returned to their devotions.

Charvet and Giresse had seated themselves in pews at the rear of the church. Giresse was thumbing disinterestedly through a prayer book that was partly in Latin, partly in German. He understood neither language. The other dragoons were either standing, gazing around at the splendour of the building or wandering about inspecting the carvings and the stained glass.

'Moreau's God has quite a house,' Giresse intoned, softly.

Lausard smiled. 'One *you* would like to share?' the sergeant wondered.

The horse-thief shook his head.

'How many francs worth of gold do you think are in here?' Rocheteau mused, gazing around at the many ornate candle holders. 'It looks like more than two years' pay.'

'The Church is the richest organisation in the world,' Bonet observed. 'Pope Pius VII has a personal fortune that exceeds that of many small countries. I understand his wedding gift to the Emperor was a twenty-two-carat solid gold vase containing solid gold flowers.'

'Then the Pope is fortunate that *we* have never had cause to visit Rome,' said Rocheteau. 'I fear that fortune would be somewhat diminished by the time we left.'

Some of the other men laughed.

A number of disapproving glances came from the worshippers towards the front of the church, Moreau among them. He glared at his companions for a moment then returned to his prayers.

'Are we staying here, Alain?' Rocheteau wanted to know.

'We have no reason to,' Lausard told him.

'Sergeant.'

Lausard turned as he heard a familiar voice.

Lieutenant Royere wandered into the church, dipped his fingers into the font and genuflected.

Lausard smiled as he saw the officer.

'What are you heathens doing in here?' Royere grinned.

'I might ask you the same question, Lieutenant,' Lausard said. 'Has being billeted with a priest for so long finally persuaded you that you may have been wrong about a god all these years?'

'I never denied the existence of God, Sergeant. I just doubted His sincerity occasionally.'

Both men laughed loudly. The sound attracted more

disapproving stares from the worshippers inside the building.

'We had better leave before we are ejected by some higher power,' said the officer, smiling.

Lausard and the others followed him out onto the cobbles of Fürstenberg's town square. The market was still in full swing. If anything, the noise had amplified. The buying, selling and bartering seemed to have increased in intensity. Karim saw the lieutenant and saluted.

'You should meet our newest recruit, Lieutenant,' said Rocheteau, patting his thigh.

At this signal, the dog hurried across to the corporal and stood beside him, looking around excitedly.

'Where did you find *this* monster?' Royere wanted to know.

'He found *us*,' Rocheteau explained. 'His name is Erebus.'

'A place beyond hell itself,' murmured Royere, looking down at the dog. 'Most appropriate.'

'You never did tell me why you were in the church, Lieutenant,' Lausard persisted.

'I saw you and your men entering and I feared for the well-being of the congregation. Or, more to the point, their valuables.'

Lausard grinned. 'Tell me, Lieutenant, is it true that God is a Frenchman?' he wanted to know.

Royere leaned close to Lausard and kept his voice to a low, almost conspiratorial whisper. 'I have it on very good authority, Sergeant, that God is a Corsican. Democratically elected to rule Heaven and the whole of Europe.'

Again the men laughed heartily as they set off across the market square, weaving their way along the rows of stalls and amongst the crowds of people.

'How are you finding life with the priest, Lieutenant?' Lausard wanted to know.

'He is a good man. Perhaps a little misguided in some of his views. A little too fond of his communion wine at times, but, otherwise, I have no complaints. What of yourself?'

'We have all been, and continue to be, well received by the townspeople here. Our only complaint is our inactivity. Three hours of drill every day are meagre substitutes for war.'

'You are the only man I know, my friend, who can make peace sound odious. Personally, I would rather spend my time in the company of generous and friendly Prussians than in the sights of Austrians or Russians.'

'Have you or Captain Milliere received any orders about what is to happen to us?'

'We are to wait here until otherwise instructed. Just as hundreds of other garrisons across Bavaria, Helvetia, Baden and Württemberg must.'

'I thought we were supposed to be returning to France,' said Rocheteau.

'I did too, Corporal,' the officer told him. 'As far as I can tell, the only formations doing so are those of the Imperial Guard.'

'You see,' snapped Charvet. 'Those bastards get to go home and we have to sit and rot in some Prussian backwater.'

'There must be a purpose to our presence here,'

Royere murmured. 'The Emperor would not leave us idle unless he had good reason.'

'Why do *you* think we're still here, Lieutenant?' Lausard wanted to know.

'There you have me, my friend,' he shrugged. 'But I am sure everything will become clear in time. I apologise if that isn't the answer you wanted but, at present, it is the only one I have.'

'War?' Lausard said, flatly.

'Against the Prussians? I wouldn't have thought so. The armies of the Tsar have withdrawn beyond Warsaw. They too are waiting.'

'So, if war comes, you think it will be with Russia, not the Prussians?' Bonet observed.

'If our Emperor wants to march on Warsaw then he will have to lead us through Prussian territory,' Lausard said. 'I doubt that King Frederick William will allow such a contravention without stirring himself or his army.'

'You may be right, Sergeant,' Royere said. 'War does seem somewhat inevitable. The only thing we don't know, as yet, is who will be our opponent. The bear or the eagle.'

Lausard nodded slowly.

'Perhaps both,' he muttered. As he did, he involuntarily touched the hilt of his sword.

Four

<hr>

Lausard walked a little ahead of his men as they made their way slowly along the dirt road that led to their quarters just outside Fürstenberg. As he drew nearer, he saw three horses moving in perfect unison in a circle around Tigana. The Gascon was controlling them with thin lengths of rope, calling encouragement to them as they walked then trotted around him. Lausard knew that Tigana, like a number of his companions, had been raised on a farm and, as he had grown older, he had bred horses. He seemed to find more in common with them than he did with men. Lausard could understand his devotion. Horses obeyed unconditionally, they were loyal and trustworthy. He had met very few men in his own lifetime who shared those attributes. Erebus ran ahead, barking loudly despite the lamb bone he still held in his jaws. One of the horses shied away slightly from the dog and Tigana rasped something at the black animal, watching as it moved away to gnaw on its prize. Only when the three horses had begun their unerring circle around him again did the Gascon turn his attention away from the animal.

'Horses are meant to be trained with kindness,' said Karim, joining the sergeant.

Lausard glanced at the Circassian. 'Did the Mamelukes teach you that, my friend?'

'They taught me the misery of slavery.'

'They also taught you how to fight.'

'That is true. For some of the things they taught me, I thank them. For others, I damn them to hell.'

'Don't you ever miss your country?'

'Egypt was not *my* country, Alain, you know that well enough. I was taken there when I was a child, a captive of the Mamelukes like so many others before me.'

'Like the rest of us you have no home now other than the army.'

'What was your home like before you became a soldier, Alain?'

Lausard hesitated, remembering the large house in the country where he had been born and brought up. A house he now knew to be empty and delapidated, inhabited only by ghosts and memories.

'My home was a cell,' he said, quietly. 'A twelve-by-twelve room with rotting straw for a carpet and slops of food for sustenance. Most of the men in the squadron will tell you the same story. I am not unique, Karim.'

'He's right, Karim,' Rocheteau grinned, joining them. 'There's nothing special about him.'

Lausard slapped his companion hard on the shoulder and the men laughed.

Behind them, Tabor was carrying a sack of potatoes in one large hand and a sack of carrots in the other. Charvet had already begun to pull feathers from the chicken he had acquired. Bonet was nursing a loaf of bread beneath one arm. None of the goods had been paid for. All had been presented to the dragoons with the best wishes of the townspeople.

'I wonder, if the roles were reversed and it was France that was occupied by Prussian troops, would *we* be so welcoming and so generous?' Bonet mused.

'We might find out one day,' Carbonne chuckled.

'You think the Prussians could defeat us in battle?' Charvet asked. 'Drive us back onto our own soil and occupy France?'

'Anything is possible,' the former executioner said.

'Not that,' Charvet told him, defiantly. 'We are invincible. With the Emperor leading us, no army in the world could match us, let alone defeat us.'

'It is God who has made us invincible, not Bonaparte,' Moreau said. 'He has smiled down upon us and allowed us to be victorious.'

'We don't need your God's help to win a war,' Rocheteau told him. 'Just courage and self-belief.'

'And this,' added Rostov, touching his sword.

'An army needs many things to win a war,' Lausard interjected. 'Good leadership. Good weapons. Good troops and some luck. Never underestimate the part *that* plays in a campaign.'

'If any of us had any *real* luck, we'd all be heading home now,' grumbled Charvet. 'Not stuck here waiting for orders.'

'Stop complaining,' Rocheteau told him. 'Get inside and prepare some food. I feel as if I haven't eaten for a week.'

'You're starting to sound like Joubert,' Bonet smiled.

Tigana looked up and saw the men approaching. He brought the horses to a halt and patted them on the neck one by one.

'Just a little extra exercise,' he explained. 'They are as bored as we are.'

Lausard nodded and reached for the muzzle of the nearest horse. He patted the animal as it nuzzled against him.

'By the way, Alain,' Tigana said, a slight grin on his thin features. 'There is someone here to see you. A visitor.'

Lausard looked at him quizzically.

'She's inside,' the Gascon told him, nodding towards the makeshift barracks. 'Roussard and Delacor are entertaining her.'

'A woman?' Giresse said, eagerly.

'She did not come to see *you*,' Tigana told him, grinning. 'She has eyes only for our sergeant.'

The other men began laughing as Lausard walked towards the converted grain warehouse.

'When you've finished with her, Alain,' Giresse called, 'tell her she only has to ask me and I will introduce her to delights she will have known only in her dreams.'

Another chorus of laughter greeted the remark.

Lausard himself chuckled and waved a hand dismissively at the other dragoons. He paused for a moment before entering the barracks then pushed the door and stepped inside.

Delacor and Roussard turned to look at him.

So too did Claudia Keppler.

She smiled enticingly at the sergeant, who returned

the gesture, allowing his gaze to rove up and down her slender form. From the gleaming flaxen hair that framed her finely chiselled features and cascaded as far as her shoulder blades, down to her slender neck and slim narrow shoulders. She wore a blouse embroidered with lace. Over that she sported a dark waistcoat. Her riding breeches accentuated her slim hips and buttocks. They were tucked into brown riding boots. Slung around her shoulders was a long black cape which hung just above the floor of the barracks.

'Fräulein Keppler,' said Lausard, softly. 'Yet again you grace us with your presence.' He bowed his head in mock reverence.

The young woman smiled appreciatively and blushed.

'I have something for you, Sergeant,' she said. 'A gift.'

'Another one? I cannot begin to imagine what any of us have done to deserve your generosity.'

She took a step towards the sergeant and swept a basket into view from beneath her cloak in the manner of a young and beautiful conjurer. Lausard peered into the receptacle as she pulled back the multi-coloured cloth that covered the contents.

'Bread and rolls,' she announced. 'Freshly baked this morning.'

'I thank you,' Lausard said, taking them from her. 'They will be as much appreciated and enjoyed as everything else you have given us.'

'I wish there was more I could give you,' she told him, gazing into his eyes.

Lausard smiled, trying to hide his amusement at the precocity of this eighteen-year-old. He held her gaze, enraptured by her gleaming blue eyes. She was indeed a very beautiful young woman. Her clothes smelled as if they had been newly laundered, her hair as if it had been freshly washed.

'Does your father know you are here?' the sergeant said, finally.

She shook her head.

'Why don't you tell him you come to visit us?' he asked. 'Would he disapprove?'

'He doesn't like me being around men. He says that they have only one thing on their minds.' She smiled slightly and gently licked her lips. 'Especially soldiers.'

Behind her, Delacor had his hooded eyes fixed firmly on her. Roussard was also leering silently at the young woman. Delacor flexed his fingers then rubbed his hands together, his gaze never leaving Claudia.

'Shall we walk?' Lausard said, ushering her towards the door.

She nodded and stepped in front of him.

'Haven't you got work to do?' he asked, looking at the other two dragoons.

Both shook their heads.

'Do you want me to find you some?' the sergeant persisted, hooking a thumb over his shoulder. 'Help Tigana with the horses.'

'Are you sure *you* don't need any help, Sergeant?' asked Delacor, still leering at the young woman.

Lausard ignored the comment and walked to the end of the barracks, where Claudia was preparing to step out into the morning air.

'Excuse my comrades,' he said, apologetically. 'But to

soldiers beautiful young women are as rare as a soft bed and good food.'

'A woman and a soft bed should go together,' Claudia giggled.

They walked slowly in the direction of the woods that grew thickly behind the buildings. The wind blew through the branches, rattling them like skeletal fingers. It whipped Claudia's blonde hair around her face.

'If your father doesn't want you mixing with soldiers then you should not be here,' Lausard told her.

'I am not afraid of him.'

'It is not a matter of fear. It is a matter of respect. He must have a good reason for wanting you to keep away from us.'

'We have a soldier living in our house. Your captain. My father finds no problem with that. But he says that *you* are criminals.'

'He only speaks the truth. We *were* criminals. Now I would like to think we are soldiers like any others.'

'What was *your* crime?'

'I was a thief,' he told her without blinking. 'So were many of my men. We have among us a forger, several political undesirables, a heretic, a horse-thief, a former executioner and a rapist. Will you be so willing to return here again now you know that?'

'If that happened in the past then I don't care. I have nothing to fear from you, do I?'

Lausard shook his head.

'As you say, that was in the past. It is just that some are not as willing as others to leave the past where it belongs.'

'Where is that?'

'Behind them.'

Claudia laughed and it had a musical sound to it. Lausard studied her features for a moment. Her skin looked as pure and unblemished as alabaster. He wondered if it was as smooth.

'When you were a thief, what did you steal?' she wanted to know.

'Food. Drink. Whatever I needed to stay alive,' Lausard told her.

She nodded.

'What would your father say if he knew you were here?' the sergeant wanted to know. 'What would he do?'

'I don't care.'

'That isn't what I asked you.'

She shrugged and pulled her cloak more tightly around her as a cold breeze buffeted them.

'He would forbid me to come here again,' she said, finally.

'And would you obey him?'

She looked at Lausard and grinned. 'Probably not,' she confessed.

'Why *do* you come here, Claudia? What is so fascinating about us? Every other day, it seems, you come with freshly baked bread or cakes. What brings you here so often, especially when you know how much your father disapproves? Or is it his disapproval that brings you here?'

'What do you mean?'

Lausard smiled.

'I was your age once,' he mused. 'I know what it is

to rebel against those who would control me. If your father gave you permission to visit us you would not even *want* to come here.'

'I am not a child. I do what I do through my own choosing. I come to see *you*.'

'You come to see a thief?'

'Until you told me, I did not know of your past. I know nothing about you other than that you are a soldier.'

'A soldier from a nation that may well soon be at war with your own. From an occupying force. Good enough reason to stay away.'

'Do you want me to go?'

He shook his head slowly. 'I appreciate what you do, Claudia,' he said, quietly. 'I thank you for your kindness.'

'It is not out of kindness that I visit you. I come here because . . . ' She turned away from him as the sentence trailed off.

Lausard took a step towards her then hesitated.

'I loved you from the first moment I set eyes upon you,' she told him.

'You are eighteen. What do you know of love, Claudia? What little you know about me you have learned this morning. You do not love me. You cannot. People cannot love unless they know each other. You can never know me.'

'Why not?'

'What you feel is some kind of schoolgirl love,' Lausard told her.

'I am not a child,' she snapped, angrily.

'And you are not a woman either. If you were older you would see the folly of this infatuation.' He saw the tears in her eyes and took another step closer. 'Do not misunderstand me. You are very beautiful and intelligent, but you still have many years left to understand the meaning of love.'

'Then teach me,' she said, tears coursing down her cheeks.

'I probably know less about it than you,' he told her, wearily. 'I would not presume to give lessons about a subject on which I am so ill-informed.'

'Have you never loved anyone?'

Lausard momentarily lowered his gaze then stared out across the fields beyond the wood as if searching for an answer in the dark soil.

'Does it matter?' he said, finally. 'What happened in the past is gone. Everything I knew is gone. A way of life. People. All that matters is *now*. Soldiers learn to live that way. Forget the past because you cannot change it. Never look to the future because you may not have one. Never love anyone, it will bring only heartbreak. To you or to them.'

'Is there no love in your heart for anything?'

'It is best that there is not. A man cannot grieve for something he has never had. People you love die and then what is left? Nothing but misery. Better not to love at all.'

'Your heart is of stone.'

'That is one of the ways I survive.'

'And what of the men you fight with? Your comrades. Do you care nothing for *them* either?'

'I would give my life for any one of them. As they would for me.'

'Is that not a form of love?'

Lausard smiled. 'Perhaps it is,' he admitted. 'One that only fighting men can understand.' He reached out a hand and touched her cheek. 'Go back to your father.'

'Do you not want me to come here again?'

'By all means, bring your bread and your cakes with you,' Lausard smiled. 'But keep your *love* for someone who deserves it.' He stepped forward and kissed her tenderly on the forehead.

'When will you leave here?' she wanted to know.

'I wish I could tell you. We are still awaiting orders from our Emperor.'

'And once you have gone, I will never see you again.'

'For that, be thankful. I fear that if I ever have to pass through this town again it will be as an enemy. The next time you see me might well be through smoke and flames.'

Night fell like an impenetrable blanket over the town and its surrounding hamlet. With the darkness came a cold that had grown steadily more severe as the day had progressed. As Alain Lausard walked from the stables leading his horse by its bridle, he pulled his green cloak more tightly around him. The frosty ground crunched beneath his boots. Lausard checked the girth strap then he put his right foot into the blackened iron stirrup and swung himself into the saddle. The first flecks of snow dappled the woollen material of his cape. He had already placed the familiar oilskin cover over his brass helmet to protect it from the elements. Lausard patted his horse's neck, its breath clouding in the freezing air. He heard snuffling close by and turned in the saddle to see Erebus wandering around outside the barracks. The dog looked up at him and jerked its head questioningly, as if to ask him where he was going at such a late hour. Lausard clicked his fingers and pointed back in the direction of the building from which the dog had emerged. It wandered back, swallowed up by the night, as black as a portion of the umbra.

The moon was battling to find its way from behind the thick clouds that scudded across the firmament but it could force only a meagre amount of cold light onto the earth below. Lausard sat astride his mount in almost total darkness but for the torches burning outside the stable and barracks. Inside the building, most of his men slept soundly, well fed and well rested after another day of virtual inactivity.

The food they had acquired at the market that morning had been consumed gratefully. There was some left for the following evening. Charvet had put a lid on the great pot he always cooked in and left the potatoes, carrots, chicken and barley to remain in the delicious wine and stock he had added.

Lausard could see the snow falling more thickly now and he prepared to guide his horse away from the building, out across the hills and fields of this Bavarian hamlet. As ever, sleep had eluded him. It was to be another of many rides he had already taken during their time here. Good food, a comfortable bed and warmth – the three things a soldier in the field dreamed of. If those things could not bring him sleep then he knew he had but one alternative. He flicked the reins of his bay and the animal whinnied quietly, pawing at the ground with one hoof.

'Do you want some company, Alain?'

He turned as he heard the voice, recognising it immediately as belonging to Rocheteau.

The corporal looked up at Lausard, almost invisible in the gloom.

'*You* don't normally have trouble sleeping,' the sergeant said 'What's wrong?'

'I could ask you the same thing. Every night you ride or you prowl about into the small hours. Not just here but everywhere we've been.'

'How do you know that if you are always sleeping?'

'The others have told me. So, *do* you want some company or not?'

'Get your horse,' Lausard smiled.

He walked his own mount back and forth as he waited for the corporal to emerge from the stable leading his own horse. It was a large, powerful animal he'd taken from a dead Russian cuirassier after his own mount had been killed by an exploding shell. Like Lausard, he checked his girth strap before mounting. Lausard looked at the corporal then, without speaking, he pulled on his reins and rode off. Rocheteau followed, the two horses carrying them effortlessly across the rapidly whitening landscape. For more than ten minutes they rode in silence, cantering across the fields and hills, occasionally breaking into a short gallop, the horses feeling the same exhilaration as their riders. The animals, Lausard mused, were obviously as grateful for this break from the daily monotonous routine of drill, grooming and stabling as their riders were. The sergeant bent low over the neck of his mount and urged it to greater speed as they crested the top of a low, tree-littered ridge. Only then did Lausard pull on the reins and bring the animal to a halt. Rocheteau did likewise and the two men looked behind them in the direction of Fürstenberg.

The town was hidden by darkness and the curtain of steadily falling snow but they knew it was there, slumbering in the blackness just as it did every night. The only thing visible, flanked on both sides by trees and hedges, was the road that led to the town. It cut through another ridge a mile or so away. There were several small houses set along this road and Lausard could see an oil lamp burning in the window of one.

'I trust these midnight rides have a purpose,' Rocheteau said, patting his horse's neck.

'They give me time to think,' Lausard told him.

'About what?'

'What goes on inside here,' said the sergeant, tapping his temple, 'is no one's business but my own.'

'Do you not trust me, Alain?'

'With my life, Rocheteau, but every man must have at least *one* secret. Don't you agree?'

The corporal chuckled and nodded in agreement. Both men swung themselves out of the saddle and secured their mounts to the nearest tree. Both animals began to scratch at the bone-hard ground with their hooves.

'Does your secret have anything to do with a certain Fräulein Keppler?' Rocheteau wanted to know. 'She seems most taken with you, Alain.'

'She is a child. I am flattered by her attention but I have no desire to experience her passion.'

'There are many men in the army who *would*. Myself among them.'

'Of that I have no doubt, and I do not blame you for your interest. She is indeed very beautiful. But war is no place for romance, Rocheteau. It breaks enough hearts as it is.'

'Do you think that war will come?' the corporal asked, reaching inside his jacket for a silver hip-flask. It was another souvenir from Austerlitz, taken from a dead Russian grenadier. The blood had cleaned off easily.

'I fear it is just a matter of time, my friend,' Lausard told him, accepting the flask and swigging from it. He savoured the feeling as the brandy burned its way to his stomach. 'But then, we all suspected as much, did we not? Our Corsican's destiny lies in war. So too does ours.'

Rocheteau considered the statement for a moment then nodded. He accepted the flask back from Lausard and drank deeply.

'Will that always be the case, Alain?' he asked.

Lausard could only shrug.

'I have no crystal ball to see into the future,' the sergeant said. 'And I cannot see into our Corsican's heart. I have no idea what he desires. But I suspect his thirst for power will not be satisfied with the destruction of the Austrian army. There are still the Russians. Prussia too and always the English.'

'Always the English,' Rocheteau echoed, gazing off across the snow-flecked fields. The frozen grass crunched beneath his boots as he walked.

'As long as Bonaparte has ambition, we will be needed. For that I am grateful.'

'What of peace? Do you not desire that as much as the rest of us?'

'And what will peace bring *us*? A return home? Back to the way of life we knew before we became soldiers? Back to scratching a living in the gutters of Paris? Is that what *you* want, Rocheteau? We have no soldier's pensions to rely on. No fortunes to enjoy like those of Bonaparte and his Marshals. No dukedoms. No grand duchies. No fine mistresses to keep us company on cold nights such as these. All we have are these uniforms. All we *are* is contained within them. Without the army, without war, we don't even have that. Now do you understand why I do not crave peace with the same appetite as other men?'

The corporal sipped from the hip-flask and regarded his companion evenly. He brushed some flecks of snow from his cloak and patted his horse's neck.

Lausard walked to the crest of the ridge, glancing up at the sky. The moon finally fought its way out from behind the thick banks of cloud, and cold white light spilled across the landscape, illuminating it like some massive phosphorous flare. He saw a fox scampering over one of the fields towards the road. However, as he watched the animal, it suddenly turned and scurried back away from the thoroughfare. The sergeant saw movement on the road and reached into his pocket for his telescope. He pulled it free and trained it on the disturbance. He counted thirty men riding in a tight column along the road, moving at a brisk pace. All were mounted on jet black horses. Even in the gloom of the night it was possible to make out their colour. The riders wore long blue cloaks but it was their headgear that made them unmistakeable. He saw the bearskins nodding threateningly, the tall red plumes at one side covered with oilskins to protect them from the weather.

'Rocheteau,' he murmured, beckoning his companion to him and handing him the telescope. 'Tell me what you see.' He pointed in the direction of the approaching horsemen.

Rochteau also recognised them immediately.

'"Big boots",' he said, disdainfully. 'What the hell are they doing here?'

Lausard took the glass back from him and studied the men once again. Horse Grenadiers of the Imperial Guard. There could be no mistake.

'Let us hope they are just passing through,' he murmured.

'If they stop, they'll scrape this town clean and leave nothing for us,' Rocheteau hissed.

The mounted grenadiers were now within a mile of the town and closing by the second. Through the silence of the chill night, Lausard could hear the jingle of their harnesses and the thundering of their horses' hooves on the frozen road. He watched for a moment longer then snapped the telescope shut. He turned and walked back to his horse, swinging himself into the saddle.

'We'd better get back,' he said, waiting until Rocheteau had also mounted. 'Perhaps we will know better tomorrow whether we are to make the acquaintance of our comrades in the Guard.'

Lausard took one more look in the direction of the approaching heavy cavalry, then he and Rocheteau set off in the direction of Fürstenberg.

Five

❧

Napoleon Bonaparte pulled tightly on the reins of his magnificent white horse, digging his knees into the animal's flanks to slow it down. The superb Arab stallion slowed its pace and began pawing the mossy ground. It contented itself with nuzzling a nearby bush while the Corsican patted its neck. He had never been the best of horsemen and his mounts were hand-picked and trained for him by his equerry, Jardin. The task was made even more difficult considering Napoleon's penchant for such Middle-Eastern stock and the fiery temperament of Arab steeds. The stallion began tossing its head and, for a moment, he struggled to control the horse. Beside him, Marshal Jean Baptiste Bessiéres thought about shooting out a hand to grab the Emperor's bridle. It was finally unnecessary. Napoleon stroked the horse's mane and sat motionless as the other riders around him also brought their mounts to a halt. Bessiéres brought his own chestnut gelding to a stop, as did Marshal Louis Alexandre Berthier. The Chief of Staff took off his plumed bicorn and wiped a hand across his forehead. Despite the chill in the air he was perspiring. General Anne Jean Marie Rene Savary tugged on the reins of his grey and allowed the animal to begin nibbling at the grass that grew on the hillside overlooking Schönbrunn.

Despite his relative ineptitude as a horseman, Napoleon enjoyed riding for exercise. It also, he told those close to him, cleared his head.

'Is it not the most glorious life a man can lead, my friends?' he proclaimed, sucking in lungfuls of fresh, clean air. 'Who would trade a place in the army for anything else?' He smiled.

'There may be some of your infantry who would disagree, sire,' Savary remarked. 'When their feet are sore from marching they may well hold alternative views on the subject.' The other men laughed.

'Savary is right, sire,' Bessiéres offered. 'We cavalry-men alone know the joy of being borne at speed on the backs of well-bred and well-trained animals such as these.' He patted his own horse.

'You forget, Savary, I learned my trade behind a four-pounder,' Napoleon remarked. 'I carried cannonballs. I helped drag guns from the mud and yet still I knew that the army was the only place I ever wanted to be.'

'Did you ever envisage you would one day be ruler of all France, sire?' Berthier asked. 'Surely you could not have done.'

'I believed in my own destiny, Berthier. What ambitious man does not?'

The Chief of Staff nodded.

'May I compliment you on the choice of such a magnificent horse, sire,' Bessiéres said, looking admiringly at the white stallion. 'It is a superb animal. Perhaps I should compliment your equerry too.'

'He is the best trainer of horses in France,' the Corsican remarked. 'I'm surprised he allowed me out this morning. Because he is so good, I never have a horse to ride. With anyone else, I would have sixty.'

'He is particular because he cares about your safety, sire,' Berthier noted. 'We all do.'

'How long does it take him to train one of your horses, your Highness?' Savary wanted to know. 'I have heard that some of his training methods are frowned upon.'

'Such as?' Napoleon said, challengingly.

'To teach the horses to bear pain, he strikes them over the ears and head repeatedly with whips. Pistols are fired near them. Drums are beaten and flags waved in their eyes. I have heard he even has live sheep or pigs thrown under their hooves.'

'That may be true, but Jardin is a good man. He demands the best from the horses I select and he knows how to get it. You, as well as anyone, know what they must endure in the heat of battle. An animal that flies at the sound of a pistol shot would be of little use to me.'

Savary nodded.

'There is supposed to be good hunting around here, sire,' Bessiéres observed, glancing around the thinly wooded slopes. 'Some of my men claim to have seen wild boar in these woods.'

'Some of your men have seen the Virgin Mary herself after drinking too much wine,' Berthier chuckled.

'If *my* men encountered the Holy Mother, I fear she

would not remain a virgin for too long,' Bessiéres laughed.

'If you wish to hunt, Bessiéres, then by all means do so,' Napoleon smiled. 'But I urge you not to extend an invitation to me. You might be disappointed when I refuse. The only kind of hunting I care to indulge in is the hunting of glory for France.'

Again the Emperor's staff broke into a chorus of laughter.

'Acquiring more glory might be a little more difficult than riding a boar to ground, sire,' Bessiéres observed. 'Especially at the moment. Austria is beaten. The Russians have fled. King Frederick William seems paralysed by the presence of our troops in Prussia. Your enemies are not eager to renew hostilities.'

'Neither am I,' said Napoleon, flatly. 'War, at this present time, is not in the interests of France, either economically or militarily. If I can avoid it, I will. There are matters of a more pressing nature regarding the economy of France. Large numbers of bonds have disappeared from the treasury, thousands of people have been ruined. I suspect that the Minister of the Treasury may have more to do with this predicament than he cares to admit. I, myself, will speak with Monsieur Barbe-Marbois when the time is right.'

'Forgive my impertinence, sire,' said Berthier. 'You say you desire peace and yet the terms you have presented to your enemies, be they actual or potential, would seem to indicate that the precipitation of war is inevitable. Particularly with Prussia.'

'King Frederick William is in no position to question

my terms,' Napoleon snapped. 'With one hundred and fifty thousand French troops encamped on his borders he would be a fool to do so.'

'Talleyrand told me that your demands were close to being excessive, sire,' the Chief of Staff muttered. 'He feels that you may push the Prussians into war.'

Napoleon waved a hand dismissively.

'Talleyrand also believes that a settlement with Russia is impossible,' he sneered. 'He is a very gifted diplomat but he conducts *his* manoeuvres within the *state* rooms of our enemies, not on battlefields.'

'Tsar Alexander did express his admiration for you when I spoke with him after the battle of Austerlitz, sire,' Savary interjected. 'He said he felt you were a man predestined by Heaven and that it would be a hundred years before his army would be the equal of yours.'

'For one so young he has learned very quickly,' Napoleon smiled. 'I cannot understand Talleyrand's reservations. I am sure that an amicable solution can be reached between ourselves and Russia without recourse to war.'

'What of Italy, sire?' Berthier wanted to know.

'The greater part of Northern Italy is already at my disposal,' the Emperor mused. 'Now would be the time to extend our possessions there. Austria is in no position to offer resistance with either diplomacy *or* force of arms.'

'Increased power in Italy will bring conflict with the Pope, sire,' Savary reminded him.

'That is to be expected,' the Corsican said, dismissively. 'To the Pope I am Charlemagne. I expect to be treated from this point of view. Whatever may have been gained by the Concordat with Rome three years ago is of no importance now. The position of France, however, is stronger. Should he voice too vehement an opposition, Pius VII may well find himself reduced merely to Bishop of Rome. But Italy is not a major concern at the moment. The reorganisation of Germany *is*. France has many allies among the states and electorates of that country, principalities who would be more than happy to pledge their allegiance to France: Bavaria, Württemberg, Baden, Hesse-Darmstadt and several smaller principalities along the Rhine. We should not be slow to use their dissatisfaction with Frederick William's incompetence.'

'With what purpose, sire?' Bessiéres enquired.

'It will consolidate our influence over German affairs,' the Corsican explained. 'It will also provide a source of men and materials for future campaigns. Secure a bridgehead over the Rhine from which our armies may be launched when they need to be. And, most importantly, it will provide France with a buffer between herself and the central and eastern powers of Europe.'

'These measures are designed for war, sire?' Bessiéres said.

Napoleon shook his head almost imperceptibly.

'It is inadvisable at this moment, but if the circumstances demand that it becomes unavoidable then I will not hesitate to act,' he said, flatly. 'I do this knowing that I can rely upon men like you. I know you will not fail me when the time comes.'

* * *

The change from line to column was completed with seamless skill, the dragoons watching either the waving sword of Captain Milliere or listening to the blasts on the trumpets that signalled each different manoeuvre. Lausard pulled gently on the reins of his horse, guiding the animal to the left at the regulation two hundred and forty paces a minute of the trot. All changes of formation were carried out at this speed or at the faster pace of the gallop when the horses reached as much as four hundred and eighty paces a minute. The green-clad dragoons, drilled for so many years in these practised movements, completed them effortlessly, and Milliere wheeled his horse away from the head of the column to watch as the leading dragoons swept past him. He was smiling delightedly. The guidon of the squadron fluttered in the cold breeze and he, like the others who made up its numbers, looked upon the red, white and blue swallow-tailed emblem with pride. Especially at the twenty centimetre-high gilded bronze eagle that topped the staff.

Lausard noticed the officer watching the movements and saw the pride on his face. The sergeant both liked and respected the captain. He was a consummate horseman and an intelligent and brave man, as dedicated to the army as any man Lausard had ever met. He often wondered if, like himself, the army had offered him some form of escape from his previous life. He knew little about the captain's background but, he reasoned, opinions were formed in the company of another, not on reputations. The two men were of roughly the same age and build, Lausard perhaps a little more powerful about the shoulders and upper body. As the sergeant watched, he saw Lieutenant Royere join the captain. The two officers watched their companions complete the drill that had become close to robotic, so faultlessly was it carried out. More than ten years perfecting the movements both on parade grounds and battlefields had made Lausard and the dragoons, and indeed the rest of the men of *La Grande Armée*, into a superbly drilled fighting machine capable of crushing any opponent sent against it. As he guided his horse through the required movements, Lausard wondered which enemy would be the next to confront them. He knew it was only a matter of time before he found out.

The dragoons moved back into linear formation with the same faultless expertise as before, slowing their pace to a walk. The horses were in good condition and seemed to relish the exercise somewhat more than their riders, who understood the necessity of the drill but disliked its predictability. Most of the horses came from Brittany, Normandy or the Jura region of France, but a large number of Russian remounts had also been acquired in the wake of Austerlitz. On the whole, the horses ridden by Lausard and his companions were strong, quick, reliable beasts capable of carrying riders and equipment with ease as long as they were well cared for. The problems on campaign were exactly the same for both the cavalrymen and their mounts. Shelter, food and warmth had to be found to prevent illness and weakness. Since the end of the last campaign, both men and horses had been blessed with comfortable quarters and plentiful food. All had thrived on it. However, as the squadron walked back and forth across the field that passed as a parade ground, Lausard wondered how long their current situation would continue. He glanced around at his companions, all dressed in their fatigues – the green surtout and reinforced grey breeches they wore for drill and stable duties. Even the normally flamboyant red and green tunic worn by Gaston was replaced by a plain red jacket for these daily exercises.

A further hour would now be given over to sword practice, both in *and* out of the saddle. When that was completed, the Charleville carbines would be employed. Speed of firing and reloading would be tested. Well-trained men, like Lausard and his companions, could be expected to fire two, perhaps three, rounds a minute. The firing would also take place from the saddle and on foot. The process of firing while mounted was infinitely more difficult, especially in the heat of battle, but it was something that every man in the squadron had done more times than he cared to remember, both in peace and war. Then, when Captain Milliere was satisfied, all the equipment would be cleaned and stored before the men were released from their duties for the day. The remainder of their time would be spent as it always was: staving off boredom with games of cards or dice, visiting Fürstenberg or simply sleeping. There were rumours that fencing competitions had been arranged, that horse races were to take place. But so far none of these promised events had transpired. Lausard remembered only too well the crushing boredom he and his comrades had endured while stationed in the camp of Boulogne just over eighteen months ago. Everything about their present situation was beginning to look decidedly familiar. It seemed that one of two things would happen: they would be sent home or they would be summoned for war. The sergeant favoured the latter of the two options. At least it would signal an end to this interminable inactivity.

'I could do this in my sleep,' Delacor grumbled.

'The way you perform some manoeuvres you look as if you *are* asleep,' Rocheteau said, grinning.

Delacor glared at the corporal as several of those within earshot laughed.

'Perhaps we should give *him* a uniform,' said Sonnier, nodding in the direction of the hillside.

Erebus was hurtling down it, barking madly. The big black dog skidded at the bottom of the slope and almost fell, but it righted itself and then trotted across towards Gaston's grey horse. The young trumpeter glanced down at the dog then across at Captain Milliere.

'I see we have a new recruit,' the officer called, pointing at the dog. 'Where did that hound of hell come from?'

'No one knows, Captain,' Lausard told the officer, 'but he seems to favour *our* side, not the Prussians.'

'He has good sense then, Sergeant,' Milliere smiled.

The captain waved his sword in the air to halt the lines of troopers. As they remained perfectly still, the officer rode back and forth between them, checking their distances. The lines were perfectly ordered, twelve paces between each, as regulations stated. Lieutenant Royere followed. The dog looked up at each of the officers as they rode past. Both men had assumed their position at the head of the column when a low rumbling sound suddenly filled the air. It grew steadily louder. Lausard realised it was coming from just beyond the crest of the ridge. He also realised that it was the pounding of horses' hooves. Erebus began barking and suddenly dashed out from beneath Gaston's horse. He hurtled towards the slope and stood at the bottom of it growling as the sound grew in volume. All eyes turned to the crest.

The detachment of Horse Grenadiers of the Imperial Guard crested the ridge and brought their mounts to a halt.

Rocheteau shot Lausard a glance.

'The same "big boots" we saw last night?' he mused.

'I should think so,' the sergeant said, quietly, his eyes never leaving the line of blue uniformed men. 'Now, perhaps we *will* find out what they want here.'

They were all astride magnificent black horses, their dark blue shabracques stirred by the cold breeze that swept across the landscape. The grenadiers had discarded the blue capes they had sported the previous night so that their distinctive blue jackets with white lapels and waistcoats were clearly visible. Their huge bearskins were ruffled by the breeze. Their red plumes, protected the night before by oilskins, now looked almost luminescent against the black of their headgear. As three of them spurred forward down the slope, Lausard could see that the leading rider sported gold, fringeless epaulettes, marking him out as an officer. He was also wearing the watered red silk ribbon and cross of the *Légion d'Honneur* on his breast. Of the two men with him, the first bore the chevrons of sergeant on his arms, the other sported a dazzling light blue jacket with red lapels and a white bearskin that marked him out as a trumpeter. The gold instrument was strapped across his portmanteau.

Erebus growled once more at the trio of soldiers then turned and scampered back towards Gaston who, like the other dragoons, sat watching the approaching riders with a combination of curiosity and distaste. The sight of anyone connected with the Imperial Guard was usually sufficient to raise the hackles of any soldier in the French army. Lausard also fixed the horsemen in an unwavering gaze, patting his horse's neck as they drew nearer.

'Captain Lucien Diomede,' the grenadier officer announced, saluting sharply. 'Grenadiers of the Guard.'

Milliere returned the salute. 'So I see,' he said, flatly. 'What brings such exalted company to this part of Bavaria?'

'Myself and my men are on our way back to France,' Diomede said.

'You are very lucky.'

'It is the orders of the Emperor that all units of the Guard should return. He feels it is just reward for our part in the last campaign.'

'The Guard were not the only men who fought. You should be thankful you are smiled upon. That still does not explain what brings you *here*.'

'We need food and quarters for a few days. Somewhere to rest. This town would seem to be as good as any. You and your men have made your homes here. We will be doing the same but on a *temporary* basis, of course.' Diomede smiled crookedly. 'How long have you been here?'

'Almost a month,' Milliere told him.

'Then you know the town well.'

'Yes we do. We were welcomed warmly by its people. They continue to extend that warmth towards us. However, should *too* many French troops descend upon them I fear their generosity may become somewhat strained.'

'Are you suggesting we move on? Find somewhere else?'

'I am merely telling you that there may not be enough room for both your men and mine to live amicably with the people of Fürstenberg.'

'And I told *you* that we would be here only on a temporary basis. Besides, I have no interest in the feelings of these Prussians. I have no interest in living amicably with them, merely with finding some food and shelter for the time being. Why should any of us care about the people of a nation that we may soon be at war with?'

The blue-coated trumpeter and sergeant laughed.

Milliere held the grenadier officer's gaze. 'What do you want from *us*?' he said, sharply.

'You can help us find barracks and lodgings,' Diomede told him. 'If you know the townspeople so well, it should be a small enough inconvenience.'

'Find your own billets,' Milliere said, flatly. 'I serve France, not the Guard.'

'The Guard *is* France,' Diomede snapped.

'It is your duty to help us,' the grenadier sergeant hissed.

'Do not presume to tell me my duty, *Sergeant*,' Milliere said, scornfully. 'And I do not care for your insolence. Guard or not, I still outrank you. Remember that.' He turned his attention back to Diomede. 'I suggest you keep your dog on a tighter leash, Captain.'

The grenadier sergeant gritted his teeth angrily.

Milliere looked at the blue-clad officer.

'My men can share the quarters of your troopers,' Diomede said. 'My officers will find lodgings with the town's officials.'

'Lieutenant Royere and myself are already guests of the burgomaster and the local priest,' Milliere told the guard officer. 'Do not presume to prevail upon *them*. As for your men, let them set up their camp somewhere outside the town.'

'You would turn away fellow soldiers?' Diomede said, quietly. 'To do so would be a betrayal.'

'Of what?' Milliere snapped. 'Of France? I think not. Find your own billets, Captain. Now, if you have nothing further to say, I and my squadron have work to do.'

The two officers locked stares for a moment longer, then Milliere wheeled his horse and rode back to the waiting dragoons.

Lausard glanced across at the watching grenadiers who, as one, turned and rode back up the gentle slope to where their companions watched. The entire mass of blue-clad troops turned their mounts and departed, the sound of their horses' hooves echoing through the cold air.

'The Guard,' sneered Delacor. He hawked and spat. 'Who the hell do they think they are?'

'They are the Emperor's personal bodyguard,' Bonet offered.

'They are still only men like us,' Delacor said, flatly. 'They fight, they bleed, they die. Just as we do. They are nothing special.'

'Do you think they will leave?' Rocheteau murmured. 'Those damned "big boots".'

Lausard shook his head.

'I doubt it,' he said, quietly. 'I may be wrong, but I don't think that we've seen the last of *them*.'

Six

———◆◆◆———

The snow had begun to fall during the night and was still falling when Lausard stepped out of the barracks the following morning. The strong wind had prevented it from doing anything other than dusting the landscape but, nevertheless, the ground was white as the sergeant walked towards the stable. His boots made imprints on the almost luminescent carpet and he glanced up at the grey sky and its swollen clouds. The snow looked as though it would continue for the rest of the day. His brass helmet was already covered by a protective oilskin and now he pulled his green cloak more tightly around him as he approached the stables.

There were sounds of movement coming from inside and as he wandered through the door he wasn't surprised to see Karim and Tigana feeding not just their own mounts but also those of the other dragoons. From the far end of the building, Erebus wandered across to the sergeant and he stroked the great black dog with one gloved hand. Its tongue lolled from one corner of its mouth. The horses were all covered by thick, woollen blankets to protect them from the cold. Some peered inquisitively over the top of their stalls as Lausard entered, as if anxious to get a look at the newcomer. He wandered over to his own horse and stroked the bay's muzzle.

'You two are showing a devotion to these animals that some might find disturbing,' Lausard grinned.

'There is little else for us to do, Alain,' Tigana said, taking a curry comb to his own mount. 'You know that. Besides, the horses appreciate it.'

'A horse deserves pampering as much as any man,' Karim added. 'And a horse that is well cared for will serve its rider better.'

'Is that more of your Eastern philosophy, Karim?' smiled Tigana.

'I do not need to be a philosopher to realise that, my friend,' said the Circassian. 'Neither should you.'

'Yes, how many years did you breed horses, Tigana?' Lausard asked. 'Ten? Fifteen?'

'I have been surrounded by horses for as long as I can remember,' the Gascon said. 'I bred them, now I rely on them to keep me alive. In the heat of battle, this horse is as important as any sword or carbine.' He patted the animal, allowing it to nuzzle against him.

'Your expertise is greatly valued by the squadron, both of you,' the sergeant offered.

The other two dragoons watched as Lausard saddled his mount. He slipped the bridle into place, arranged the green shabracque on the back of the bay then fastened the girth strap. The horse pawed the ground as Lausard worked. Erebus looked on silently, his head cocked quizzically on one side.

'It is a Sunday, Alain. God's day,' Tigana observed. 'Are you going to church?'

All three men laughed.

'I expect Moreau will,' the sergeant said. 'Let him enjoy the day.'

'I heard the church bells in Fürstenberg when I woke,' said Tigana. 'I wonder if those "big boots" will be attending the service.'

'The Guard worship at their own altar,' Lausard said, quietly. 'Their God is Bonaparte.'

'There is only one God,' Karim murmured. 'And that is Allah, all Praise to Him.'

'I fear that even He would suffer from an inferiority complex were He ever to meet Bonaparte,' Lausard smiled.

The other two men laughed, watching as the sergeant led his mount out into the snow. The dog followed, forsaking the relative warmth of the stables. It watched as Lausard swung himself into the saddle and, once more, glanced up at the sky. More cloud gathered in premonitory banks, scudding like gun-smoke across the heavens.

'Come on,' he said, grinning down at the waiting dog. 'You can join me.'

The sergeant flicked the reins and rode off in the direction of Fürstenberg.

Erebus followed, bounding along delightedly beside the trotting horse.

The main road leading into the town was deeply rutted by the comings and goings of carts and wagons – further testament to the profusion of farms that surrounded the Bavarian hamlet. However, as he rode, Lausard noticed that the road was still relatively white with snow. Very little traffic had passed along it on this Sunday morning, the ruts were still full of the white flakes. Trees crowded in on the road, in some places locking branches above it, making the highway even darker beneath the natural canopy. When the summer arrived and the branches were thick with leaves, Lausard wondered if any natural light at all would penetrate from above. He rode at a steady pace, allowing his horse to savour the extended exercise. The bay tossed its head extravagantly but Lausard had it well under control and he smiled at the animal's natural exuberence. Erebus ran alongside the sergeant, occasionally darting between the legs of the bay but the horse seemed relatively unconcerned and continued without protest.

There was a small stream up ahead, frozen solid by the winter temperatures. The bridge that spanned it was wood and the bay's hooves beat out a tattoo as Lausard guided it across, glancing down at the ice-crusted stream. Erebus scurried to the bank of the stream, thought about descending to the frozen water itself then bounded after Lausard instead. The dog ran ahead, a great black blot against the whiteness of the fallen snow.

Another mile or two and the road turned gently to the right. As it did, the trees at either side of the road thinned out and Lausard could see the town sprawling beneath him in the hollow formed by the two ranges of hills that flanked it. Like everything else in the countryside, the hillsides were covered in snow. If temperatures continued to drop, Lausard reasoned, the terrain would become more treacherous. Already the ground was unyielding beneath his horse's hooves. By morning, it could be as hard as steel. Drill would be impossible. If the horses couldn't keep their footing then costly accidents could occur both to animals and men. The thought of a day without even the tedium of drill to enliven it was one Lausard tried not to entertain for too long.

Up ahead, Erebus was barking loudly and Lausard wondered if the dog had scented a rabbit or fox. He urged his horse on a little faster and found the big black animal standing in the middle of the road. A grey horse was facing Erebus, its nostrils flared, its rider looking fearfully at the dog. Lausard recognised the rider immediately and a smile creased his face.

'He is a little overzealous,' Lausard called. 'Please forgive him. Either that or feel free to let your horse trample him.'

Claudia Keppler looked at the sergeant and smiled as he brought his mount to a halt beside her.

Erebus stopped barking and loped off into the woods where he began to urinate against a tree before snuffling around some dead leaves.

'The dog has spent too much time around myself and my companions,' Lausard explained. 'He has lost what little manners he ever had.'

Claudia looked at the sergeant silently for a moment and Lausard thought how small and vulnerable she looked astride the grey she rode, but she controlled it effortlessly, yanking hard on its reins when it tossed its head.

'I did not expect to see you again, Fräulein,' he confessed.

'Why? Because you told me to keep away from you?' she said, sharply. 'I did not realise it was an order, *Sergeant*. Are you so used to giving instructions you expect *everyone* to obey them?'

It was Lausard's turn to look on silently.

Her expression softened. 'I'm sorry,' she said, quietly. 'I would not have come back but . . . ' She allowed the sentence to trail off.

Lausard could see that she was trembling slightly and he feared it was not merely the result of the weather. She ran a hand through her long blonde hair and looked into his eyes.

'I need your help,' she said. 'I would not have come to you otherwise.'

'What's wrong?'

'What kind of men are the soldiers who arrived in our town yesterday? All morning my father has been forced to deal with the problems they have created. They have stolen from us, invaded the houses of my people. There have been fights. People have been injured. We are powerless to stop them. You warned me of war. I fear it has already begun.'

'What do you expect me to do, Claudia?'

'Stop them.'

'I have no control over these men. They are of a different regiment. They *have* a commander. A man called Diomede.'

'A man who is as guilty as his men of transgressions against my town and its people,' Claudia blurted, tears welling in her eyes. 'They might not be of the same regiment as yours but they are still French soldiers. They are men like you.'

Lausard shook his head. 'They are nothing like me,' he said, flatly.

She fixed him in her imploring gaze once again and the sergeant saw a tear trickle down her cheek. She wiped it away, as if fearing that the cold would freeze it on her soft skin.

'So you will not help us?' she murmured.

'I didn't say that,' he told her. He reached out and wiped another tear from her cheek. 'Now, show me.'

She wheeled the grey and rode back towards Fürstenberg. Lausard cantered up alongside her. Erebus emerged from the woods, barking loudly and loping along ahead of the two horses.

High above, the clouds grew darker.

Lausard and his companion had already reached the outskirts of Fürstenberg when they saw the first of the Guard grenadiers. Two men were knocking on the door of a wooden house, one of them leaning against the wall chewing some tobacco. Every so often, he would project a stream of brown juice from his mouth, usually against the wall of the house. Dressed in dark blue surtouts, forage caps and grey breeches, they appeared to have walked from their makeshift encampment – Lausard could see no horses nearby. As he and Claudia drew nearer, Lausard saw the first of the two men take a step through the door when it was opened. The woman inside moved back, a look of fear on her face. Lausard reined in his mount. Erebus began to growl, baring his teeth in the direction of the blue-clad troopers.

'What do you want here?' Lausard called.

'What business is it of yours?' asked the second grenadier, spitting more juice from his mouth. Some droplets hung from his bushy moustache.

'We need food,' the first grenadier told him, turning away from the woman. 'These peasants can supply it for us.' Both men laughed.

'Are you too inadequate to find it yourselves?' Lausard snapped. 'Would you have a woman do the work of a soldier? There is game in the woods around the town. Have you not the wits to catch it?'

'Why should we chase rabbits when we don't have to?' snarled the first grenadier. 'There is food in all these houses. We are entitled to some of it.'

'This is the way it has been since they arrived,' Claudia said.

'Did Captain Diomede order you to steal from the people of the town?' Lausard wanted to know.

'We have to eat,' the second man told him. 'What we eat and where we get it is none of your business. You *or* the little filly.' He looked at Claudia and licked his lips exaggeratedly. 'I'll bet *you* could give me more than food, couldn't you, my little chicken?' Both grenadiers laughed. 'You could keep one of the Emperor's body-guards warm at night, couldn't you?' He took a step towards Claudia. Erebus continued to growl menacingly.

'Perhaps we could eat *that* black devil,' the grenadier rasped.

'He is more likely to make a meal of *you*,' Lausard said.

The grenadier grinned and lunged at the dog.

With devastating suddenness, Erebus launched himself at the trooper, teeth bared. The dog's heavy body slammed into the man, knocking him to the ground. As he tried to rise, the animal snapped at his hands and arms, finally sinking its teeth into the man's forearm. Erebus bit through the tunic easily, tearing a large piece of material free. The first grenadier turned to help his companion, who was now howling madly as he tried to beat the furious dog off. Lausard saw the first man's hand fall to the brass hilt of his sword.

With lightning speed, the sergeant pulled one of his pistols from its holster on the front of his saddle and aimed it at the grenadier.

'Leave the sword where it is,' he snapped, noticing that Erebus had now drawn blood and that the second grenadier was trying to scramble away from the gnashing teeth of the frenzied black dog. The animal bit him again, this time on the buttocks, then turned and scampered back towards Lausard, still carrying the torn portion of blue material in its jaws like a trophy.

The first grenadier still had his hand rested on his sword.

Lausard thumbed back the hammer of the pistol.

'You would fire on one of your own?' said the grenadier.

'Not on one of my own. But you are *not* one of my own, are you?'

'You will not fire,' said the grenadier, his hand hovering over the hilt.

'Pull the sword and find out,' Lausard murmured.

The second grenadier looked down at his savaged forearm to inspect the damage.

'What kind of monster is that?' he snarled, looking first at Erebus then at Lausard. 'I will gut it.'

'Be thankful he is choosy about what he eats,' Lausard said. 'He tasted your flesh. He obviously has an aversion to rotten meat.'

The two grenadiers stood defiantly before the dragoon sergeant, who was making no move to lower his pistol.

'If you shoot me, my friend will kill you before you have a chance to reload,' said the first man.

'An interesting theory. If you would care to put it to the test then go ahead,' said the dragoon. 'If not, I suggest you walk back into Fürstenberg.'

'I will remember you,' said the first grenadier, finally allowing his hand to drop to his side. 'You *and* that stinking dog. I will kill you both if I ever see you again.' Both men trudged towards the road and began walking. Occasionally they would glance behind them.

Lausard re-holstered the pistol then wheeled his horse and headed off down the road, Claudia close behind him, Erebus bounding along excitedly beside the two horses, the torn and chewed blue material gripped in his jaws. They passed the grenadiers, Lausard bumping into the first man with his horse, almost knocking him off his feet.

'I said I will kill you and I will,' the man shouted.

'You are welcome to try,' Lausard called over his shoulder.

He and Claudia rode on, drawing ever nearer to the centre of Fürstenberg. The spire of the town church was clearly visible now, thrusting upwards towards the mottled heavens. Another minute or two and the horses' hooves clattered on the cobbles of the main square. The church loomed ahead of them and Lausard could already see people spilling out of the large building, some in groups, others in ones and twos. Several women were crying. One looked up at Lausard and yelled something angrily in German.

'She says you are all heathens,' Claudia told him.

Lausard swung himself out of the saddle and headed for the church, the scabbard of his sword clanking against the steps as he ascended. Erebus stayed close to him. Claudia hurried after them.

As he entered the church, Lausard heard the noise. Amplified by the high, vaulted ceiling of the building, the cacophony of voices seemed to coalesce into one, fearful, strident wail. He heard shouts, screams and coarse laughter but, at first sight, none of the sounds seemed to have any discernible source. Then, as his eyes became more accustomed to the gloom inside the church, he saw that most of the activity was coming from the pulpit and chancel at the far end of the building. He saw the unmistakeable black bearskins of the Guard grenadiers and, among them, he spotted another, more welcome sight: the brass helmets of his fellow dragoons. It took him only seconds to recognise Captain Milliere and Lieutenant Royere. Close by was the town priest, alternately ringing his hands and pressing the palms together in prayer. Claudia saw her father. A rotund man with thinning hair. He was remonstrating with both dragoons and grenadiers. While, all around the church, the people of Fürstenberg either sat silently in their pews, entranced by the spectacle before them, or slipped away from this scene of blasphemy and irreverance.

Lausard strode down the nave, the sound of his boot heels echoing within the walls of the building. As he drew nearer he saw more clearly what was taking place.

Captain Diomede and three other grenadiers were standing with their backs to the altar. The sergeant who Lausard recognised from the other day was holding one of the golden candlesticks the dragoon had last seen on the altar. Another grenadier held the other. A third man was clasping the huge Bible he had taken from the lectern of the church. Seemingly oblivious to the noises around him, he was gently tracing the outline of the magnificent gold-leaf script on the cover of the holy book.

Claudia rushed after him and Erebus trotted, unhurriedly, along in her wake, sniffing the air and wondering what the strange, unfamiliar odours were that hung so thickly in the heavy air.

'Did you send for reinforcements, Captain Milliere?' Diomede chuckled as he caught sight of Lausard.

The sergeant saluted his own officers then turned to look at the grenadiers.

'What are you doing here, Claudia?' Burgomaster Keppler wanted to know.

'I went to this man for help, father,' she said, moving to the rotund man's side.

'How touching,' Diomede intoned.

'I have already encountered some of your men this morning, Captain,' Lausard told him. 'It seems their lack of respect and ill discipline comes from their commander.'

Diomede glared at the sergeant. 'I will have you arrested for speaking to an officer like that,' he rasped.

'Sergeant Lausard is under *my* command,' Milliere snapped. 'You have no authority over him. Only over your own rabble. And I suggest you instruct them to return those holy artifacts immediately. I thought the Guard was supposed to be the cream of the French army, not the dregs.'

'You would steal from a church,' the priest interjected. 'God will punish you for that.'

'Shut up, you old fool,' hissed the grenadier sergeant, pushing the priest away. 'God can spare these things. His kingdom is richer than any we have yet encountered.'

'Put them back,' Milliere said, flatly.

'This is none of your business, Captain,' Diomede told him, dismissively. 'Sergeant Merle, take these things away now. From this moment onwards, they are the property of the French army.'

'They belong only to God,' the priest persisted. 'I beg you, in His name, to return them.' He tried to drag one of the candlesticks from the grenadier's grip.

Merle pulled away angrily from the priest. Lausard stepped across the aisle blocking the way.

Merle met his gaze and held it. 'Step aside,' he hissed.

Lausard didn't move.

'You are not with your little German whore now,' the grenadier sergeant rasped. 'Get out of my way before I cut you down. Then, when I have dealt with you, perhaps I will have some fun with the girl.'

Keppler shot the grenadier sergeant an angry glance.

'If you want to pass me, you will do so with a sword in your hand,' Lausard said, evenly. 'If you have the courage to draw it. But I doubt if you will. Should you try, be grateful you are in a church. You are close to God. Try to pass *me* and you will be able to speak with Him in person very shortly.'

Merle dropped the candlestick and roared angrily, dragging his sword from its sheath in one fluid movement. Lausard imitated the action and steadied himself for the onslaught.

The other grenadiers also reached for their swords, but Milliere and Royere drew their own and held them close to the Guard cavalrymen.

'Keep your hands away from your swords,' Royere insisted.

Merle struck savagely and Lausard parried the blow, throwing the grenadier's blade off to one side, unbalancing him. He then stepped forward and drove his own sword at the Guard sergeant's unprotected side. Somehow, Merle managed to swing his own blade back in time to divert the thrust. The sound of steel on steel echoed around the church and those who had remained were now hurrying towards the main doors in a desperate bid to escape the insanity before them.

Claudia held tightly to her father and watched the fight, her breath coming in gasps.

Merle drove at Lausard again, powerful, accurate thrusts designed to pierce his chest or stomach, but each one was parried expertly. Lausard struck back with hammer blows that sent vibrations ringing the full length of the three-foot blades. Sparks erupted from the cutting edges upon each contact. Merle found himself backing towards the lectern. He stumbled and fell, the savage downward swipe Lausard had aimed at him cutting through the wood of the lectern and shaving a lump off. Lausard pressed his advantage and drove his sword down, intending to spear Merle through the throat, but the grenadier sergeant rolled to one side and the point of Lausard's blade screeched harmlessly across the cold stone floor of the church. The two men faced each other like gladiators. Lausard looked first at Merle's eyes, trying to see the direction from which the next attack would come. But he was also careful never to allow his gaze to stray too long from the gleaming sword his opponent held. An expert swordsman would often glance in a different direction to that at which he intended to strike purely to confuse his opponent. But Lausard was well versed in these techniques and tricks and, when the next wave of blows came at him, he met them with ease. Each powerful swipe and thrust was diverted. As Merle moved in close, Lausard ducked under a swipe and used his weight to slam his shoulder into the other man's chest, knocking him backwards. He then brought his head up under the Guard sergeant's chin. The impact cracked Merle's jaws together, forcing him to bite the side of his own tongue. Blood burst from his mouth as the collision sent him reeling. Lausard saw his opponent stumble and cut at his flailing arm.

The blade bit easily into the flesh of the forearm, the pain and severed tendons forcing Merle to release his weapon. It fell to the ground with a clang, blood spraying across the cold stone floor.

Diomede moved to retrieve the blade but Captain Milliere pressed his own sword gently against the Guard officer's chest and shook his head almost imperceptibly.

Merle dropped to his knees and reached for the sword with his other hand.

Lausard brought the heel of his boot down with incredible force on the grenadier sergeant's outstretched fingers. Two of the digits splintered under the impact and Merle's shriek of pain reverberated around the church.

He knelt helplessly in front of Lausard, who rested the wickedly sharp tip of his sword against the other man's throat.

'Finish it,' Merle hissed, defiantly.

'You cannot take a life in the house of God,' the priest implored.

'I have no wish to,' Lausard told him. 'I would not pollute my sword with the blood of one such as *this*.'

As he spoke, he drove one boot hard into the side of Merle's face, almost breaking his jaw. Two teeth fell from his bloodied mouth and skittered across the floor. The Guard sergeant lolled helplessly onto his back, his eyes rolling upwards in their sockets. The other two grenadiers made to help him but Royere waved his sword before them menacingly.

'Before you help him, put back what you have taken,' said the lieutenant.

The two men looked first at each other then at Diomede. He swallowed hard then nodded.

'A very wise decision, Captain,' Milliere said, withdrawing his sword and sheathing it. 'The next time you and your men decide to steal something, you should ensure there is less *capable* opposition.' He smiled thinly.

'You have not heard the last of this,' the Guard captain snarled. '*Any* of you.' He looked across at the other two men who were dragging the unconscious Merle to his feet, supporting him between them. 'If there were not army regulations forbidding duels, I would challenge you here and now.'

Milliere took a step forward. 'Do not feel constrained by those regulations, Captain,' he said, through clenched teeth. 'I am sure they could be overlooked just once.'

Diomede held his gaze for a moment longer, then pushed past, striding angrily towards the door.

Erebus growled at him as he passed.

The grenadiers stalked out of the church, and relative silence descended once again.

'Thank you,' said the priest. 'I thank you and so does God. I will ask Him to watch over you.'

'I do not need His thanks,' Lausard said, quietly. 'Or His protection. Let Him keep it for one who does.' He slid his sword back into its sheath.

Seven

—◆◆◆—

'I have been in Paris for less than six months of this new year and yet still the country teeters on the edge of a financial abyss. I have rarely left my apartments in the Tuileries, such has been the workload I have been forced to surmount. My *wife* has seen less of me than my ministers.'

Napoleon hurled a sheaf of papers furiously across the room and turned away from the other men in the chamber, who could only look on in silence as their Emperor's rage exploded with the ferocity of a November storm. Despite the heat outside the building, the windows were firmly closed and a number of the men in the room felt uncomfortable in the cloying atmosphere. It seemed as if the temperature was rising as steeply as the Corsican's temper.

Talleyrand coughed unobtrusively. 'We are all thankful that your brilliance in matters of state has rectified so many of the problems that were visited upon the country in your absence, sire,' the Foreign Minister said. 'A brilliance matched only on the field of battle.'

'I have no time for your platitudes, Talleyrand,' Napoleon barked. 'Save them for the state rooms of our enemies.'

The Foreign Minister nodded almost imperceptibly. 'I am at your Highness's command,' he said, sipping from a glass of water.

'Sire, much has been achieved since your return,' offered Nicholas Mollien. The Paymaster-General was a fox-faced man with a high forehead and small eyes and, when he spoke, he glanced at the others in the room as if seeking their approval for his words. 'France is in a much more financially stable condition now than she was when you first returned.'

'And at what cost, Mollien?' Napoleon said. 'The bankruptcy of thousands of businesses? It has taken the passing of new laws to regulate the flow of money and a revision of the system of accountancy. Undertaken, I might add, by yourself.'

'But those measures have been successful, sire,' Mollien offered. 'I fail to see why you continue to be so fearful for the financial future of France.'

'A balance of sixty million francs is still owing,' Napoleon reminded the Paymaster. 'You were present when I was forced to threaten merchants with their lives unless they handed over all of their assets to you.' His tone softened. 'When I left France in September last year I did not expect to return to find her in such dire straits. Perhaps I myself was to blame. I appointed the wrong men to the wrong offices. I placed my trust in those who were not fit to hold it.'

'But the money that is outstanding *will* be collected, sire,' Mollien insisted. 'From Spain. From the Pope. From Church properties.'

Napoleon wandered across to one of the closed

windows and finally pushed it open. A warm breeze swept into the room, sending some papers spinning to the floor. Mollien stooped to retrieve them.

'The problems that face France now, sire, are not *in*ternal,' Talleyrand added, watching the Paymaster shuffling the papers as if they were huge playing cards. 'But I am sure you do not need me to remind you of that.'

'No, Talleyrand, I do not. I do not need *anyone* to remind me that England once again is intent on war with France,' Napoleon said, wearily. 'Why is it always England? That wretched country has troubled me like some kind of persistant insect for more years than I care to remember. Nipping away. Causing discomfort and irritation. Now, since May of this year, she has blockaded French ports. Agitated within Europe. I thought when Pitt died I would no longer be troubled by that perfidious Albion, that nation of shop-keepers. It was always Pitt who sought war against us. Others in the English government would have been content to remain aloof from the struggles that did not concern them but there was always Pitt to encourage and goad them to war against France. Yet now, even though I am no longer plagued by him, his heritage lives on.'

'I feel the greater threat in Europe is from Russia, sire,' Talleyrand said, 'not from England. The treaty between ourselves and Russia, conducted by myself and Count d'Oubril at the beginning of the year, has yet to be ratified by the Tsar. Until it is, we have no guarantee that there is peace. And there is still the question of Prussia.'

Napoleon looked at his foreign minister quizzically.

'The territorial changes you initiated were not well received in Berlin,' Talleyrand continued.

'Then let King Frederick William mount some kind of opposition to my plans. The Prussian court is weak. Its king the weakest of all. There is more fight in his wife than there is in him.' The Corsican grinned.

Talleyrand did not share the joke.

'All I have done is what I said I would do,' Napoleon stated. 'When we spoke of these measures last year you offered no opposition to them. Why do you now suddenly fear the reactions of so weak and spineless a man as Frederick William?'

'You yourself declared a desire for peace in Europe, sire. To enable France to reassert herself financially. Should Prussia opt for war then that will be impossible.'

'Prussia has neither the desire nor the stomach for war,' Napoleon said, dismissively.

'As long as the Russians remain uncommitted to peace there is danger, sire. All I ask is that you consider that possibility. King Frederick William might see a strong possible ally in the Tsar and he would be correct in his assumption. The Prussians could field over two hundred thousand men, the Russians perhaps twice that number. It would be a powerful alliance should it see fruition. Once the Tsar has ratified our treaty of mutual non-aggression then I would also discount Prussian desire for war but, as you know, he has yet to do so.'

'The Prussians could not fully mobilise for three months even if they were to start today,' Napoleon sneered. 'The Tsar is no more anxious for war than I am myself.'

'Then why has he not made that fact plain, sire?' Talleyrand said, challengingly. 'All it would take for him to secure that peace would be a signature and yet still he refuses to supply it. To my mind, this is not the action of a man desperate to avoid hostilities. More so of a man biding his time. Perhaps he is waiting for the Prussians to make the first move before he commits his forces against France.'

Napoleon shook his head.

'I do not agree,' he said, flatly. 'The Tsar has nothing to gain from a war against France and the Prussians have neither the time nor the inclination to open hostilities.'

'But your proposals may push them into such a position that they find themselves with war as their *only* option, sire,' protested Talleyrand, vehemently. 'Your intention to dissolve the Holy Roman Empire removes even more power from Austria but they offer no threat anyway. The presence of French troops in Branau makes resistance unthinkable for them. But there is a growing antipathy towards the soldiers who still remain in Prussia. They are living at the expense of that country, sire. To begin with that was not a problem but your men have been there now for over seven months. Except most units of the Imperial Guard, not one single corps has been recalled to France since the war against Austria and Russia ended.' He reached into his pocket and pulled out a letter that he unfolded. 'Correspondence from a friend of mine, Madame de Monteglas,' the Foreign Minister said as he read aloud: '"I was fond of the French who drove out our enemies and who returned our legitimate rulers, but I detest those who live like leeches at the expense of our poor country."' He folded the letter and replaced it inside his jacket. 'There is a groundswell of anti-French feeling in Prussia, sire. It cannot and *should not* be ignored.'

'We have many allies within Prussia and along her borders, Talleyrand,' Napoleon said, quietly. 'Sixteen princes have already announced their willingness to separate from the Holy Roman Empire and enter into the formation of the Confederation of the Rhine. They have further promised to supply a military contingent of sixty-three thousand men. Thirty thousand from Bavaria, twelve thousand from Württemberg, eight thousand from Baden. Berg will supply five thousand, Hesse-Darmstadt another four thousand. Four thousand more troops will be drawn from other smaller states. Furthermore, Bavaria has already agreed to fortify Augsburg and Lindau. Should Prussia arm, the Confederation will immediately do likewise, but only upon *my* order.'

'With respect, sire, more than 150 years ago, Cardinal Mazarin formed the League of the Rhine,' Talleyrand reminded the Emperor. 'It was a failure. Even the Directory experimented along broadly similar lines. They, too, failed.'

'What are you saying, that my plans are doomed to fail also?'

'I am merely making a point, sire.'

'The Confederation is to be formed for the security of France,' said Napoleon, with an air of finality. 'I have suggested that Prussia will be allowed to form a confederation of its own northern states, should it feel that necessary. The northern confederation will look to Prussia for protection as that of the south looks to France.'

'And if that eventuality transpires, what of Saxony and Hesse-Cassel. Would they be allowed to choose which of the two confederations they joined?'

'It would be in the interests of Hesse-Cassel to join that of the south. I would tell their elector as much.'

'But he favours Prussia, sire. Some of these rulers are proud men. They would fight rather than see their country controlled by France. I fear they would rather go to war than lose their national identity to an army led by yourself.'

'That is their choice, Talleyrand. If they wish to fight then so be it. But they have more to gain by *joining* France than making war against her. Better to serve than to rule a kingdom of ashes.'

'Let us hope that the electors of Hesse-Cassel and Saxony can be tempted by the same bait that landed their brother sovereigns of Bavaria and Württemberg,' Talleryrand mused. 'With any luck, the lure of a crown may be sufficient to colour their judgement.'

'Saxony is fiercely independent,' said Napoleon, flatly. 'She has no wish to be drawn into the northern confederation and, should the Prussian court insist too vehemently on her allegiance, then they will serve only to drive her into *our* arms. Should Saxony join the Prussian cause, it would be as an *unwilling* ally. A man needs to know he can rely upon his allies, not fear their true intentions.'

'And what of England, sire?' Talleyrand said, finally. 'She will not be pacified so easily. If you wish to avoid war in Europe then some common ground must be found between France and England.'

'Between France and a country who already blockades our ports,' Napoleon snapped. He let out a long sigh and gazed once again out of the open window. 'Her king is German. What better way to appease him than by offering him part of his own homeland?'

Talleyrand looked puzzled.

'I will offer him Hanover,' said the Corsican.

'Sire, you gave Hanover to Prussia.'

'Then I will take it back.'

'With respect, sire, should you do that, then I can see no way of avoiding war with Prussia. There will come a time when they will feel compelled to strike back. You cannot continue to heap insults upon King Frederick William and not expect him to respond with force. I fear that the retrocession of Hanover would be the final indignity and one that even Prussia could not ignore. War would be the only possible outcome of such action.'

Napoleon did not answer. He merely gazed out of the open window, the light breeze gently ruffling his hair.

The town of Fürstenberg boasted an inn just off the main square and another on the road that led out of town to the west. Both were similar in appearance and size. Both offered six rooms to weary travellers as well as food and a good selection of wines, ale and spirits. Some were brewed on farms close by and, during their time in and around the town, Alain Lausard and his men had found the locally fermented drinks to be not only the most palatable but also the most potent. One stein of beer was enough to floor even the most prolific drinker. Lausard had seen it happen on more than one occasion since the dragoons had arrived in Fürstenberg. He had stood around sipping schnapps, laughing and joking with the locals as his companions had drunk themselves into oblivion. More than once, troopers had been taken back to the makeshift barracks strapped across their saddles, incapable of sitting upright. Captain Milliere had encouraged rather than frowned on the activities of his men, feeling that the more contact they had with the locals, the less antagonism would be generated against them. It had been sound reasoning in the beginning. Songs had been sung, both in French and German. Songs about the Revolution. Songs about Frederick the Great. Both sides had joined in with gusto, eager to learn the words sung by those who would normally be their enemies. So it had been when the dragoons first arrived. During the past few months so much had changed.

Lausard tethered his horse to a wooden rail outside the inn on the main road and waited for Rocheteau and Sonnier to do the same. A little further down the road, Delacor and Roussard urged their horses on through the dusk to join their companions. Erebus bounded along beside them, occasionally barking in the direction of birds returning to their nests in the sky above. Only when all five dragoons had dismounted did Lausard make to open the door.

'They don't want us here,' said Roussard. 'Why do we come?'

'To drink,' said Delacor, impatiently. 'If you didn't

want to come you should have stayed behind.'

'Everything was fine until those stinking "big boots" arrived here,' Sonnier hissed. 'Why are they still in the town? I thought they were supposed to be going back to France.'

'So did *they*,' Lausard reminded him. 'They must be here for a reason. Every order Bonaparte gives has a purpose. He would not merely have forgotten about them.'

'And as long as *they* are here, they poison the townspeople against *us*,' Sonnier protested. 'Before they arrived we were welcomed. Now we are hated as much as they. Yet they are the ones who have treated those who live here so cruelly. The ones who have stolen and cheated. They are the ones who have brought dishonour upon the French army.'

'I wonder what our Emperor would have said had he seen their conduct these past five months,' Delacor sneered.

'Whatever *they* have done there is nothing *we* can do to change it,' Lausard reminded his companions. He patted the head of the great black dog and the animal sat down contentedly close to the door of the inn.

'And they're still threatening to kill us,' Delacor chuckled. 'I'd like to see them try.'

Lausard pushed open the door of the inn and the dragoons wandered into the building.

There were already a dozen locals inside, drinking and talking. Some were sitting around a small table playing cards. As the dragoons entered, some heads turned in their direction but, for the most part, they were ignored. Roussard nodded a greeting towards a large man near the fireplace but the man merely sipped at his beer and ignored the gesture. The innkeeper, an overweight man with huge hands and a rotund face, looked indifferently at the troopers then continued wiping the bar surface with a damp cloth.

'Beer for us all,' Lausard said, attempting a smile. He dug in the pocket of his jacket and pulled out several coins, which he spread on the bar while the innkeeper filled five steins from a barrel behind him. He put each one down on the counter and the dragoons retrieved them.

'*Prost*,' said Lausard, raising his own drink in the direction of the watching locals.

No one responded to the toast.

'To hell with them,' Delacor murmured and drank deeply.

Lausard took a long swallow of beer, wiping his mouth with the back of his hand.

As he turned, he was aware of the innkeeper pushing something across the bar towards him. When he glanced down he saw that it was a sheet of paper. It was roughly printed, some of the letters askew, but it was still clear enough to read.

'Your Emperor may have murdered the man who wrote this but there are many who agree with his sentiments,' said the innkeeper, sharply.

'You would do well to burn that,' Rocheteau said, indicating the piece of paper, 'otherwise you may meet the same fate as its author.'

'What is this rubbish anyway?' Delacor snatched the paper from Lausard.

'It was printed by a bookseller called Palm,' Lausard explained. 'It preaches Prussian nationalism. It exhorts the people of this country to rise up against us. Bonaparte ordered Palm arrested and shot. He was taken from neutral territory under the command of Marshal Berthier.'

'Just as the Duke of Enghien before him,' Rocheteau murmured.

'A Bourbon prince was more of a threat than a German bookseller,' Sonnier chuckled.

The other dragoons laughed.

'He was not alone in his feelings,' the innkeeper stated. 'What he writes is true. This country is ours. You have no right to be here.'

Delacor screwed up the piece of paper and tossed it contemptuously away.

'We do not *want* to be here,' he snapped, 'any more than you would have us. If we had a choice we would all rather be in our own country.'

'Then why don't you leave us?' asked the big man beside the fireplace. 'You *and* those other bastards who infest our town.'

'They are nothing to do with us,' Lausard told him. 'We await their departure as eagerly as you and your countrymen.'

'The time may come when you are *driven* out,' said the innkeeper. 'Not just from here but from all over our country.'

'Would you do as Palm suggested?' Lausard wanted to know. 'Would you fight if you had to?'

'This is my country. I would die for it.'

'Very few things are worth dying for,' Lausard told him. 'But many are worth *killing* for. The difference is a subtle but important one.'

The other dragoons laughed once more.

'We are already at war with England,' said the man beside the fire. 'Seven hundred of our ships have been impounded in English ports. Our own Baltic ports are blockaded by the English navy. What difference does it make if we go to war with France too?'

'If you go to war with France, you will lose,' Rocheteau said, flatly. '*That* is the difference.'

'Your king has no desire for war,' Lausard interjected. 'If he had then we would already be fighting. I doubt that Frederick the Great would have waited as his son does.'

'He shames the memory of his father by his inaction,' said one of the men playing cards. 'I served under "old Fritz" at Rossbach. I helped destroy your army then and I would do so again if called upon.'

'Your king has none of the qualities of his father,' Lausard said, dismissively. 'On *or* off the battlefield.'

'I have heard that our Emperor admires Frederick the Great,' Roussard noted. 'He says that his ghost still looks down upon this country.'

'If all the Prussians have to send against us are ghosts then we have little to fear,' sneered Delacor.

'Our time will come,' the innkeeper said, angrily. 'And when it does, we will kick you and all those like you back across our borders to where you belong. Those of you who are still alive. Now, why don't you finish your drinks and get out?'

'Yes,' intoned another of the men playing cards. 'The burgomaster's whore of a daughter might be waiting for you.'

Lausard glanced at each of the men in turn, then he downed what was left in his stein and pushed it across the bar.

'Do not return here,' said the innkeeper as the dragoons made their way towards the door. 'You are not welcome.'

Rocheteau slammed the door behind them.

'To hell with them,' grumbled Delacor.

Lausard and the other men swung themselves into their saddles and set off. Erebus loped along after them, occasionally dashing off into the long grass at the edge of the road when he scented a hare or a fox. Sometimes they heard barking out of sight in the night-shrouded woods. Each time the dog scurried back to join the dragoons as they rode on. High in the sky, the moon was struggling to fight its way from behind banks of scudding cloud.

'Why doesn't the Emperor just give the order for us to go home?' Roussard muttered, his voice barely audible above the jingle of harnesses and the clatter of hooves.

'Because this is obviously where he wants us to be,' Lausard offered. 'Us and so many more like us.'

'It makes no sense to have trained men sitting on their arses in a country where they are neither useful nor where they wish to be,' snapped Delacor.

'On the contrary,' Lausard told him. 'It makes perfect sense. Bonaparte has the finest army in Europe within striking distance of Berlin.'

'Do you think that is his plan, Alain?' Rocheteau asked.

'I do not pretend to know the way Bonaparte's mind works, but it is a thought that cannot be ignored.'

'War with Prussia,' murmured Roussard.

'We have fought everyone else in Europe,' grunted Delacor. 'It would appear *their* time has come at last.'

Up ahead, Erebus was barking furiously. The dog was standing in the road looking into the dark mass of trees to the right of the highway, alternately snarling or growling at something as yet invisible to the dragoons. Lausard watched the dog for a moment then pulled on his reins and slowed his horse. The other men did the same, not really knowing why but puzzled at the reactions of the sergeant who was gazing almost fixedly between the dog and the woods at which it barked. Had the animal scented another fox or rabbit, Lausard mused? If so, why did it not just chase off into the undergrowth as it had done before? Erebus continued to bark furiously, the sound reverberating through the stillness.

'That dog is insane,' Delacor murmured.

'Just like the rest of us,' Lausard muttered, still not taking his eyes from the animal.

The gunshot that rang out startled them all.

Lausard heard the air close to him part as the heavy lead ball sped past him before slamming into a tree on the other side of the road.

Rocheteau pulled a pistol from the holsters on the front of his saddle.

Lausard drew his sword.

Sonnier quickly slid his carbine from its boot and hefted it up against his shoulder.

The other dragoons also armed themselves, now

looking to right and left trying to detect the source of the shot.

Erebus suddenly bolted into the bushes, still barking loudly.

'There,' Lausard snapped, pointing to a steadily growing pall of smoke that was drifting from the trees in the direction the dog had gone.

Another shot rang out.

Roussard's horse reared wildly and it was all he could do to keep the animal under control, but he dug his knees into its sides and gripped the reins firmly in his free hand until his mount calmed.

Lausard leapt from his saddle and crashed through the undergrowth, sword held before him. Rocheteau followed, thumbing back the hammer of his pistol. Sonnier slipped the bayonet onto the muzzle of his carbine and joined his two companions.

'We'll watch the road,' Delacor called as he rode in one direction and Roussard the other.

As he left the highway, Lausard found that the undergrowth was thicker than he'd first realised. He had to push his way through bushes that, in places, were as tall as he. Low branches also grabbed at him like skeletal fingers and he used the blade of his sword to push the thick undergrowth aside. He could hear Erebus ahead of him, still barking loudly. Behind him, his two colleagues also advanced, weapons at the ready. Rocheteau slipped on some mossy ground and almost overbalanced but, cursing under his breath, he moved on. For fleeting seconds, Lausard questioned the wisdom of hurtling into the bushes and trees. It was dark; they could see barely two feet ahead. If someone was trying to kill them, then he and his companions might well be aiding them. Even now he may be walking into the sites of a musket. The thought passed quickly. All that mattered was reaching their assailant. No more shots had been fired since they dismounted. Whoever had fired had either fled or was reloading. Or waiting? Again the thought passed through Lausard's mind. There could be one attacker or half a dozen but, he reasoned, six or seven men would have kept up a steady fire until the dragoons had been hit or driven off. The shots that had been fired had been random.

He heard the movement of his companions close by him. Trained to operate in any terrain or surroundings, they were ducked low to the ground and hurrying through the undergrowth, causing the minimum of disturbance. Sonnier pushed branches aside with the bayonet of his carbine. Lausard used the blade of his sword. All three men had slowed to a walk now, wary of any sounds or movement ahead of them. The sergeant glanced up into the trees that rose above them. There was always the possibility that the sniper might have sought refuge there. Hidden by the darkness and canopy of leaves, a man could remain virtually invisible. Even now, someone might be up there, preparing to fire on them again. A small bead of perspiration trickled from beneath Lausard's helmet. He told himself that it was the warmth of the night.

Up ahead, Erebus began barking furiously.

Lausard and the other two dragoons hurried in the direction of the sound and found the animal standing

over a patch of muddied ground and flattened grass.
The sergeant knelt, examining the terrain. When he stood
up he had something gripped between his fingers.
Rocheteau took it from him.

'Cartridge paper,' he murmured, sniffing the blackened material.

'There's another,' Lausard said, crushing it into the
ground with his boot.

'Alain, look,' Sonnier murmured, indicating the base
of the tree close to them.

There were several unused cartridges lying there and
he rested his own carbine against the trunk as he
inspected them.

'Prussian?' Rocheteau asked.

Sonnier fumbled in his cartouche and pulled out one
of his own cartridges. He laid it on his palm next to one
of the others. They were identical.

'French,' Lausard said, flatly. 'It looks as if someone
on our own side is trying to kill us.'

Eight

◆◆◆◆◆

Sound travels on still air. The slightest noise is amplified by solitude – a fact that Lausard had found advantageous over the years. The still of the night made it difficult for an enemy to approach too closely without detection. But, in an army billet, the small hours are filled with many sounds and now, as he lay awake on his bunk, he listened to those he had grown so accustomed to during the last ten or eleven years. The chorus of grunts, snores, breaking wind and dream-murmurs that the men around him made. All these sounds rose to greater volume during the blackness of night. Especially for a man like Alain Lausard for whom sleep was such an elusive commodity. It was little wonder that he was the first to hear the steadily rising thunder of horses' hooves approaching from the direction of Fürstenberg. The sergeant swung himself out of bed and pulled on his boots, reaching immediately for one of his pistols. The sound of hooves was growing louder. At the far end of the barracks, Erebus also stirred and got to his feet, standing close by the door as Lausard approached. He rubbed the dog's head and it nuzzled up against him, as puzzled by the intrusive sounds as the dragoon himself. For a moment, Lausard wondered if the war they had all anticipated had finally broken out. Were the horses heading towards them light cavalrymen bringing news of the outbreak of hostilities? Were they indeed Prussian cavalry, ready to sweep Lausard and his invaders from their homeland? Thoughts tumbled through his mind as he walked to the door, the sound of hooves now even louder.

Others had now woken, some disturbed by Lausard's movements, more by the sound of the approaching horses. Joubert, however, continued to snore. So too did Rostov. Only when Lausard kicked their beds as he passed did they find themselves ripped from the blissful oblivion of sleep.

'What's going on, Alain?' Rocheteau said, rubbing his eyes and sliding the knife from his belt.

'Horses,' said Giresse, aware of the sound.

Others also heard. Sonnier thumbed back the hammer of his carbine.

'No more than two,' Karim said, quietly.

'How the hell can you be so sure?' Delacor wanted to know, reaching into his portmanteau for the axe he always kept there. 'There could be hundreds of them.'

'If there were hundreds we'd have been shaken out of our beds,' Tabor offered.

'Shut up, you half-wit,' Delacor snapped, padding towards Lausard in his threadbare socks.

'There are just two,' the Circassian said with an air of finality.

'It's three-thirty in the morning,' Bonet said, glancing at his watch.

'We can all tell the time, schoolmaster,' Delacor said, 'but it seems whoever's out there *can't*.'

Lausard had edged the door open slightly and peered out into the blackness. Sentries were rarely posted. The dragoons were on foreign soil but, until the past few months, there had been no signs of hostility. Captain Milliere had advised the sergeant to post sentries only if he felt it necessary. He was beginning to wish that he'd done so this particular night. Several of the other dragoons had retrieved their carbines and were positioned at the windows, ready to fire if the need arose. Sonnier pulled the Charleville in tighter to his shoulder and squinted down the sight.

'Maybe it's the bastards who shot at us earlier,' Rocheteau offered. 'They might have come back for another try.'

'If that's the case, they wouldn't have come on horses, would they?' Lausard murmured, his gaze never leaving the direction from which the onrushing hooves came.

'I can see them,' called Sonnier. 'Karim was right. There are just two.'

Lausard thumbed back the hammer of his pistol.

He too could see the horsemen now. They were riding fast. He was sure there was something familiar about them. When he spotted the flowing horsehair manes on the crests of their helmets he realised what it was. They were dressed in the uniforms of dragoons. He took a step outside, followed by two or three of his companions. It was only as the two riders came within twenty yards that Lausard recognised them as Captain Milliere and Lieutenant Royere. The presence of the officers served only to inflame his curiosity. Both men brought their mounts to a halt and the sergeant could see that both horses were slightly lathered. The ride from Fürstenberg had obviously been completed with great speed and urgency.

'Sergeant, bring six of your men into Fürstenberg immediately,' Milliere said. 'Fully armed. Those who remain are also to arm and stand ready.'

'May I ask what is happening, Captain?' Lausard said. 'Has war been declared against Prussia?'

'Nothing so simple,' Milliere told him, wearily.

'There has been a murder in the town,' Royere informed the sergeant. 'Our troops are suspected. The burgomaster is threatening to arm the local *Landwehr*.'

'You and six of your men,' Milliere said, wheeling his horse. 'As quickly as you can. Meet us at the church.'

'Who is dead, Captain?' Lausard called after the officers.

'The burgomaster's daughter,' Milliere told him.

As the seven dragoons rode into the town square of Fürstenberg, it seemed as if a light burned in the window of every house. Lausard felt as if eyes were watching them from every corner of the square, from every secret vantage point. The sound of their horses' hooves echoed on the cobbled square but there were other noises filling the gloom too. Shouts occasionally came from houses, furious, angry bellows directed at the dragoons. They kept their faces to the front as they rode, only too aware of the ferocity of the words flung in their direction. From the upstairs window of a house nearby, someone spat at them. From another, the contents of a chamber pot were hurled towards them. Bonet's horse neighed as the foul-smelling fluid splashed it, but the former schoolmaster kept a tight hold on the animal's reins and it continued along without breaking stride. Lausard saw figures moving about in the gloom, passing across the square. Dozens of men, some carrying muskets, some holding shovels or pitchforks. Every so often, one would stop to glare up at the cavalrymen. Lausard met their gaze, his face belying no emotion. Two men stood in the path of the dragoons, one of them shouting something in German. Lausard waved a hand, signalling to the men to step aside. Neither moved until the sergeant's horse gently bumped them, and only then did they reluctantly allow him to pass. Both of them continued to yell angrily as the green-clad troops rode on.

As they drew nearer the church, Lausard saw more of the townspeople gathered on the steps leading to the main doors. As the dragoons came within twenty yards, all faces turned in their direction. As the cavalrymen dismounted, they were aware of the furious expressions etched on the faces of those watching them.

'Rostov. You and Sonnier stay with the horses,' the sergeant instructed.

'Come to take another look at your crime?' shouted a voice from the crowd.

'Alain, what do we do if they attack us?' Rostov wanted to know.

'Draw your swords. Protect the horses. Don't retaliate unless you have to. If there is direct danger to either of you then defend yourselves.'

Rostov looked unsure.

'Don't kill anyone unless you have to,' Lausard said, flatly. 'But if it's unavoidable then do it.'

'Murdering bastards,' someone else shouted as Lausard and the other four dragoons mounted the steps to the main doors of the church. The sergeant pushed the wooden partition and the men stepped inside.

There were candles burning at the far end of the high-ceilinged building but few other places. The shadows they threw were long and dark. It looked as if the night air had seeped across the stone floor of the church like some kind of indelible stain. Lausard could see that there were several figures huddled around the altar. As he and his companions walked along the nave, the sound of their boot heels echoed through the stillness. Sword scabbards scraped the stone floor like blades against sharpeners.

As they came closer, the sergeant could see Captain Milliere and Lieutenant Royere standing close to the altar. With them were the priest, the burgomaster and another man whom Lausard recognised as the town doctor, Heide. A tall, thin man with a shock of red hair, he was crouched over something that lay on the altar itself. A shape shrouded in a blood-stained white sheet.

'Come and see what your butchers have done,' shouted the burgomaster as Lausard and his companions drew nearer. The older man's face was wet with tears, his eyes puffy and red. He took a step towards the sergeant but Milliere put out a restraining hand. He also shook loose of that, glaring at the captain and not allowing himself to be restrained until Doctor Heide put a hand on his shoulder.

'Your anger will do your daughter no good now,' Heide said, softly.

The priest crossed himself.

Keppler took a step back, his gaze never leaving the faces of the dragoons.

'What happened?' Lausard wanted to know.

It was Lieutenant Royere who lifted the sheet, exposing the shape beneath.

Lausard and the other dragoons stepped forward. Keppler finally turned away, his anguished sobs rising to the very heights of the church and beyond. The huge wooden figure of Christ, suspended above the altar, looked on impassively.

The body of Claudia Keppler was naked but for some shreds of material – all that remained of her tattered dress. Lausard could see the savage gash across her throat that had ended her life. There were a dozen more lacerations around her face, hands and arms. Bruises disfigured her once beautiful features. There were more on her breasts and the inside of her thighs. Lausard even saw one close to her left little toe. It was as if every single detail of her mutilation was imprinted upon his vision. Seared into his retina like a brand.

'Who found her?' he wanted to know, his eyes never leaving the ravaged corpse.

'What do *you* care?' Keppler called. 'If she had done as I ordered her and stayed away from you and your kind, this would not have happened.'

'She was found by one of the townspeople,' Milliere said. 'They brought her here.'

'They brought her back to the house of God,' said the priest, looking around at the dragoons. 'They brought her to rest in His arms once more.'

'And where was your God when *this* was being done to her?' Lausard snapped, nodding towards the corpse.

'She was also raped,' Heide said, walking across to the altar. 'I realised that upon my first examination.'

'Raped and murdered,' Keppler rasped.

'What has this to do with us, Captain?' Lausard asked.

'She was always with you,' the burgomaster interrupted. 'No matter how many times I forbade it. She would return to see you and your men. And now it has cost her her life.'

'She brought us gifts, she treated us kindly. Why would any of *us* want to do her harm?' the sergeant enquired.

'Because you are animals,' Keppler snarled. 'You and all of those like you. Not content with occupying our country, now you resort to this. To an act so foul even a monster would not countenance it.'

'Where was the body found?' Lausard asked.

'On one of the roads leading from town,' Milliere told him. 'The road that leads to your barracks, Sergeant.'

'Is that how you repay her kindness,' Keppler said, bitterly, 'by raping and murdering her? You should *all* be hanged.'

'For a magistrate you seem to have forgotten that a man is innocent until proven guilty, Herr Keppler,' Lausard said. 'Believe me, I share your sorrow for what has happened to your daughter. If I thought my sympathy would aid your suffering then I would offer it. But I fear it will not.'

'I do not want your sympathy,' Keppler hissed. 'I want your confession.'

'For what? A crime that I did not commit?'

'You are in the house of God,' the priest reminded him. 'You cannot lie now.'

'I have no need to lie, priest,' Lausard said, flatly. 'In the presence of your God or not. I nor any of my men.' He looked at Milliere. 'Do you doubt my word, Captain?'

The officer shook his head.

'I know it was not you or any of your men, Sergeant. I have known you too long to think otherwise. I know you for the man you *are*, not the man Herr Keppler would have you be.'

'*You* have not lost a daughter tonight,' Keppler shouted, jabbing an accusatory finger at the officer. 'I do not expect you to stand against one of your own, no matter what they have done.'

'Do you think I would tolerate any of my men doing something like *this*?' Milliere hissed, pulling the sheet back further. 'If I thought for one second that any of them were guilty of such a crime, I myself would knot the rope that would hang them.'

Rocheteau continued to gaze down at the body, shaking his head almost imperceptibly.

Bonet turned away and wandered across towards one of the stained-glass windows, gazing up into the multi-coloured panels as if seeking solace there.

Karim bowed his head reverentially. 'Would that her suffering was short,' the Circassian whispered. 'In the name of Allah, all praise to Him.'

'What a waste,' Giresse murmured. 'What kind of

man could do that to so delicate a blossom?'

'You are all killers,' the burgomaster said, accusingly. 'How many men have you murdered? Why would any of you find it so difficult to slaughter a woman the way my child has been slaughtered?'

'We kill on the battlefield because we have to,' Rocheteau said. 'Because we are soldiers. No other reason.'

'It is in your blood. Your instincts are to kill. When my daughter resisted your vile advances you butchered her.'

'Someone did,' said Lausard. 'But not one of us. Believe it if you wish but we know the truth of the matter.'

'I have only your word. Why should I believe it?'

'Because it is all you have.'

'The word of an invader is worth little. Your oaths are as empty as your souls.'

'How close to home have you looked, Herr Keppler?' Lausard wanted to know. 'How many of the local men did your daughter know? How many of *them* wanted her? How many would be capable of doing this to her if she refused their advances? How many had *already* enjoyed her company?'

'You seek now to besmirch her memory,' Keppler said, sniffing back tears. 'You would brand her a whore?'

'I said nothing of the kind,' Lausard reminded him. 'I would simply ask you how well you knew your own child.'

'Have you ever lost anyone close to you? I doubt it. If you had you would know the pain I am feeling. Pray that you never have to experience the torment I now endure.'

'I have felt and seen enough suffering to last me *two* lifetimes,' Lausard rasped. 'Do not presume to lecture me on loss, Magistrate.'

Lieutenant Royere lowered the bloodied sheet back into place, hiding the body from view.

'So, how do we find her killer?' the officer said, quietly.

'It is no business of yours,' Keppler snapped. 'The only way you can help is by handing over the men who did this.'

'None of my men were responsible for your daughter's death,' Milliere said, flatly. 'If you want to find her murderer you must look elsewhere.'

'Already your townspeople are infected with the same hatred that afflicts you,' Lausard added. 'Stop this contagion before it spreads beyond control.'

'Are you threatening me now?' Keppler wanted to know.

'One innocent life has been lost. Let us ensure it is the only one,' Milliere said. 'Speak to your people. Make them understand that we abhor this crime as much as they. We will do all in our power to help you find your daughter's killer, but we cannot do so if we are to be treated as if we were already guilty.'

'I cannot answer for the reactions of the townspeople,' Keppler said. 'Most of them have known my daughter since she was a child. I might not be able to control their rage.'

'Then I will take the necessary steps to ensure that none of my men are injured by your lynch mobs,' Milliere told the burgomaster. 'If they are attacked, they will retaliate. I can assure you of that.'

'You seem very certain, Captain.'

'I am. Because *I* will give them the order to do so.'

'Why do you presume to blame us when there are other French troops in Fürstenberg?' Rocheteau wanted to know.

'My daughter has been seen with you,' Keppler snapped. 'I know what kind of men you are. I have heard talk in the town that you are all criminals. You cannot hide who you are behind your uniforms.'

'We have neither the *need* nor the desire to hide,' Lausard told the older man. 'Any of us.'

The two men locked stares until finally Keppler turned away and glanced up towards the huge wooden figure of Christ as if seeking guidance.

'Have you spoken to the others?' Lausard wanted to know. 'To Captain Diomede and his grenadiers?'

Heide shook his head.

'Then I suggest that you do,' the sergeant continued.

'You seek to put the blame on others now,' Keppler snapped. 'You know that it was *you* my daughter was infatuated with.' He pointed at Lausard. 'Her body was found on the road leading to *your* barracks.'

Lausard suddenly drew his sword and stepped towards the burgomaster. The metallic hiss as the steel left the sheath echoed around the church.

'Is your daughter's blood on my blade?' he rasped.

Keppler moved backwards.

'Look at it,' Lausard snarled, pushing the three-foot sword towards the burgomaster. 'Her blood is *not* there but soon *yours* may be.' He sheathed the weapon as swiftly as he'd drawn it. 'I would not have hurt her, you have my word. But then, the value of a man's word is best measured by the worth of the one he *gives* it to.'

Lausard turned and looked at Milliere.

'Is there anything else, Captain?' he asked.

The officer shook his head. 'You may go,' Milliere said. 'But be careful. Remember what I said. If you are attacked, you have my permission to defend yourselves.'

'Let us hope it does not come to that,' Royere added.

'Give me a day and I will find the killer,' said Lausard. He looked at Keppler. 'That *is* what you want, isn't it?'

The burgomaster nodded almost imperceptibly.

'Where will you look?' Milliere called as Lausard and his companions headed for the doors of the church.

'Whoever killed Claudia was vermin,' the sergeant answered. 'I intend to visit the nest.'

Nine

The linen cloth was as white as freshly fallen snow. It covered the long dining table from one end to the other. The table itself was of polished oak and it needed to be strong to bear the amount of food piled upon it. Silver dishes, wine glasses, porcelain plates and solid silver cutlery festooned the table from end to end, despite the fact that there were only two diners at the table. Both were shrouded in deep shadow. The room was lit only by the light of two large gold candlesticks. The flames flickered occasionally as breezes caressed them. The sound of cutlery against china echoed around the stillness of the room.

Napoleon jabbed his fork into a piece of chicken, scraping some of the rich, aromatic sauce from the fowl before he pushed it into his mouth. He looked up, to the far end of the table, and watched the other occupant of the room for a moment. The Empress Josephine saw him looking at her and afforded him a smile.

'Dunan will be angry if you send back his food again as you did last night,' she said, quietly, dabbing at the corners of her mouth with a napkin.

'I will risk his anger,' Napoleon grinned. 'He knows all too well what I like to eat. That my tastes are simple. Chicken with garlic. Lentils. Eggs. Tomatoes. Langoustines. Yet he serves me up these complex dishes knowing full well I am unable to stomach them.'

'He expects meals to be serious, unhurried affairs. Accompanied by rich sauces and a lavish variety of desserts.'

'He makes me overeat.'

'You eat like a soldier, my husband. Quickly and with little appreciation of what you consume.'

'How else do you expect me to eat? What am I if not a soldier?'

'Emperor of France.'

'A man's position in life does not alter his eating habits,' he observed, sipping his Chambertin. As ever, it was diluted with water from a jug close to the Emperor's elbow. 'I ask my own chef for sausages and he refuses, saying they are vulgar. What am I to do with this man?' He pushed his plate away from him.

'You have not eaten very much,' Josephine observed. 'Is the food *so* unpleasant?'

'I have other things on my mind,' he told her. 'Matters that are unaffected by either a full or an empty belly.'

'War?'

'Why should my thoughts be concerned with war?'

'Aren't they?'

He sipped more of his burgundy and reached for a piece of bread, pulling it apart and chewing small pieces.

'I sought to avoid conflict,' he said, quietly. 'Had the Tsar ratified the peace treaty made between France and

Russia back in January then I would have achieved my aim. Yet, only today, I was informed of his refusal to do so. News of this has spread to the Prussian court too. King Frederick William may well seek war against France knowing that he has the backing of Russia. He is a weak man with strong allies. Perhaps even now he would not be so foolish as to send his armies against me.'

'And what if he does?'

'Then I will destroy them as I will any force arrayed against me. I seek to make France strong; if it brings me into conflict with other nations then that is the price I am willing to pay.'

'You speak of peace and yet your every action is designed to provoke war. Do you love it so much?'

He regarded her silently for a moment.

'I am not the one who is threatening war,' the Corsican said, finally. 'I am not the aggressor.'

'And what of your brothers? How quickly will they come to your aid? How happy will they be to risk their new-found kingdoms? Kingdoms that you have bestowed upon them. Your brother Joseph sits grandly on the throne of Naples. Louis is King of Holland. You fought so long to rid France of the tyranny of Kingship and yet now you create new monarchs wherever you wish.'

'I have the right to reward members of my family as I see fit,' Napoleon told his wife. 'Did I not reward *you* with the title of Empress?'

'When you placed the crown upon my head I thought that you did it as a token of love, not to reward me as you would reward a faithful pet. I understood that you wanted me to rule at your side. Do you buy my loyalty with jewels and crowns? With regal promises? I never asked you for that honour, unlike your family, who follow you as jackals follow a beast of prey. They argue and fight over the scraps you throw them and still they are not satisfied. They will not be so until I am no longer their Empress. They despise me. They always have.'

'That is not true.'

'It is all too true and you know it to be so.'

'Their jealously blinds them to our love,' the Corsican told her, lowering his gaze.

'Still you defend them.'

'They are my family,' Napoleon shouted, angrily. 'What would you have me do? Abandon them?' He poured himself some more burgundy and sipped slowly from the glass.

'They feed from you like parasites,' Josephine mused, brushing some strands of her gleaming, long dark hair from her shoulder. 'And I know what they whisper to you when you are alone with them.'

The Emperor looked quizzically at his wife.

'They tell you of your need for an heir,' she said, quietly. 'An heir that *I* cannot give you.'

A heavy silence descended, finally broken by Napoleon, who sat forward in his chair. 'We have discussed this matter before,' he murmured. 'Many times. You know how important it is that what I have created must *not* die with me. Too many men have given their lives to make France what she is today. I will not see her returned to the hands of the Bourbons. I need to know that, when I die, my bloodline will continue. That everything I have striven and suffered for is not lost.'

'And the only way you can do that is if I give you an heir, and you know that is impossible. What future is there for us? Or for France if I am unable to fulfil my duties not only as a wife but as a *woman*? How do you think that makes me feel? I am incomplete. There will be no children from this marriage. You have known that for some time. Yet you still pretend to love me.'

'It is no pretence,' he snapped. 'I married you because I wanted to spend my life with you, not for you to act as some kind of brood mare for me.'

'You have a love for France that I know *I* can never taste. You are devoted to this country.'

'As I am to you,' he said, flatly.

'France is your mistress,' said Josephine. 'I can never hope to compete with her.'

Napoleon opened his mouth to speak but the Empress pressed a finger to her lips as if to silence him. 'I know well enough your *true* thoughts,' she told the Corsican. 'I understand your needs. I realise the consequences should France be left without an heir. Not one night passes that I do not pray for the fulfilment of that dream. But it would appear that God has seen fit to ignore my pleas.'

In the candlelight, Napoleon thought he could see tears in her eyes.

'If our marriage is to be childless then so be it,' he murmured, finally.

'And you would accept that?'

He drained his glass then sighed. 'What choice would I have?'

The Corsican got to his feet, dropping his napkin

onto his plate. Josephine watched as he headed towards the double doors that led out of the dining room. He paused for a moment, his back to her. For fleeting seconds she thought he was going to speak but, instead, he merely pulled open the doors and walked out, his footsteps echoing away down the corridor. She considered following him or at least calling out but she realised it would serve no useful purpose. She sat motionless in the massive room, alone but for her thoughts.

Alain Lausard sat astride his horse and watched as the mounted grenadiers of the Guard rode back and forth in regulation formation and at the specified pace. He ran a hand through his long brown hair and glanced up briefly at the sun, which had risen high in the cloudless sky. Hidden in the thick woods that overlooked the field where the grenadiers drilled, Lausard watched the elite horsemen as they performed manoeuvres which had become so commonplace to himself and his companions over the years. From line to column and back again. All changes of formation performed at the trot or the gallop. Captain Diomede rode at the head of his troops, his long straight sword held before him, the blasts of the trumpet signalling those orders he could not communicate by shouting over the rattle of so many harnesses and the pounding of so many hooves. Lausard watched impassively, counting every trooper as they passed back and forth.

'Thirty-five including Diomede,' he said, finally.

Rocheteau nodded and patted the neck of his own mount to steady it.

'What they do they do no better than us,' Delacor hissed. 'The Guard.' He hawked loudly and spat. 'They are the Emperor's toy soldiers.'

On a branch above them, a bird sang, cocking its head to one side as it gazed down at the green-clad men. It watched them for a moment longer, then, seemingly tiring of their presence, it flew away. Lausard watched it soaring out over the field where Diomede and his grenadiers continued to drill. Erebus also watched the bird, resisting the temptation to bark at it. The sergeant turned his horse and led it back through the undergrowth towards the road. Waiting there were a dozen more of his companions. All eyes turned towards Lausard as he led the bay to the head of the small column, pausing a moment until Rocheteau joined him, Erebus trotting along unhurriedly beside him. Then the dragoons set off.

Dust rose in thick clouds from the dirt road that wound its way through the hills to the south of Fürstenberg. The summer months had delivered little rain and the ground was parched. Rostov, Tigana and some of the other men who had been brought up on farms had remarked that the men who worked the land in this part of Bavaria might well find themselves with slim pickings come the autumn. Crops such as wheat, maize and corn flourished in the arid conditions but other arable products needed the nourishment that only wet or damp soil could provide. Even as they rode, some of the men spoke of the unbearable dryness of the land. Others contented themselves with coughing through the almost blinding dust that clogged both their own and their horses' nostrils. Erebus ran along the side of the road, through the wild flowers and bushes. The dry weather brought flies too. An irritant to man and beast alike. Blowflies would seek open wounds to lay their eggs. Horseflies were content to feed from the blood of mounts leaving sores in their wake, particularly beneath the saddle. Lausard and his men were especially careful during grooming to ensure that none of the troublesome insects caused their horses any undue suffering. Muzzles and docks were sponged with even greater attention during hot weather. Lausard and his companions had seen too many horses lost over the years to saddle sores. In that condition they were unrideable and cavalry horses unable to accommodate a rider were worse than useless. Some could be used to pull limbers or caissons but most were despatched by the regimental farriers. As the dragoons moved along the road, they could see swarms of midges hovering like living clouds over the vegetation at the side of the thoroughfare. Bees fed on the pollen from wild flowers. Wasps and hornets buzzed around menacingly. Erebus snapped playfully at the insects as they flew around him. High above, the sun continued to blaze away.

The road veered slightly to the left, and the dragoons followed the curve, increasing their speed slightly as they drew nearer to one of the narrow wooden bridges that spanned a small stream just ahead. Lausard saw more insects darting about in the dust-choked air. Mosquitos and dragonflies, drawn by the tepid, rancid water, swooped and hovered. Rocheteau angrily swatted one of the blood-sucking insects as it landed on his unprotected neck.

'If it isn't fleas it's mosquitos,' he said, irritably. 'And rats when we're in the field. We live our entire lives with parasites.'

Some of the other men laughed.

'The only reason Joubert hates rats is because they want to share his food,' Delacor offered. 'Isn't that right, fat man?'

There was more laughter.

'At least rats can be eaten if a man is hungry enough,' Carbonne offered.

'*Anything* can be eaten if a man is hungry enough,' Lausard said, flatly. 'How many of us have eaten horse meat? Dog?' He glanced down at Erebus, who was still running along, his tongue lolling from his mouth.

The men nodded sagely.

'A plague of rats would mean good eating then?' Charvet chuckled.

'I say a plague on those bastards in the Guard for what they have done,' Moreau interjected.

The mood of the men suddenly changed.

'What's wrong with you, your Holiness?' Delacor wanted to know. 'Doesn't your God preach forgiveness?'

'He also teaches that it is wrong to kill.'

'Then all of *us* are damned,' Rocheteau mused. 'How many have we killed in our time? Tens? Hundreds? Women? Children?'

'We have never killed women and children,' Moreau said.

'You have a short memory,' Lausard told him. 'What about back in Italy in '96? In Egypt in '98? We killed those who *you* would call innocent.'

'Because we were *ordered* to kill,' Moreau snapped. 'Not because of some wanton blood-lust. Whoever killed the burgomaster's daughter did it because of carnal desire and the animal need to spill blood. We are not men like that, Sergeant.'

'You sound very sure of that, Moreau,' the sergeant mused.

'Because I know it is true.'

'What makes you so certain the grenadiers murdered Claudia?' Rocheteau wanted to know.

'I am not *certain*, but we know it was none of us,' said Lausard. 'I doubt if any of the locals would have the stomach for such an act. To rape and murder a woman like that takes a certain kind of man. A man with feelings hardened to suffering. A man who holds the life of another in such contempt he would think nothing of snuffing it out as he would the flames of a candle.'

'Until they came to Fürstenberg everything was fine,' Roussard offered. 'Now the locals hate *all* of us.'

'I fear we had outstayed our welcome anyway,' Lausard mused.

'But they didn't look upon us as enemies before,' Bonet said.

'Don't be naïve, schoolmaster,' Delacor snapped. 'We were *always* their enemies. We are invaders in their homeland. They tolerated us to begin with. Now they hate us. They want us gone as much as we wish to leave.'

'Delacor is right,' Lausard echoed. 'Our place is no longer here. Perhaps the least we can do is find the murderer of the daughter of their chief magistrate. They will look upon us no more favourably but at least we can clear our own names in their eyes.'

'Who cares whether they believe us or not?' Delacor grumbled.

'*I* care,' Lausard told his companion. 'They may hate us but they will not be able to deny that we are honourable men. That is all that matters now.'

The dusty road split into two forks, one leading directly to the town, the other to a disused farm a little under half a mile away. Lausard urged his horse on and the other dragoons followed, the outbuildings of the farm coming into sharper focus as they drew nearer. The farmhouse, two of the barns and a derelict granary had been used as barracks for the thirty Guard horsemen. The other barns and storehouses had been converted into makeshift stables.

Erebus ran ahead into the yard and Lausard watched the great black dog as it hurried towards a trough close to the entrance of one of the stables. The animal dipped its snout into the trough and began drinking. It suddenly turned as it detected a fresh scent and the sergeant saw the dog dash off out of sight around one of the barns. There was a loud snorting, the unmistakeable sound of pigs. Erebus began to bark at the snuffling animals and Tabor swung himself out of the saddle to quieten the dog. Other dragoons also dismounted and wandered across the yard, peering round cautiously, watching the doors and windows of the buildings for any sign of movement. Lausard scanned the dwellings but saw nothing. It appeared that, as he had counted, every one of the Guard grenadiers were at drill. The farm was deserted.

The sergeant swung himself out of the saddle and strode towards the main farmhouse.

He tried the door and was surprised to find it unlocked. He put his weight against it and pushed. The door swung open and he stepped inside, closely followed by Rocheteau and Charvet. There were a dozen makeshift beds inside the ground-floor room. The stairs, eaten through by woodworm, looked unstable. He placed one boot on the first step and pressed down. It confirmed his suspicions. The stair snapped with a loud crack. Charvet crossed to a large iron pot suspended over the remains of a fire and peered inside. He sniffed hard then reached in and pulled out some pieces of carrot that he popped into his mouth. Rocheteau was already overturning the pallets, searching under the makeshift straw mattresses. He slid the knife from his belt and slit them open one by one. Straw spilled onto the floor but he continued with his work.

Lausard left his companions inside the house and wandered back out into the yard. Tabor was dragging Erebus away from the pigs by the scruff of his furry black neck. Joubert and Roussard were inspecting the pigs with expert eyes. Several chickens also scuttled about in the yard and it was all Tabor could do to prevent Erebus from hurtling after the clucking fowl. Lausard watched as Gaston caught one of the chickens then expertly broke its neck and carried it back to his horse, where he stuffed it into his portmanteau. Joubert drew his bayonet and clambered into the makeshift pig pen, intent on claiming his own, more substantial, prize.

The stables smelled of horse sweat and urine. Lausard

walked into the first, blinking myopically as his eyes became accustomed to the gloom. Motes of dust turned silently in the shafts of sunlight that managed to poke through the odd hole in the roof. There was a hayloft, and two pallets had been established on this higher level, which was accessible only by a wooden ladder nearby. The sergeant leaned against it, testing its strength, then started to climb. The rungs creaked menacingly under his weight but he continued upwards until he reached the loft, the scabbard of his sword clanking against each rung of the ladder. There were chicken bones scattered among the straw. Flies crawled over them then buzzed somnolently in the air around the dragoon.

Karim watched from below as the sergeant overturned the two beds, using the toe of one boot to separate the debris. He turned and climbed back down the ladder, heading out into the yard once again. He glanced across in Tabor's direction and whistled. Erebus came running and the sergeant patted the dog's head as it nuzzled against him, apparently no longer concerned with the chickens in the yard. Lausard dropped to one knee and reached into his pocket, pulling out something that he shoved in the dog's direction. It was a portion of light blue woven material.

'What is that, sergeant?' Tabor wanted to know. He nodded in the direction of the soiled linen Lausard held.

'A key, hopefully,' the NCO said without looking at him.

Karim also saw the piece of material. He knew that the dark stains on it were dried blood. 'You took that from the dead girl?' the Circassian asked.

'It's a piece of her skirt,' Lausard told him.

'How did you do it without anyone in the church seeing?' Bonet wanted to know.

'I was a thief, remember,' Lausard smiled. 'I still have fast hands.'

He patted Erebus once again then pushed the dog away, watching as it scurried off across the yard, occasionally stopping to sniff at the ground. The sergeant pushed the piece of bloodied material back into his pocket and wiped his hands on his breeches.

'What *we* cannot find, he may,' Lausard mused, watching as the black dog loped towards the farmhouse then changed direction and made for the other temporary stable. The animal began to bark as it drew nearer, again stopping to sniff at the dusty ground. The watching dragoons saw him disappear inside the building. The barking became louder. Lausard and his companions hurried over to the stable. As they stepped inside they were again enveloped by the cloying odour of sweat, urine-soaked hay and leather. A familiar smell to any cavalryman. As with the other temporary stable, portions of the structure had been transformed into makeshift stalls and, as before, a wooden ladder led up to a hayloft and some more pallets. Erebus was standing at the foot of the ladder barking madly. However, as Lausard entered, the dog suddenly dashed into one of the stalls, where he began digging furiously at one corner, sending damp hay flying in all directions. Lausard pulled the dog away and took his sword from its scabbard. He prodded the sticky floor of the stall, raising one eyebrow slightly when he heard the sound of metal against metal.

He dropped to one knee and pulled more of the reeking bedding away.

The knife was about eight inches long. Double-edged. Wickedly sharp. There was blood on the blade. Lausard picked up the weapon by the hilt. Close to it was a small scrap of sodden material. Soaked in horse urine but, like the piece he himself held, stained darkly with blood. Lausard lifted the fragment on the tip of his sword and held it close to his own prize. They were identical in colour. Without question, both had come from the same garment.

'So, it would appear that one of Diomede's men killed the burgomaster's daughter,' Bonet murmured.

'Do you think the captain knows?' Giresse asked.

Lausard said nothing. He was still gazing at the piece of bloodied linen on the end of his sword.

'What do we do now, Alain?' Bonet wanted to know.

'Tell the burgomaster,' Tabor said. 'He must know who murdered his daughter.'

'Is this enough evidence to prove the guilt of one of the grenadiers? I think not,' Bonet mused.

'A piece of her dress and the knife used to cut her throat, what more evidence do you want, schoolmaster?' snapped Giresse. 'You saw her body. What they did to her. Something must be done.'

'It is still our word against theirs,' Lausard noted. 'If we take the knife to the burgomaster why should he believe us when we say we found it here? He will assume we brought it from our *own* barracks, not those of Diomede's men. It does nothing to confirm our innocence in *his* eyes *or* in the eyes of his people. He had made up his mind before we arrived at the church that night that we were guilty. This,' he held up the knife, 'will not change his opinion.'

'So what was the point of coming here today, Alain?' Giresse wanted to know. 'If we are not to tell the burgomaster then who will know what has happened?'

Lausard remained silent, his eyes fixed on the end of his sword and the bloody material there. He finally took the cloth and pushed it onto the sharp end of the knife. The sergeant turned and strode out of the stable, across the yard towards the door of the farmhouse. Watched by his companions he drove the knife into the wooden door, the blood-stained material hanging from it like some kind of miniature flag.

'Someone will know we were here,' he said, quietly. 'Claudia's murderer will know he cannot hide his secret any longer.' He glanced once more at the rag and the knife that skewered it to the door. 'It is enough.' The sergeant turned and wandered back towards his horse. Others watched as he swung himself into the saddle, their expressions ranging from bewilderment to surprise. Lausard flicked the reins of his horse and guided the animal back towards the road.

On the farmhouse door, several bloated black flies were already crawling over the blade of the knife.

Ten

Lausard swigged from the bottle of wine and looked around at the other men crammed into the barracks with him. They were sprawled on their beds, seated on the floor or gathered around the sputtering fire warming their hands. Bonet was carefully sewing up a tear in the arm of his surtout. Like most of the men's, his uniform was virtually in tatters. None of the men had been issued with new equipment or clothing since the summer of the previous year. What they had they did their best to keep clean but, despite their efforts, the thick woollen tunics they wore were grimy and holed. Lausard himself still had gunpowder stains on his own tunic that had resisted the most persistent washing. The horsehair mane of his brass helmet was home to a family of fleas. His socks were full of holes, his breeches torn in several places. Three of the pewter buttons were missing from his tunic. Boot heels were worn down and many of the men had no soles on their shoes. Lausard had patched up his own with pig-skin. The shoes were primarily worn for stable duties but Lausard wore his boots most of the time. He felt more comfortable in them, as did many of his companions. They might be the finest army in Europe, but *La Grande Armée* was also the most unkempt. Even their officers were dressed in rags. Lausard noticed that Captain Milliere's jacket was held together by several lengths of thin string, threaded through the button holes and tied tightly. The cuff of Lieutenant Royere's right boot was missing and one of his spurs was rusted, despite his best efforts to prevent the corrosion. The men's horse furniture was in somewhat better condition. Saddles and harnesses were polished on a daily basis. Shabracques were washed and dried with monotonous regularity. Weapons too were kept in good repair. Flints in carbines were changed every week. Swords and bayonets were kept sharp and well-oiled to prevent them rusting. To Lausard, it seemed the army had at least got its priorities right. It didn't matter if men looked like scarecrows as long as they could fight, and there were no soldiers in the world who were the equals of the French.

While Bonet continued with his sewing, Karim sat cross-legged sharpening his curved scimitar. The Circassian was puffing away at his pipe as he lovingly worked on the wickedly curved blade, finally wiping it down with a cloth, turning it so that the firelight caught its gleaming steel.

Sonnier was cleaning his carbine. Delacor, Charvet, Giresse and Roussard were playing cards, using cartridges as currency. The other men were relaxing or talking quietly. Joubert was nibbling on a biscuit. Gaston and Tigana were sitting on the floor, Erebus stretched out between them, his large brown eyes half closed. Gaston was stroking the dog's back.

'A toast,' said Lausard, raising his bottle. 'To a wasted year in Bavaria.'

Some of his companions raised their own drinks to echo the words.

'Not quite a year, Sergeant,' Milliere reminded him. 'It is October now. We arrived here in December last year.'

'What are two more months, Captain? We could be here for *another* year. Sitting around waiting as we have been since we first arrived.'

'I do not think so,' the officer remarked. 'The rumours of Prussian mobilisation grow stronger day by day. Although I fear, by now, they are more than just rumours.'

'Word is the Emperor himself is en route to Bamberg,' Royere added. 'We ourselves may shortly be called upon to mobilise. War with Prussia seems inevitable.'

'Better a war than another year of such intolerable inactivity,' Lausard murmured.

'I wish I could agree with you, Sergeant,' Milliere said, swigging his wine. 'But I prefer the monotony of peace to the fury of war. Does that surprise you?'

'I blame no man for choosing peace over conflict, Captain,' Lausard said, smiling. 'But we are soldiers. War is our destiny. Our reason for being.'

Milliere nodded. 'Forgive me if I do not share your desire to rush headlong into the jaws of death, Sergeant,' the officer grinned.

'I do not want to die, Captain. No more than you or any man in this room. But I have no fear of death because I have nothing to live for. We are all living on borrowed time. Life is like a debt to be repaid. One day we will all be called to settle our accounts.'

Milliere chuckled. 'I know you are right, Sergeant, but I will avoid paying that debt for as long as I can.'

Some of the other men nearby joined in the laughter.

'Here's to survival,' Milliere said, raising his own bottle.

Lausard also joined him in the toast.

'Here's to the Emperor,' Royere offered.

'Once a revolutionary and now a royalist, Lieutenant,' Lausard smiled. 'Your ethics have become twisted.'

'On the contrary, Sergeant. I supported our Emperor when he was a humble general, a figurehead for the ideology I supported. He turned France into the power she is now. He drove out the lawyers who were destroying her. He has my loyalty whether or not he wears a gunner's uniform or the Imperial purple.'

'Is there not a conflict in your reasoning, Lieutenant? You supported a regime sworn to remove royalty. Bonaparte did just that then crowned himself Emperor and created another autocracy. Did he not merely replace one dictatorship with another?' Lausard wanted to know.

'Every country must have a figurehead, Sergeant. Better one who epitomises the views of his countrymen. I have told you before, these past ten years I have lost many things, at least allow me to retain my idealism.'

Lausard and many of the other men laughed.

'So, where do we go from here, Captain?' Rocheteau wanted to know. 'To Vienna? To Berlin? On to Poland or Russia?'

'Not back to France,' sighed Giresse.

'Not France,' Lausard echoed.

'Your guess as to our destination is as good as mine, Corporal,' Milliere admitted. 'But I fear we will soon be seeing more of Germany than we have seen of it these past ten months. Most of it from the end of a sword.'

'We won another war for the Emperor and what is our reward?' hissed Delacor. 'To sit in some mudhole for ten months waiting for the *next* one.'

'Is there truly to be a war?' Tabor wanted to know.

'Of course there's going to be a war, you half-wit,' snapped Delacor. 'How many years of peace have we known in our lives? Three? Four?'

'Our Emperor has left the Prussians with little choice but to fight,' Royere murmured. 'The formation of the Confederation of the Rhine and the dissolution of the Holy Roman Empire has done much to antagonise his enemies within Europe. None more so than Prussia.'

'He has offended God by his politics,' Moreau interjected. 'He wants to rule the Pope as he rules every other man.'

'What is the Pope if he is not a man?' Rocheteau wanted to know. 'He eats, drinks and breaks wind the same as the rest of us.'

'He is the direct descendant of St Peter, our only link with Christ,' Moreau protested.

'So you believe,' Delacor said, dismissively. 'If your God objects to Bonaparte then why doesn't He do something? He could strike him with a thunderbolt or cause the ground to open beneath him.'

'You will pay for your blasphemy when you face Him on Judgement Day,' Moreau said, crossing himself. 'And so will Bonaparte.'

'Will we be judged for following him?' Tabor wanted to know.

'Everyone will be judged according to their sins,' Moreau said, with an air of superiority.

'We might as well put pistols to our heads now then,' chuckled Giresse. 'Perhaps the rest of you should let me confess first. By the time I have finished telling God of *my* sins, he will have neither desire nor time to hear *yours.*'

The entire barrack room exploded with the sound of laughter. Even Erebus barked loudly, as if infected by the fleeting moments of merriment within the room.

Lausard raised his bottle. 'To Judgement Day,' he said, grinning. 'And to our Emperor for hastening us all towards it.'

The men cheered and laughed and drank.

Napoleon Bonaparte stood with his back to the open fireplace, warming himself as the flames danced behind him. He was wearing the green uniform of a guard chausseur. Occasionally he would turn and stare into the flames as if seeking something there. His eyes, alert as ever, darted back and forth, tracing patterns in the blazing coals and crackling wood. There were those, like the gypsies he had met while growing up in Corsica, who believed that the future could be seen in a fire. Napoleon was convinced that the future of Prussia lay in fire. He smiled, the thought amusing him. He wondered about sharing it with the other men in the room then decided not to. Flames had been seen in this German town before – the flames of retribution and execution. In the fifteenth century, Bamberg had been the centre of a massive witchcraft trial, and dozens of men and women had been immolated alive for their supposed allegiance to the forces of darkness. Many had been held prisoner in the cellars of the very building in which the Corsican now made his headquarters. He took a sip of wine and turned to face his companions, holding a piece of paper before him.

'Prussia's ultimatum,' he said, flatly. 'It arrived in Paris the very day I departed.'

'It was inevitable they would react eventually, sire,' said General Savary. 'Perhaps too many demands had been made upon them. With all due respect, war has become unavoidable.'

'I agree, Savary,' the Emperor conceded. 'And it is the Prussians who have initiated this coming war by their subterfuge. Their lies and their deceit. It is they who have armed and mobilised when I instructed my ambassador in Berlin to inform them there was no need for such a course of action. It is they who have conjoined against me with Russia. They who have tried to compel Saxony to arm against France. They who have sought to persuade Hesse-Cassel to join them against me when I was willing to allow that state to maintain neutrality. And now, this.' Again he held up the piece of paper. 'They threaten me with *this*,' he snarled. 'These are their terms. Firstly, that all French troops should be immediately withdrawn beyond the Rhine. Secondly, that France is not to put any hindrance in the way of the construction of a North German Federation embracing all states not already included in the Confederation of the Rhine. And thirdly, they demand the immediate opening of negotiations for the permanent settlement of all remaining points of dispute.' His voice took on an even more disdainful tone. 'And, as a preliminary condition, that Wessel should separate from the French Empire and Marshal Murat should evacuate the three abbacies he has seized. They seek an affirmative reply to reach Berlin by October the eighth.' The Corsican balled up the piece of paper and hurled it across the room. 'That is what they demand of *me*.'

'They are empty threats, sire,' offered Marquis Armand Augustin Louis Caulaincourt. 'The Prussian army is no match for *La Grande Armée*. They are little more than walking muskets, steeped in the traditions of Frederick the Great but without any men capable of leading them so brilliantly. Tactically, the Prussian army is a museum piece. They are dependent upon their supply trains. Incapable, it seems, of living off the land as our men do. If they cover ten miles a day during a march this is viewed as a major achievement. They cannot match the speed and flexibility of *La Grande Armée*.'

'I agree with Caulaincourt, sire,' added Marshal Berthier. 'They are automatons commanded by failing old men, and you yourself know of their king's weakness both as a soldier and as a man.'

Napoleon nodded. 'Who is in command?' he wanted to know.

'The Duke of Brunswick,' the Chief of Staff said. 'He fought in the Seven Years War. He is seventy-one years old. Von Mollendorf, the Senior Royal Advisor, is eighty-two. He fought under Frederick the Great but his ways are cautious. Of the lesser generals, the ablest is Blücher who is already sixty-four. Prince Hohenlohe and General Schmettau are both sixty. Hohenlohe has some military talent but he is inclined to rash and hot-headed decisions. There are younger generals such as Tauenzien who is forty-five, Weimar who is forty-nine and Prince Louis himself is just thirty-three. But these men have little say in the overall control of the army. In their line infantry, out of a total of sixty-six colonels, twenty-eight are over sixty years of age. Similarly, of two hundred and eighty-one majors, one hundred and ninety of them are over fifty. They are well disciplined, that much may be said for them. But the Prussian definition of good discipline seems to require the abandonment of all initiative.'

Napoleon chuckled.

'Some of their disadvantages might be overcome were they not so lacking in an adequate staff corps, sire,' Caulaincourt offered. 'Three soldiers share the duty of Chief of Staff. Generals Phull and Scharnhorst and Colonel Massenbach. They have more interest in their own personal advancement than in the proper running of the army they purport to serve.'

'And beneath them?' Napoleon asked.

'There are no corps headquarters and even divisional staffs are poorly organised,' the Master of the Horse said, shrugging his shoulders. 'Orders issued from general headquarters are often out of date and useless by the time they reach divisional and regimental level.'

'What news have we of their strengths and dispositions?' the Emperor demanded, crossing to a large map on a table in the centre of the room.

'There are, as far as we can ascertain from intelligence reports, sire, three field armies,' Savary said. 'The first, under the Duke of Brunswick, comprises some seventy thousand men. Current intelligence has them concentrated between Leipzig and Naumburg. The second, commanded by Hohenlohe, is of similar strength but twenty thousand of those troops are Saxons, forcibly incorporated.'

Napoleon nodded. 'Unwilling allies,' he mused. 'Where are they concentrated?'

'Around Dresden, sire,' Savary continued. 'The third army is under the joint command of Blücher and Ruchel. Stationed, respectively, at Göttingen and Mülhausen. They command thirty thousand men between them.'

'So, arrayed before us we have around one hundred and seventy thousand men, neither fully concentrated nor ready for immediate conflict,' the Corsican mused, his eyes flicking back and forth over the map and the pins that were stuck into it, each signifying a force of troops. 'Of that number, how many are cavalry and artillery?'

'Thirty-five thousand are cavalry, fifteen thousand are gunners serving five hundred and fifty cannon, sire,' Savary informed him.

Napoleon stroked his chin thoughtfully as he regarded the map. 'Is there any indication of their plans?' he said, quietly.

'Not as yet, sire,' Savary said, almost apologetically. 'We have had word that there is a possibility King Frederick might wait until the Russians can assist him before committing his troops. Fifty thousand of the Tsar's men are assembling at Brześć on the river Bug under the command of General Bennigsen.'

'Then speed, as ever, is of the essence,' the Emperor exclaimed. 'We must move quickly and annihilate the Prussians before Alexander has the chance to send his men to their aid.'

'The Prussians could trade space for time, sire,' Berthier remarked. 'Fight delaying actions until Bennigsen reaches them.'

'Let them squabble over their own course of action,' Napoleon snapped. 'The fate of this campaign is in *our* hands, let us seize the initiative. The surest way of inducing the Prussians to fight is to drive on Berlin. The river lines of both the Rhine and the Main are controlled by us. As far as I can see there are three avenues of approach open to us.' He stuck a pin into the map. 'An army concentrated around Wesel, on the Rhine, could advance directly on Berlin and, other than a series of river crossings on the way, there would be no natural obstacles to slow their progress. However, this would mean redeploying the bulk of the army. It would take time and I have no wish to give the Prussians any more time than I have to. It might also enable Bennigsen to reach them from the east.' Napoleon shook his head. 'A concentration in the vicinity of Mainz, at the junction of the Rhine and the Main, is a possibility. We could advance on Berlin through Frankfurt, Fulda and Erfurt.

This area is also closer to *La Grande Armée*'s cantonments, which would make concentration easier.'

'But, sire,' Caulaincourt interjected, 'the greater part of a march along that route would have to be made through mountainous regions.'

'We have crossed mountain ranges before, Caulaincourt,' Napoleon observed.

'I agree, sire, but once those obstacles have been surmounted there is the problem of the Thüringer Wald to consider. The roads through the forest are poor and would not allow the quick passage of troops or equipment. Certainly not at the speed that is required.'

'Also, sire,' Savary offered, 'once the Prussians were defeated, they would naturally be driven back to the East, *towards* their supplies and reinforcements, and they would still be in a position to defend Berlin.'

The Corsican nodded again. 'That is true,' he murmured. 'There is a third course of action and it would seem to be preferable. An advance north, through the easier stretches of the Franconian forest, towards Leipzig or Dresden and then on to Berlin.'

'Again, the terrain does not favour us, sire,' Caulaincourt noted. 'The forest is dense and hilly and there appear to be only three good roads to the north and no lateral communications at all.'

'I appreciate that,' the Corsican said. 'Just as I realise there are numerous water obstacles to face, not least of which is the Elbe itself. However, several valleys run parallel to our proposed line of march. These could accommodate cavalry and artillery and make their passage easier.'

'But, sire, if the weather turns against us then it would be just another problem to be surmounted,' said Caulaincourt. 'Roads that are already difficult could become totally impassable.'

'It is a risk I am willing to take,' Napoleon said, flatly. 'The compensations outweigh the objections. To begin with, the concentration area is the most convenient, given the present positions of the army. We could set up fortified bases of operations at Mainz, Würzburg, Mannheim and Bamberg. Others could be set up running south towards Ulm and westwards along the Upper Danube as far as the Black Forest and Strasbourg. Most importantly, this line of advance could use the Saale, the Elster or the Mulde as a strategic barrier and give us the possibility of making a manoeuvre to the rear of the Prussian army. A rapid movement from Bayreuth towards Berlin would threaten the Prussian lines of communication, outflank their field forces, put us in a central position between Frederick William and his Russian allies *and* threaten the Prussian bases and their capital.' He jabbed another pin into the map. 'The area between Dresden and Leipzig is the key. Once we take that we are in an invincible position. I will concentrate two hundred thousand men on the same battlefield and sweep these antiquated, bickering children of Frederick the Great from the face of the earth, once and for all.'

The Corsican moved back and forth around the map, eyes studying it so intensely it seemed his stare would burn a hole in the paper.

'We will advance in three columns,' he said, finally. 'The first, to the right, will be composed of the IV and

VI corps commanded by Soult and Ney, respectively. They will be supported by seven thousand Bavarians. This column will total just over fifty-nine thousand men, supported by ninety cannon.'

Berthier began scribbling furiously, his quill scratching over the paper noisily within the confines of the room.

'Instruct Soult that, should he encounter an enemy force not exceeding thirty thousand, he and Ney should attack it,' the Emperor continued. 'Upon reaching Hof, he must open communications between Lebenstein, Ebersdorf and Schleiz.'

Caulaincourt moved more pins on the map to coincide with the locations the Emperor had designated.

'The central column will be led by Bernadotte, who has command of I corps. To be supported by III corps under Davout, the Imperial Guard under Lefebvre and the reserve cavalry under Murat. A total of nearly seventy-six thousand men and one hundred and forty-four guns. I myself will travel with that formation. The left column will be led by Lannes and V corps, closely supported by Augereau with VII corps and sixty-four guns. Just over thirty-eight thousand men.'

'Sire, the columns will be spread over a thirty-eight-mile front,' Caulaincourt remarked. 'Is there not the danger the Prussians will attack them piecemeal as they emerge from the forest?'

'Each column will be more than able to cope with an opposing force of up to thirty thousand men,' Napoleon said with assurance. 'In the event of such an eventuality, the column under attack will fight a holding action until it can be supported by the other two formations. If necessary, ground must be given but this will serve only to expose the Prussian flanks and rear to the other columns. Our enemies would be very foolish to attempt such a manoeuvre.' The Emperor smiled to himself, his words apparently not directed at anyone in particular. 'An entire army moving in battalion square formation. One hundred and eighty thousand men able to meet an enemy attack from any direction. Each column within supporting distance of the other.'

'Frederick the Great himself would be proud, sire,' smiled Caulaincourt.

'Indeed,' murmured the Emperor. 'Until we know the exact positions of our enemy, this formation is both practical *and* prudent.' He clapped his hands together. 'Berthier, instruct the reconnaissance squadrons of each column to empty every letter-box and interrogate every peasant they come across during their advance. We must discover the exact whereabouts of our foe.'

'When we do, it will be a bloody day, sire,' Savary mused.

'That is true,' said Napoleon, turning back to gaze into the flames of the fire. 'But one cannot gain victory without spilling blood and, make no mistake, victory is what I will have. A victory so crushing and so final that Prussia will beg for peace.'

Eleven

Lausard swung himself into the saddle and looked around at his companions. Their expressions ranged from weariness to resignation. From concern to anticipation. He had seen all this before and had no doubt he would see it all again. He reached into his pocket and glanced at his watch. It was approaching five a.m. From every hamlet and village where the men of the first squadron had been stationed for the last ten months, they had congregated at this one place and joined thousand upon thousand of their comrades in readiness for the journey across the borders of Saxony into territory that belonged to Prussia. A country that was now their sworn enemy. Ahead of them lay nothing but an endless mass of trees. For as far as he could see in all directions, Lausard saw nothing but forest. The road that cut through them was wide enough to accommodate troopers riding six abreast and easily allowed the passage of cannon and other vehicles but, in places, it narrowed to half that width. His horse pawed the ground, as eager as its rider to be on the move.

Several units of light cavalry had already passed through. Lausard himself had sat and watched as a group of hussars had cantered past the dragoons' camp and been swallowed up by the dark woods. Erebus, sitting with him by the remains of a dead fire, had barked at the brightly uniformed horsemen, who had waved back as if in greeting. How long it would take to pass through the forbidding environs of the Franconian forest he didn't know. What awaited him and his companions on the other side was not so much of a mystery. There could be only one outcome. Battle. It was just a matter of time as to how soon that battle came and, when it did, what its scale would be. Lausard wondered if it would match the carnage of Rivoli, Lodi, Marengo, Elchingen or Austerlitz. He suspected it would. During his time in the army of Napoleon he had seen both French and opposition armies grow in size. Every battle, it seemed, was contested by larger numbers of men and each one left more dead upon those bloodied fields. He had no reason to believe that what awaited them on the other side of the stifling Franconian forest would be any different. But then, a man had as much chance of being killed in a skirmish as he did in a full-scale battle. Death had no compunction about when or where to take a man when his time came.

The sergeant reached into his portmanteau and pulled out a sheet of paper. He unfurled it and scanned it once again. It was a proclamation from the Emperor himself. Duplicated a thousand times by the mobile printing presses that accompanied the army on its travels, it had been read aloud a thousand times by aides-de-camp to men along the length and breadth of the waiting French lines. Greeted, Lausard had little doubt, by cheers of

furious exultation for the most part. Most of the men
who fought in Napoleon's army still reserved an uncon-
ditional love and respect for their leader and to hear his
words, for many, was like being touched by the hand of
God. Lausard himself had slightly more faith in the
Corsican than he had in any greater, more ethereal power.
But he knew that once on a field of battle there were
many factors to be considered if a man was to survive,
not the least of these being luck. Bravery was immaterial.
The bravest, most fearless man in the world could be
struck down as easily as the most spineless coward.
Roundshot, bullets, swords and bayonets made no distinction. And, on a battlefield, there were a hundred
different ways to die. He knew, he had seen most of them.
Men trampled by horses, crushed by wheels. Burned alive
in tinder-dry grass. Hit by cannister fire. Blown apart by
howitzer shells. Impaled by ramrods fired from muskets.
Beaten to death with the pommels of swords or the butts
of carbines. Inadvertently shot down by the fire of their
own side. Even those who survived the rigours of the field
itself might find themselves embraced by death many days
or weeks later. Blood poisoning. Gangrene in a wound.
Shock from the loss of a limb. Starvation. Dehydration.
Lausard smiled to himself. It was a wonder anyone ever
survived a campaign. But they did and they rushed headlong into the next. All at the behest of their Emperor.
Like all those around him, Lausard would follow
Napoleon to the ends of the earth but, perhaps, for different reasons. He glanced at the proclamation once again.

'Read it, Alain.'

He turned to see that Rocheteau had walked his horse

up alongside him. The corporal was chewing on a piece of salt beef. He tore off a lump and threw the rest to Erebus. The dog caught it and chewed hungrily. The other men, formed up in perfectly straight lines behind the sergeant, listened intently as he began to read.

"'Soldiers. The order for your return to France had already issued, you had drawn nearer to it by several marches. Triumphal fetes awaited you and the preparations for your reception had begun in the capital,'" he began, then looked at the men and smiled. 'Why do you wish to hear these words again?'

'You read them so beautifully, Alain,' Giresse chuckled.

The other men laughed.

Lausard raised a hand for silence then continued. "'But, just as we became too confident of security, fresh plots were being woven under the mask of alliance and friendship. Warlike utterances were heard from Berlin. For the last two months we have been subjected to daily increasing provocation. The same faction, the same giddy spirit which, fourteen years ago, favoured then by our internal dissensions, led the Prussians to the midst of the plains of Champagne, still rules their councils.'"

'What does that mean?' Tabor asked.

'It means that the last time the Prussians went to war with France, *we* were all in prison,' laughed Rocheteau.

'Perhaps we'd be better off there now,' Roussard offered. 'At least in prison we couldn't get shot.'

'No,' Lausard said, raising one eyebrow. 'Just guillotined.'

The other men laughed.

'What else does it say, Sergeant?' Moreau insisted.

'"If it is no longer Paris that they seek to burn and destroy,"' Lausard continued, '"it is today their standard which they boast that they will raise in the capitals of our allies."'

'I didn't know we had any,' mused Sonnier. 'It is usually the rest of Europe who are united against France.'

'"It is Saxony that they seek to compel, by a disgraceful transaction which would range her among their provinces, to renounce her independence,"' Lausard read.

'But isn't it Saxony *we* are about to invade?' Rostov said.

'*We* come as liberators, my friend,' Lausard told the Russian. 'In Bonaparte's eyes, every country we invade, we liberate. We bring with *us* the ideals of the Revolution and the Empire.'

'We bring the sword,' Bonet muttered. 'Nothing more.'

'Shut up, schoolmaster,' hissed Delacor, taking a swipe at his companion.

'"In a word, it is your laurels which they seek to tear from your brows,"' Lausard continued, unfurling the paper a little more as he scanned it. '"They wish us to evacuate Germany at the sight of their arms! Madmen! Let them know that it would be a thousand times easier to destroy the great capital than to tarnish the honour of the great people and its allies. In days gone by their schemes were confounded; they found in the plains of Champagne defeat, death and dishonour."'

'My father fought against the Prussians at Valmy,' said Sonnier.

'You never knew who your father *was*,' Delacor said, sarcastically.

'Then he is in good company, is he not, Delacor,' Lausard offered, looking directly at the other dragoon.

Many of the other men laughed.

'"But the lessons of experience fade from memory, whilst there are men with whom the sentiments of hatred and jealously never die,"' Lausard read. '"Soldiers! None of you would wish to return to France by any path other than that of honour."'

'I will return by the safest path,' Roussard said.

'And I by the quickest,' Rocheteau added with a grin.

'"We must re-enter it only under triumphal arches. What! Have we braved seasons, the ocean, the deserts, have we conquered Europe, several times united in coalition against us, have we carried our glory to the East and the West only to return to our country today as fugitives, abandoning our allies, to hear it said that the eagle of France has fled terrified by the aspect of the Prussian armies?"'

'We lived our lives as fugitives before we joined the army,' Giresse observed.

'Would you want to be one again?' Lausard asked.

The former horse-thief shook his head.

'"Already they are at our outposts. Forward then, since moderation has failed to calm this astonishing intoxication. Let the Prussian army suffer the fate which met it fourteen years ago! Let them learn that, if it is easy with the friendship of the great people to acquire an increase of power and of territory, that people's enmity, which can be provoked only by abandoning the spirit of wisdom and reason, is more terrible than the ocean's tempests."' The sergeant folded the proclamation and smiled. 'The Emperor's words,' he said, with an air of finality.

'*Vive l'Empereur*,' shouted a man from further down the column and the shout was rapidly taken up by others. Even Lausard himself raised a fist into the air and shouted the words. Erebus barked loudly at the sound of so many raised voices and, as Lausard rode his horse back and forth before the waiting dragoons, the dog ran alongside, seemingly as infected with patriotic fervour as the green-clad men before him.

Lausard recognised a familiar figure riding towards him. The pock-marked face. The hooked nose and deep-set eyes. The other man also bore the three chevrons of sergeant on the sleeves of his jacket.

'Reading to your bastards before you send them off to die,' said Sergeant Delpierre, scathingly.

'You should have joined us,' Lausard told the other NCO. 'Perhaps then you too would understand these words.' He balled up the proclamation and threw it in Delpierre's direction.

'I understand them well enough,' snarled the other man. 'Just make sure you and your scum heed them.'

'Don't tell me how to fight, Delpierre.'

'Perhaps I should *show* you.'

'I look forward to it.'

'I told you that one day I will kill you, Lausard, and I meant it.'

'And I told *you* that you are welcome to try.'

Delpierre wheeled his horse and trotted back into position in the column.

'Re-acquainting yourself with an old friend?'

Lausard turned in the saddle as he heard the words.

Lieutenant Royere brought his horse to a halt alongside the sergeant, a slight grin on his face. Erebus looked up at the officer, barked once then scampered off towards the waiting column.

'When do we move, Lieutenant?' Lausard wanted to know.

'Everything is ready, my friend. Every unit is furnished with enough supplies for four days. There is no need for us to stop until we reach the plains beyond this accursed forest.'

'Is that how long it is expected to take to traverse it, four days?'

Royere nodded. 'Longer if the weather turns against us,' he mused.

'We've marched with mud on our boots before. And sand. And dust.'

Both men smiled.

Captain Milliere rode to the front of the column and waved a hand in Gaston's direction. The young trumpeter blasted out the first notes of the advance and the dragoons moved off at a walk, the sound of so many harnesses filling the still morning air. Lausard glanced at his watch. It was almost six a.m. The trees gradually swallowed them up.

Despite the lateness of the season, the trees of the Thüringer Wald still sported most of their leaves, and the dragoons found that they rode beneath a dark green canopy only occasionally penetrated by the weak sunlight from above. Erebus ran ahead of the column, occasionally barking but, on the whole, reluctant to disturb the cloying silence inside the woods. The air smelled of moss, mud, horse sweat and droppings. Smells Lausard and his companions had grown used to during the past ten or eleven years. They moved at a steady pace, occasionally breaking into a trot when the road was wide enough and the terrain sufficiently flat. However, for the most part, the ground inside the forest was uneven. More than once it rose sharply to form ridges and inclines and Lausard wondered if one of these higher points would lead them up and out of the trees, albeit momentarily. They never did. No matter how steep the slope, trees clung to it and maintained the natural umbrella of leaves over the heads of the advancing dragoons. Countless small streams also bisected the wooded area and, as more horses passed through them, the waterways were transformed to little more than liquid mud at the places where the cavalry crossed.

By midday, many of the mounts were already lathered from the effort of crossing such inhospitable and difficult ground. However, Lausard mused, compared to some of the terrain they had crossed in the past, the confines of the great forest were relatively benign. He guided his horse across another narrow stream, water splashing up all around him. The rest of the column followed and, not too far behind them, a battery of horse artillery trundled along, dragging their four pounders. To their rear came caissons laden with ammunition and following were the infantry, toiling along roads and across fords transformed into quagmires by the passage of the cavalry and artillery. Lausard thought how fortunate the French were that the weather had stayed fine. Any kind of downpour would transform the terrain into a swamp and slow their advance. He peered upwards, trying to see through the canopy of leaves, hoping that the relatively calm autumn weather would continue. He was surprised at the warmth and felt sweat running down his face from beneath his helmet. On more than one occasion he removed the brass casque to run a hand through his long sodden hair.

'There must have been an easier way to reach the Prussians,' said Rocheteau, digging his knees into his horse, urging it up a sharp incline.

Lausard said nothing. He merely snapped the reins of his bay as it continued along the road at a steady pace.

'We always seem to be hurrying to our deaths,' Roussard complained.

'I am sure the Emperor would have us gallop everywhere if he could,' Joubert offered. 'I just wish we were hurrying towards food.' He rubbed his mountainous belly with one hand.

'Ten months of easy living has made us soft,' Delacor said.

'Ten months of good food,' Joubert said, wistfully. 'How long before we can say that again?'

'If you spent less time thinking about your gut and more time thinking of other things you wouldn't have so much to complain about,' Roussard said.

'Yes, you should be thinking of things more important than food,' Giresse interjected.

'*Nothing* is more important than food,' Joubert snorted.

'God is the most important thing in my life,' Moreau interjected.

'Shut up, your holiness,' rasped Delacor.

'A fine horse,' Tigana said, 'is a true treasure.'

'Freedom is to be valued more than anything in the world,' Karim noted. 'If any of you had been a slave as I have, you would know. I thank Allah, all Praise to Him, that I have my freedom now.'

'A good woman is worth more than any feast or any god,' Giresse countered. 'Any horse or freedom. I would go without food for a week, renounce any god, walk instead of ride and give up my freedom if it meant spending time with a woman.'

'If you went without food for a week you wouldn't have the strength to satisfy a woman,' Bonet chuckled.

'We've all been without food before,' Rocheteau reminded them. 'We've been without our freedom too.'

'That's true,' Giresse agreed. 'Besides, you can eat anything if you're hungry enough. You can't find a *woman* just anywhere. If you could, I would lift one of these rocks and pull a fine maiden free right now.'

'Joubert would probably eat her,' the corporal grinned.

The other men also laughed.

'What do you think is the most important thing in life, Alain?' Rocheteau asked.

'Honour,' said the sergeant without hesitation. 'If a

man has no honour then he may as well be dead.'

'What of other virtues?' Bonet said. 'Such as bravery. Fortitude. Temperance.'

'I fear none of us has any need for temperance,' the sergeant said. 'Especially when it comes to liquor. As for fortitude, we have all shown that in our lives. Bravery is a different matter.'

'Do you think it is important?' Bonet persisted.

'There are many kinds of bravery,' Lausard said. 'Not just on a battlefield. For instance, it takes courage to stand by a belief. To uphold a principle. That can sometimes require more courage than looking down the barrel of a cannon. Charging headlong into the fire of the enemy is not always the sign of a courageous man but of a fool. Valour must be tempered with discretion. A truly brave man knows when the time is right to withdraw. What shows the most courage? To cling to a lost cause or fall back and regroup in readiness for another onslaught?'

'So you are saying that men who run are sometimes heroes?' Delacor asked.

'Not heroes perhaps but, under certain circumstances, they show more wisdom than those who stand and wait for death.'

'Would you ever run, Alain?' Rocheteau wanted to know.

'From an enemy? Who can say? It depends upon the nature of that enemy. Some of the most ferocious adversaries come from in here.' He tapped his temple. 'There is nowhere a man can run to hide from *them*.'

'Sergeant Lausard.'

He looked up as he heard his name and saw Captain Milliere beckoning to him. The NCO urged his horse on to where the officer waited. Lausard saluted then noticed the captain was looking in the direction of a small wooden hut about fifty yards away, connected to the main road by just a narrow dirt track that was virtually obscured by thick undergrowth. Lausard glanced down at the muddy ground around them.

'No tracks, Captain,' he said.

'The light cavalry must have ridden past without even seeing it,' Milliere observed.

Lieutenant Royere rode up to join the two men, accompanied by Karim.

All four sets of eyes gazed in the direction of the hut.

Karim suddenly swung himself out of the saddle and walked three or four yards along the side of the track, occasionally ducking low to the ground. At one point he even ran the flat of his hand over the earth.

'No one has been along here for days,' he murmured.

'It's probably empty,' Royere offered. 'It looks deserted.'

'There's only one way to find out,' said Milliere, pulling his carbine free. He quickly loaded it then stepped down. Lausard followed his example, pulling one of the pistols from the holsters on the front of his saddle.

'Our orders were to interrogate *every* peasant we came across in this forest,' said Milliere. 'I suggest we do so.'

Royere called Tabor to him and the big man took hold of the reins of the other horses, holding them steady as his dismounted companions walked slowly along the edges of the pathway, hidden by the thick undergrowth and densely growing trees. Lausard was reasonably sure that, even if the hut was occupied, the occupant would be unable to see the approaching dragoons due to the natural cover. Also, as far as he could see, there didn't appear to be any windows in the front of the small dwelling. He could see a door but nothing else. The sergeant heard the low hiss of metal against metal as Karim eased the scimitar from its scabbard and turned the wickedly sharp curved blade in his grip, his eyes never leaving the hut as he continued to advance. Even though the main road was still relatively close, Lausard marvelled at how quiet it was near the hut. Only fifty yards away a constant stream of troops was passing by on the thoroughfare and yet their passage seemed somehow muted by the profusion of trees and bushes that surrounded them. It was as if someone had encased the hut and its closest surroundings in an invisible glass bubble which shut out all extraneous sound. He became aware of his own footsteps and was anxious not to step on any dry, fallen branches. The solitude was beginning to become oppressive, and Lausard could draw only two possible conclusions. Either the hut was empty and had been for some time or its occupant was waiting with a stealth the dragoons themselves would have envied. He eased back the hammer on his pistol as they moved to within ten yards of the hovel.

Karim tapped his scimitar three times gently against the cuff of his boot to attract the attention of the others, then used the point of the weapon to indicate the area around the front of the hut. Lausard nodded. There were several bones lying there, scattered before the entrance.

At least one looked like the jaw bone of a large animal, possibly a pig. But there was neither sight nor sound of any livestock around this secluded dwelling. Lausard wondered if the jaw bone might even belong to one of the wild boars that roamed the wood. He took a step nearer the hut, watching as Captain Milliere scurried across to the other side of the small building and pressed himself up against the wooden wall. Karim advanced through the undergrowth. Lieutenant Royere kept low to the ground, his own sword drawn. He pushed branches aside with the three-foot steel and watched as Lausard edged nearer the door.

The sergeant paused, listening for any sounds of movement from inside.

He could hear nothing.

Milliere steadied himself, swinging the Charleville up to his shoulder and sighting it. Karim took four or five large strides across to where Lausard waited and hefted the scimitar before him. Royere moved to the other side of the door. Lausard waited a moment then, as Milliere nodded, he drove his foot against the flimsy partition.

The door crashed inwards and Lausard and Karim squeezed quickly through the narrow entrance and into the hut itself.

It was almost pitch black. Impossible to see more than a foot or two ahead. Lausard collided with something he couldn't see and stumbled. Karim looked around, trying to squint into the Stygian blackness to pick out shapes. Both men were immediately struck by the stench. An overpowering odour of sweat, excrement, charred wood and animal fat. Lausard was aware of something moving in the darkness. A large shape that loomed up at them as if a portion of the umbra had detached itself. Lausard heard a sound like animalistic growling but this was deeper and more guttural. He heard words he didn't understand being barked angrily at him. Then came the impact that knocked him off his feet. Something hard was driven into his side with such force that he staggered sideways then fell to the reeking floor of the hut, the pistol spinning from his grasp.

Karim turned in the direction of the collision, swinging the scimitar through empty air. He too felt a thunderous impact between his shoulder blades and the Circassian too went sprawling. Lausard dragged himself to his feet and pulled his sword clear of its sheath. He struck blindly in the blackness then finally saw the huge shape filling the doorway, silhouetted there like something from a child's nightmare.

'Don't shoot,' shouted the sergeant, chasing out after the shape.

Karim struggled back to his feet and hurried after his sergeant. Both men emerged within seconds of each other. There in the dull grey light of the forest, they caught sight of their attacker. The man was enormous, fully six and a half feet tall, and he was broad too. Shaggy haired and clad in what looked like animal skins, he looked like some hulking relic of the time when men still lived in caves. In hands as big as ham-hocks, he gripped a large wooden club that, to Lausard, appeared little more than a shaved down lump of tree trunk. The giant of a man wielded the weapon with ease, his hooded eyes darting from one dragoon to another.

'Put it down,' Milliere told him.

The man merely looked disdainfully at the officer and raised the club again, as if to strike at him.

Lausard and Karim moved around the man like hunters stalking a wounded bear, fearing its final furious assault. The sergeant rubbed his injured side, wondering if this collossus before him had broken any of his ribs.

The man said something, the words clipped and spoken rapidly.

'What did he say?' Milliere asked Royere, not taking his eyes off the man-mountain before him.

'I don't recognise the language,' the lieutenant mused, puzzlement etched on his face. 'I think it's German, but it's unlike any dialect I've ever heard before.'

'Tell him to put the weapon down or we'll attack,' Milliere instructed.

In impeccable German, Royere relayed the instructions.

The huge man merely glared at the four dragoons.

Royere repeated the words.

The man snapped something back and Royere could only shake his head.

'I can't be sure,' the officer began. 'But I think he wants to know who we are.'

'I'm surprised he doesn't know,' Milliere mused. 'After all, we are at war with his country.'

The huge man rasped the words once more.

Royere nodded. 'It *is* German he's speaking,' he said. 'But the dialect must be peculiar to these parts.'

'Can you understand him and make *him* understand *you*?' Milliere wanted to know. 'Ask him if any Prussian

troops have been seen in this area in the last two or
three days.'

Royere did as instructed.

The big man shrugged then spat out a few guttural
words.

Lausard looked on silently.

'He asks why soldiers would come to this place,'
Royere said, falteringly. 'To *his* forest.'

'Captain, I don't even think this man knows that there
is a war on,' Lausard murmured.

The big man looked at Lausard then spoke again.

'He asks again who we are,' Royere translated.

'Tell him we come from the Emperor Napoleon,'
Milliere said.

Royere did so.

Lausard heard more of the harsh words from the large
man.

'He says he has never heard of such a man,' Royere
told the other officer. 'He says he lives in the forest. He
hunts its animals. He lives off its fruits in the summer.
He knows nothing of a war or any soldiers from any
country. This is *his* forest. His home. He says it has been
all his life.'

Milliere eyed the large man impassively.

'I think he speaks the truth, Captain,' Royere said.

'You can barely understand him and yet you believe
what he tells you, Lieutenant,' Milliere mused.

'We have ridden for more than half a day into this
forest, Captain,' Lausard offered. 'We face another three
days at least within it. I doubt we will find another man
like this.'

'You are probably right, Sergeant,' Milliere conceded. 'I certainly *hope* that you are.'

'What would you do with him, Captain?' Lausard continued. 'Orders called for us to interrogate the local peasants, not slaughter them.'

Milliere nodded and finally lowered his carbine.

'We will move on,' the officer said. 'Leave this man to his own means.'

The big man watched silently as the dragoons moved away, back towards the road where the procession of French troops was still filing past. When Lausard turned round, the man was gone. Swallowed up once again by the trees and undergrowth.

'Did you find anything?' Tabor wanted to know as the dragoons mounted their waiting horses.

'A man to be envied,' Milliere said. 'A man who knows nothing of war or conflict. Within the next few days, I fear there will be few in this country who will still be able to lay claim to such blissful ignorance. And fewer still who will not know, and curse, the name of Napoleon Bonaparte.'

'Not all of those who curse his name will be Prussian, Captain,' Lausard offered.

'That may well be,' Milliere agreed.

'Let us hope that *we* are not among that number,' Lausard added, quietly.

During the daylight hours, the confines of the Thüringer Wald, Lausard had found, were at best gloomy. Night brought a darkness so total that men could barely see their hands in front of them. A combination of moonless skies and the thick canopy of leaves and branches transformed the forest into a veritable sea of blackness. A number of small camp fires had been lit but officers and NCOs constantly patrolled the bivouacs of the French troops to ensure that these islands of light within the ocean of darkness never became too large. For the most part, troops were forced to eat dry rations or consume any captured rabbits raw. It was a prospect to dampen even the fiercest appetite. Lausard and his companions were thankful, at least, for the fact that the weather had remained unusually temperate for the time of year. They did not need the warmth of a fire to drive the chill from their bones, only to cook and see by. Men huddled around the fires they were allowed, as much for companionship as anything else. The night hours brought a completely different set of sounds from those of daylight. The almost serene stillness the dragoons and the other troops had passed through earlier that day had been replaced by a virtual cacophony of noises as the nocturnal denizens of the great forest emerged. Lausard himself had heard a number of snortings and sniffings, which he attributed to everything from hedgehogs to badgers, all drawn by the warmth of the fires or the scraps of food the men had discarded. Foxes also roamed the night. Bats wheeled in the air, one occasionally swooping a little too low. When that happened, the high-pitched squealing of the creatures could be heard clearly. He heard an owl somewhere. The sergeant wondered what other creatures roamed the forest. Sonnier, asleep with his carbine cradled in his arms like a slumbering child, had wondered if wolves might patrol the Thüringer Wald.

Even bears had been mentioned but Lausard doubted the presence of such redoubtable predators in this part of the world. Despite the chorus of derision Sonnier's musings had provoked from some of the other dragoons, a number of the men sat close to the fire, their weapons near at hand should any predator larger than a fox decide to show its snout.

Lausard was amused by the irony of the situation. Men who would soon be facing the hideous varieties of death a campaign held in store for them seemed more concerned with the unlikely appearance of a wolf or wild boar than they did with the certainty of facing cannon spewing cannister at them. Even Erebus seemed on edge, constantly getting to his feet to pad back and forth whenever he heard a sound from the undergrowth but careful never to stray too far from the meagre light of the camp fire. It was as if he too was nervous. The large black dog was almost invisible in the gloom, only its eyes glowing in the night as if its skull had been lit from the inside by candles. It patrolled a small area of the camp once again then returned to lie between Gaston and Tigana. The trumpeter began stroking the dog's back as he lay with his head propped on his saddle. Tigana swigged from a bottle of wine then passed it to Lausard.

'How long before we're out of this forest?' the Gascon wanted to know.

'Two or three days,' Lausard told him, accepting the bottle.

'And then?' Roussard wanted to know.

'Then we fight,' the sergeant murmured.

'Why the hell can't we have camp fires?' Delacor muttered, irritably.

'We've *got* a camp fire,' Lausard reminded him, nodding towards the crackling embers before them. 'This is sufficient for our needs. Captain Milliere said that orders had been issued that fires were to be kept to a minimum.'

'I'll bet the Emperor has a fire,' Delacor said. 'And cooked food. And a comfortable bed. What do we have to sleep on? This damp moss.' He touched the ground beneath him then wiped his hand on his tunic. 'We'll all have piles and rheumatism before we meet the Prussians.'

'A forest is the worst place to camp, I grant you,' the former schoolmaster said. 'But what choice do we have?'

'The *worst* place,' grunted Joubert. 'Is there a *good* one?'

'The ideal campsite has dry, sandy soil,' Lausard murmured, robotically. 'Sloping a little toward the east or south, with a river and a forest nearby. That, at least, is what any good officer will tell you.'

'Does that come straight from the rule book, Alain?' chuckled Rocheteau.

'So where are *we*?' Delacor muttered. 'In the middle of a forest. Damp. Cold. Unable to cook. Unable to find fresh water. While our glorious leader eats his fill and warms himself at a roaring fire.'

'The Emperor has suffered deprivations as we have,' Bonet commented. 'He has lived in tents and camped in fields before. He has tasted the discomfort we know so well. He's entitled to a little luxury. He *is* the ruler of our country, after all.'

'And we follow him blindly because of that,' Roussard added.

'We follow him because we are soldiers in his army and we obey the orders he gives,' Rocheteau snapped. 'If he says we go without fire then that is what we do.'

'Bonaparte doesn't want the Prussians to discover our positions too early,' said Lausard. 'Thousands of roaring camp fires are likely to alert them, don't you think?'

'Are there Prussians in these woods then?' Roussard asked, glancing around into the gloom.

'No one knows *where* the Prussian armies are,' Lausard mused. 'My guess is they will wait until we emerge from the forest before they attack us.'

'Perhaps they've all run away,' Roussard offered, hopefully.

'And left their country to the mercy of an invading army? I doubt it. What would you do if France was in peril? Run and hide or fight?' The sergeant took another swig from the bottle then handed it to Rocheteau.

'I would die for my country if I had to,' Roussard said. 'It's just that I wish the Emperor wouldn't keep giving me the opportunity to do so as *frequently* as he does.'

The other men laughed.

'First it was the Austrians,' chuckled Rocheteau. 'Then the Russians. This time the Prussians. Who could be next?'

'The English,' offered Charvet. 'I heard from a corporal in the seventh that they have landed troops in Italy and armed the local population there. The whole of Calabria has risen against us.'

'That is not our concern presently,' Rocheteau said.

'It may be after *this* campaign,' Carbonne added.

'That depends how long the war against Prussia takes,' Lausard reminded them. 'It is October now. Soon the weather will begin to worsen. We could be up to our knees in snow and mud within a month. Perhaps then we will all long for the sunshine of Italy again.'

'The dog-faces will be hoping the war is over before winter sets in,' Delacor grinned. 'I heard that they were not issued with overcoats before the campaign began. Nor extra shoes.'

'It will be hard on all of us if the war continues through the winter,' Lausard murmured. 'Let us hope Bonaparte has made provision for that eventuality. If we are to strike we need to do so fast. This war must be concluded quickly.'

'At what cost in lives?' Roussard wanted to know.

Lausard had no answer for him.

All around them, the symphony of night sounds continued.

Twelve

———— >○< ————

Drawn by eight magnificent white horses, the Imperial post-chaise trundled along the road, occasionally lurching to the left or right dependent upon the ruts in the thoroughfare and the nature of the terrain. It was an imposing and impressive transport. Used by the Emperor for long journeys, it contained a folding bed, a desk, bookshelves and lockers, enabling the Corsican to work while he was on the move. Marshal Berthier sat at the desk, quill in hand, gazing expectantly at his commander, awaiting the first deluge of instructions and orders that would inevitably begin to spill forth once the Emperor had finished his musings. Inside the vehicle, Napoleon glanced at a series of despatches that he had received during the last hour. The Emperor seemed oblivious to the sometimes wild rocking of the carriage, so absorbed was he with the scribblings before him. Beside him sat Caulaincourt. The Master of the Horse was gazing out of one window at the German countryside as it sped by. Opposite, Marshal Bessiéres sat brushing dust from the sleeves of his gilt-embroidered uniform. Ahead of the transport, two orderly officers rode. Beyond them, another officer and twelve green-clad chausseurs of the Imperial Guard, the Emperor's personal bodyguard, cleared the way through any other traffic that might be on the road. One thousand metres behind the coach rode the main escort, another four squadrons of the elite cavalrymen.

The dense masses of trees that comprised the Thüringer Wald had given way to more open country-side. Although, still heavily wooded, it was now possible to see relatively long distances across country in all directions and, for that, Napoleon was grateful. The first and most difficult part of the journey had been successfully negotiated both by the Emperor himself and also by the bulk of his army. He finally slapped the despatches down and grinned broadly at the other men in the coach.

'Gentlemen, it is going well for us,' he declared. 'We have negotiated the hazards of the forest and emerged unscathed. These,' he held up the despatches, 'confirm our progress. Soult is at Münchberg with light cavalry towards Hof. Bernadotte has reached Ebersdorf. He is supporting Murat who is at Saalburg. Lannes is presently just beyond Coburg.'

'Is there any news on the Prussian dispositions, sire?' Bessiéres wanted to know.

'The reports are still vague as to the precise where-abouts of their *main* strength,' the Emperor said, a slight frown creasing his brow. 'Current intelligence puts Tauenzien at Schleiz with six thousand Prussians and three thousand Saxon troops under his command. There is also cause to believe that there are another eight or nine thousand Saxons on the right bank of the Saale towards Auma.'

'But still no news of the main armies?' Bessiéres persisted.

Napoleon shook his head.

'Is it prudent to continue the advance without knowing our enemies' whereabouts, sire?' the Marshal asked. 'If you concentrate your forces in the wrong place . . .'

'I am not in the habit of making mistakes like that, Bessiéres,' Napoleon told him, the hint of a rebuke in his voice. 'Have you forgotten so soon that the formation of the army is such that *wherever* the main Prussian force is concentrated, I can bring the full weight of my troops against them within a matter of hours?'

'I did not doubt your reasoning for one moment, sire. I have served under you for too long as to be so foolish. I am merely expressing a concern that I know you share.'

'Yes, you are right, Bessiéres. I would be happier if I knew *exactly* where our enemy intended to confront us, but that is a luxury I must do without for the present.'

'Will they attack us, sire?' Caulaincourt wanted to know.

'Another secret I am not yet privy too, my friend,' the Emperor smiled. 'I have no idea how the minds of these old men work. I cannot begin to fathom their strategies, only to press ahead with my own.'

'But if you do so without knowing their whereabouts, sire, you take a risk,' Bessiéres observed.

'One must take risks in any campaign, Bessiéres. If I had not taken risks at Austerlitz our triumph would not have been so complete. The burden is upon the Prussians, not us. It is their country we have entered. It is incumbent upon *them* to respond to our invasion. To attempt to drive us back. I suspect they will choose to attack. An action prompted by pride as much as necessity.' He looked across at Berthier. 'An order to Bernadotte,' the Corsican began, and the Chief of Staff dipped his quill into the ink before him, steadying himself as the post-chaise lurched over a large bump in the road. 'He is to attack what lies before him.' The quill began scratching across the paper as Berthier wrote. 'Drive Tauenzien back towards Auma and open the road to Gera.'

'And what of Marshal Soult, sire?' the Chief of Staff enquired. 'Is he to continue with his advance alongside the river Elster?'

'Yes, and Lannes is to push on towards Saalfeld and Rudolstadt,' the Corsican continued. 'We will soon flush out this Prussian fox,' he murmured more softly. 'It seems to have gone to ground for the time being. When it finally emerges it will find French hounds ready to taste its blood.'

Alain Lausard peered through the telescope and swept it back and forth across the terrain before him. The road rose gradually along the gently sloping hills. He could see blue-coated French infantry advancing unhurriedly towards a large wood that grew thickly on either side of the thoroughfare. They had been moving into the mass of trees for close to three hours now and the crackling of musket fire still filled the air as the Prussians fighting inside the woods strove to keep them back. Every now and then, Lausard would see darker uniformed Prussian troops run from the enveloping trees, some supporting wounded comrades, a number hurling their packs and bicorns away as if losing the added weight would help them in their flight. The sergeant finally handed the telescope to Rocheteau, who also watched the unfolding manoeuvres with a slight smile on his face. To the right of the road, dozens of French skirmishers ran ahead of their infantry, sheltering behind the many natural obstacles between themselves and the enemy as they fired their muskets. Trained to aim for officers and NCOs, they scuttled across the undulating terrain firing, reloading with lightning speed then firing again.

There were two Prussian six-pounders on a hill away to the right and, periodically, the guns would send round-shot hurtling towards the French but, for the most part, their efforts were token. Geysers of earth flew into the air as the solid shot struck the ground but, as far as Lausard could see, the Prussian gunners were doing little damage. Wreathed in sulphurous black smoke, they loaded and reloaded slowly and with apparent disregard for the troops arrayed before them.

Erebus ran backwards and forwards in front of the watching dragoons, more excited by the prospect of confronting the Prussians than many of the cavalrymen were. Occasionally the dog would bark loudly in the direction of the Prussians. Every discharge of the six-pounders brought a fresh bout of snarling from the animal.

'How much longer are we going to have to sit here?' Rocheteau murmured, snapping the telescope shut and handing it back to Lausard.

'Until we're told to move,' the sergeant told him, noticing Captain Milliere and Lieutenant Royere in conversation with two officers from a French hussar regiment. The men were pointing animatedly towards the woods on both sides of the road. The hussar captain, a tall man with long plaited sideburns hanging as far as his shoulders, was puffing contentedly on a pipe.

'We could charge through those sauerkraut eaters in no time,' Delacor offered.

'They are fighting inside woods,' Lausard said, disdainfully. 'Not the best terrain for a cavalry charge.' He patted the neck of his horse and glanced at his watch.

During his time as a soldier, Lausard had found that waiting was one of the most intolerable factors in a battle. To sit helplessly while fighting went on before you or, in the worst cases, around you was something he hated. Much better the shrill notes from the trumpet to sound the advance or the charge. The shouts to draw swords. Then the movement towards the enemy. Even though it meant facing death again, it was preferable, in Lausard's eyes, to this interminable inactivity.

There were clouds of smoke hanging over the woods on both sides of the road, the accumulation of musket fire from both armies that had been going on sporadically all morning. The acrid stench that Lausard and his companions had come to know so well stung their nostrils, despite the fact that they must have been a good eight or nine hundred yards from the perimeter of the densely wooded area. Joubert pulled his canteen from his saddle and drank a couple of mouthfuls.

'Don't waste that,' Lausard said. 'You may need every drop in the coming days.'

'Where are we anyway?' Roussard wanted to know. 'What is the name of this place?'

Bonet pulled a map from his portmanteau and traced one finger across it. 'The woods to either side of the road are the woods of Oschitz,' he said. 'There is a village beyond them called Schleiz. I suspect that is our objective.'

'Does it matter where we are?' asked Sonnier. 'Or what our objectives are? Everywhere looks the same through smoke anyway.'

'Roussard wants to know the name of the place where he's going to die,' chuckled Carbonne.

The other men laughed.

Moreau crossed himself.

Horses, as impatient as their riders, pawed the ground or tossed their heads. The ever present smell of droppings reached the men's nostrils as strongly as the sulphur smell of gunpowder.

Lausard heard a loud bang as one of the six-pounders fired off another shot. The metal projectile struck the earth, bounced high into the air then spun on another eight or nine feet before ricochetting once more off a low undulation in the ground. It finally rolled to a halt about thirty yards ahead of the group of officers, who seemed completely unworried by the fact that the Prussian gunners now seemed to be turning their fire in the direction of the stationary French cavalry. The hussar officer merely puffed even more frantically on his pipe, practically disappearing within a noxious cloud of fumes. Lausard glanced across at the squadron of brightly uniformed light horsemen to the left of the road. Dressed in cornflower blue surtouts and reinforced leather overalls, even in their field dress they still carried the air of flamboyance associated with their kind. Every single man, it seemed, sported a large bushy moustache, most of them waxed at the ends and curling upwards like the horns of a demon. Some of the men had removed their shakos and were preening their long plaited hair with a vanity that caused Lausard to smile.

'Peacock bastards,' hissed Delacor, also glancing across at the hussars but somewhat less impressed by their show of self-absorption.

'Perhaps you should join them, Alain,' Rocheteau smiled. 'If *your* hair gets much longer you'll have to start plaiting it. It's all the fashion among our companions there.'

The other men laughed.

'Fashion is the least of my concerns as a soldier, Rocheteau,' the sergeant said, his eyes now drawn back towards the Oschitz wood. Again he looked at his watch, as if that simple act would precipitate movement.

Another six-pounder round came arcing across the fields towards the waiting cavalry. It landed with a loud thud, sent a huge spray of earth and dust into the air and buried itself in the ground. Lieutenant Royere gripped his reins to control his horse, the animal suddenly startled by the lumps of earth that rained down on the men. He patted its neck to calm it, wiping dust from the sleeve of his already filthy uniform. It hardly seemed worth the effort.

'They're getting the range,' Rocheteau remarked.

Lausard didn't answer. His attention had been caught by another sound, coming from the rear of the stationary cavalry. He turned in the saddle to discover the source of the steadily growing noise. The unmistakeable rhythm of marching feet and beating drums filled the air. The sergeant saw several Eagles being held aloft, pennants fluttering in the wind. He heard shouts of '*Vive l'Empereur*' and now more of the dragoons found themselves gazing towards the steadily approaching mass of French infantry. They were formed into a column fifty ranks wide and double that number deep, on the road. Behind came another similar formation. And another. Led by mounted officers and two ranks of drummer boys, the infantry moved along at the regulation seventy-five paces a minute. Lausard knew that pace would be increased to one hundred and twenty a minute when the infantry reached the open ground before the Oschitz wood. They would also more than likely reform into line to assault the mass of trees where many of their comrades were already engaged.

'So, the dog-faces are finally earning their pay,' Delacor said as the head of the leading infantry column passed. He hawked and spat.

Lausard was surprised to see the infantry continue along the road, taking the gentle slope in their stride. They seemed uninterested in the fighting going on within the wood.

The Prussian gunners took the opportunity to open fire on the column as it passed and Lausard saw a roundshot smash into the ground close to the road. It spun skyward then dropped harmlessly back into the dirt. The second shot was more successful. The solid round ploughed into the column, took out six men then hurtled on until it thudded into a slope some fifty yards further on. The sergeant looked on impassively as one infantryman reeled away from the column clutching at the stump of an arm that had been severed at the shoulder by the metal ball. He stood helplessly, blood jetting from the wound, looking almost imploringly at his companions as they continued to march by. He finally dropped to his knees and remained in that position. NCOs shouted orders and the column closed up.

A horseman was thundering up alongside the column, shouting something. From his gold-trimmed blue uniform, Lausard could see that he was an ADC. His horse was lathered, indicating that it had been ridden hard for some time and some distance. The aide hurtled towards the clutch of cavalry officers gathered near the road and handed a piece of paper to the hussar captain, who read the order as he puffed away at his pipe. Moments later, the hussars wheeled away and returned to the head of their waiting troops. The aide pulled sharply on the reins of his horse and hurtled back the way he had come. Lausard saw that Captain Milliere and Lieutenant Royere were also guiding their mounts back to where the dragoons continued to wait.

'The infantry are to assault the village of Schleiz,' the captain said. 'The hussars will support them.'

'What about us, Captain?' Lausard asked.

'We wait,' Milliere told him. 'If we are needed, we will be sent for. We are to act as support for the infantry and the hussars.' He pulled his watch from his pocket. 'We are to advance towards the village two hours from now.'

Lieutenant Royere checked his own timepiece against that of his commander, nodding when he saw that they shared the same hour.

The air was suddenly filled with the shrill notes of trumpets, followed by the jingling of hundreds of harnesses and the thudding of many more hooves as the hussars moved off in perfectly regulated formation. Clouds of dust rose around the cavalrymen as they advanced. The light horsemen formed a column alongside the infantry and Lausard watched as the entire formation continued up the slope in the direction of the village that lay beyond the crest. On either side of the road, gunfire still crackled as the fighting in the woods continued. The sporadic cannon shots from the two Prussian six-pounders rang out periodically.

'Your eagerness for battle is undiminished, Sergeant,' Milliere grinned.

'It is preferable to sitting around helplessly, Captain,' Lausard answered.

'That is true,' Milliere conceded. He was gazing across at the corpses of the infantry lying on the road, blown to pieces by the Prussian roundshot. 'But are you so keen to join *those* men?' He nodded in the direction of the bodies. The infantryman who had lost an arm had now slumped forward at the roadside, unconscious from the combined effects of blood loss and shock.

'I have no wish to die, Captain,' Lausard said. 'But I accept that it is a possibility. What soldier does not?'

'Are we not supposed to look upon dying for our Emperor as an honour?' Milliere mused.

'The lieutenant would,' Lausard smiled. 'What would your last words be, my friend? Long live the Republic? Glory to the Revolution?'

Milliere chuckled and glanced at the other officer.

'It seems your politics are well known, Lieutenant,' he said. 'I hope you consider them worth dying for.'

'I would die for France if I had too,' Royere admitted. 'Wouldn't we all?'

'It appears we have very little say in the matter,' Milliere answered. He glanced at Lausard. 'And you, Sergeant, what would *your* last words be before you departed this world for another?'

'I would hope my final words would be "we are victorious",' the sergeant mused.

'An admirable sentiment,' Milliere echoed.

'And yours, Captain?'

'I have no plans to speak any final words on a battlefield, Sergeant, surrounded by dead men and horses, covered in blood. Deafened by artillery fire. Choked by the smoke from fifty thousand muskets and cannon. No. I plan to speak *my* last words from the comfort of a bed when I am a *very* old man.'

The other men laughed.

'I would speak but one word,' said Giresse. 'Women.'

There was more laughter.

'Just as Joubert's last word would be food,' Rocheteau added, chuckling.

'I would tell God that I was on my way to join Him,' Moreau intoned, crossing himself.

'My last words would be to Allah, all Praise to Him,' Karim offered.

'Mine would be "Why does it have to be me?"' said Roussard, flatly.

The men nearby laughed uproariously, the sound peculiarly alien as it mingled with the ever present popping of musket fire from the woods and the dull booms of the Prussian six-pounders.

'Let us hope that none of us is speaking our last words today or at any time in the near future,' Milliere said, quietly. He glanced in the direction of the Oschitz wood. The smoke from so many weapons wreathed the trees like a shroud. Beyond the ridge, in the direction of Schleiz, more musket fire could now be heard. Within minutes, the sky above the village also began to fill with writhing smoke.

Rocheteau was the first to spot the rider. The man was mounted on what had once been a grey horse, but it was so spattered with blood, dust and gunpowder that the animal now looked dappled. Its rider looked similarly ravaged. A portion of his left jacket sleeve had been torn open to expose a savage wound, which was pumping blood furiously, darkening the material of his light blue tunic. Lausard also saw the man and noticed that part of his blue shabracque had been ripped away and was badly singed. There were several bullet holes in his shako, including one that had dented the brass front plate. As he drew nearer, the sergeant could see that the hussar's face was a mask of blood and gunpowder.

Captain Milliere and Lieutenant Royere, like many of the dragoons, had dismounted to relieve the weight on their mounts as the interminable wait continued, but now, as the officers saw the approaching hussar, both of them swung themselves in their saddles and spurred towards him. Milliere beckoned Lausard forward to join them as the bloodied figure of the light horseman drew

nearer, his horse stumbling in one of the deep holes left
by a Prussian roundshot. For precious seconds, it seemed
as though the exhausted animal was going to fall, but
its rider kept control of the grey and guided it on towards
the oncoming dragoons. He pulled hard on the reins
and the horse reared wildly. Weakened by loss of blood
and the wound in his arm, the hussar was unable to
retain his position. The horse whinnied and toppled over
to one side, spilling the rider into the dirt. He landed
heavily on his injured arm, his shout of pain echoing
across the fields. Lausard jumped from his own horse
and helped the hussar to sit up, ignoring the blood that
spilled onto his own hands.

'An order from Marshal Murat himself, Captain,'
gasped the hussar.

Milliere also swung himself from the saddle. Pulling
his canteen free, he offered it to the panting hussar, who
gulped down the water, much of it spilling down the
front of his tunic.

'Bring your men at once to his aid,' the hussar continued, gritting his teeth against the pain. 'If you do not
then he cannot push the Prussians out of the village.'

'Are they in great strength there?' Milliere wanted to
know.

'They have heavy cavalry support,' the hussar gasped,
reaching again for the canteen. 'If we are not reinforced
we will be overrun.'

'I have two squadrons. Does Marshal Murat believe
they will make a difference?'

'There are two *divisions* of dragoons further back, they
are to be ordered forward too.'

'You are in no state to relay that order,' Royere said, flatly. 'I will send one of our own men back to execute it.'

'What of the infantry?' Lausard asked.

'They are making progress but Marshal Murat demands reinforcements immediately,' said the hussar.

Lausard allowed the man to sink back onto the earth then stood up. He reached immediately for the reins of his horse.

Milliere and Royere did likewise.

Other dragoons were running across towards the wounded man, helping him to his feet.

'Lieutenant, you take the second squadron,' Milliere said. 'I will lead the first myself.' He turned towards the waiting horsemen, many of whom were already mounting their horses. Milliere smiled. 'They seem as eager as you, Sergeant.'

The men rode back towards the dragoons, Milliere taking his place at their head.

'Single column,' he roared. 'Trumpeters, sound the advance.'

Lausard felt his heart thudding more quickly against his ribs as the shrill notes blasted from the instruments.

'Walk, march,' bellowed Milliere and the green-clad horsemen moved off en masse. The sound of harnesses filled the air once more. The pace gradually increased from a walk to a trot, dust clouds rose around them like smoke. Then, on more shouted orders and the blaring of trumpets, to a canter. The entire column picked up speed. Horses tossed their heads wildly and chewed frenziedly on their bits, as if anxious to reach the fighting, infected with the same frenzy as their riders. Lausard gritted his teeth, his breathing now quicker. Moreau crossed himself. Karim touched the hilt of his scimitar. Sonnier almost unconsciously tapped the butt of his carbine. Tabor did likewise. He had already fixed the needle-sharp fifteen-inch bayonet to the end of the weapon. Delacor reached back to his portmanteau and felt the handle of the axe sticking out. It was ready for him to use when he had to. To Lausard's left, the swallow-tailed guidon of the regiment fluttered in the breeze – the three-coloured standard topped by its sculpted brass eagle. The sergeant felt a shiver run the length of his spine as he saw the gleaming bird, a symbol of regimental pride, of Empire. Of conquest.

He tried to swallow but his mouth was as dry as chalk. Every sense seemed sharpened. Each smell was more acute. Every sound amplified. The odour of sweat, both human and animal. The rattling of sword scabbards against boot cuffs. The jingling cacophony of harnesses which now sounded almost deafening. He could even hear Erebus barking as the dog ran alongside the cantering horses, unworried by the dust and earth they threw up with hooves that churned the ground to silt.

They were approaching the crest of the rise now, passing between the two tree-choked expanses of the Oschitz wood, where the fighting still continued, and on towards the village of Schleiz itself. The sounds of battle grew ever louder. The smoke that from a distance had appeared like thin mist now looked and smelled like noxious fog. Lausard heard cannon fire. Detected the clash of sword on sword. He heard the screams of dying men. The sounds had an almost welcome familiarity about them and he touched the hilt of his sword with one hand, urging his mount on to greater speed as the dragoons crested the ridge.

The scenes around the village of Schleiz were of utter pandemonium.

Many of the buildings were already ablaze, smoke belching from their gutted shells. Inside the others, Prussian troops fought manfully to keep out the ferocious French infantry, who were storming the buildings with furious ease. Wounded men spilled into the streets, some supporting injured comrades, others emerging with their hands held high in the air, more eager to surrender than to return to their own army. To the left, more French troops were emerging from the stifling confines of the Oschitz wood, in most places pursuing the darker uniformed Prussians, some of whom were attempting to retire in good order while others were hurtling madly away from the inexorable advance of their enemies, hurling packs and weapons in all directions. A battery of Prussian six-pounders, on a rise to the left of the main road, was sending roundshot into the village itself, killing friend and foe alike. It was to the right of the collection of buildings that Lausard saw the most savage exchanges. The blue-clad French hussars were hacking away at hundreds of white-uniformed Prussian cuirassiers. Bigger men on bigger horses, the German cavalry had already caused considerable casualties and Lausard could see that the ground was littered with dead and dying hussars. Riderless horses bolted in all directions. Wounded men, desperate to escape the melee, clung to their horses' manes and allowed the animals to carry them in whichever direction they wished. Many of the horses were also injured. Lausard saw one magnificent black horse pawing the ground pathetically as blood spurted from a huge wound in its neck. Other animals lay like so many hunks of bloodied meat, many with their riders resting against them. Some actually lying on those who had once ridden them.

'Draw swords,' roared Milliere, and the loud hiss of hundreds of weapons leaving their scabbards filled the air. 'Trumpeters. Sound the charge.'

The staccato notes rose high above the cacophony of sounds, ringing in the ears of the dragoons and all those nearby. Gaston even stood in the stirrups as he blasted out the familiar refrain that would send his companions hurtling forward at a gallop.

'Charge,' bellowed Milliere and put spurs to his horse.

The dragoons hurtled down a slight incline towards the battling hussars and cuirassiers. French infantrymen, emerging from the woods to the right, cheered wildly as they saw the horsemen thundering to the attack.

Lausard felt the wind rushing past his face. It carried with it the stench of blood, death and gunpowder. Smoke and dust stung his eyes but he kept them fixed on the tangle of horsemen before him and gripped his reins more tightly. His horse barely needed coaxing. Driven on by the infectious fury of the other mounts, it rolled its eyes wildly in their sockets as it charged, hooves pounding the ground, every muscle straining. Erebus hurtled along, barking insanely, teeth bared.

The dragoons crashed into the melee like a battering

ram. Lausard drove his sword forward and skewered the nearest cuirassier through the chest, dragging the weapon free and striking again, this time catching the man in the throat. Alongside him, his companions also found their targets and struck with similar savagery. He saw Captain Milliere parry a blow from a Prussian trooper then cut upwards, driving his sword through the man's chin with such ferocity that the first twelve inches of the blade erupted from the top of the man's skull. Milliere tore it free and rode on. Rocheteau struck to his left and right, narrowly missing a wounded French hussar. He caught a cuirassier officer with a powerful backhand swipe that left a crimson gash across the front of his white tunic. The man toppled from the saddle, his white-plumed bicorn toppling from his head. Delacor swung the axe with one hand and his sword with the other. He parried a sword cut with his own blade then swung round to bury the axe in the shoulder of his attacker. The man shrieked as his collar bone shattered and Delacor finished him off with a sword thrust to the stomach. Karim ducked beneath a blow then sliced his assailant's hand off with a cut of his scimitar that sent the severed hand spinning skyward with the heavy sword still gripped in it. As the cuirassier sat transfixed in his saddle, the Circassian struck again, cutting him so violently across the stomach that he disembowelled him. Even Erebus leapt at a cuirassier, sinking its teeth into the man's thigh and tearing his breeches. He beat at the dog with the pommel of his sword but the animal's attack distracted him enough to leave him helpless as Moreau drove his sword into him. As the cuirassier hit the ground, Erebus was upon him, biting madly at his arms and face.

Many of the French hussars, seemingly beaten by their larger opponents, now found the renewed strength to fight on. Encouraged by the arrival of reinforcements, they swung their sabres at the cuirassiers and the tide of battle began to turn.

Lausard drove his horse on through the melee, dragging a pistol from its holster in time to shoot a cuirassier in the face. The man slumped forward in the saddle. He saw Tabor grab a Prussian by the head and with one powerful twist snap his neck effortlessly, dropping the body with all the disdain of a greyhound that has killed a hare. Sonnier pulled his carbine from its boot and swung it up to his shoulder in time to shoot down an enemy officer. He reloaded with incredible speed, tearing the top from his cartridge, pouring the black powder down the barrel then spitting the ball after it before ramming it home. Bonet and Joubert fought on either side of him, giving him the time he needed.

The second squadron now thundered into the fight and it was the final straw for the Prussians. The cuirassiers wheeled their mounts and, where possible, rode hell for leather towards the flaming inferno that was Schleiz and the safety of their own lines beyond it. Many of the hussars were too exhausted to pursue them but Royere led several ranks of dragoons after the fleeing heavy cavalry. Lausard, his face splashed with blood, put spurs to his horse and joined the pursuit. He saw Captain Milliere just ahead of him, the blade of his sword smeared crimson. A wounded Prussian corporal was trying to escape the French officer. He was bleeding from a sword cut that had laid open the upper part of his right arm, and the private who rode alongside him was holding his reins with his free hand, desperate to escape Milliere who was closing rapidly.

He drove his sword forward into the unprotected back of the wounded corporal, who slumped to one side, his foot sliding from the stirrup. The private reached for his pistol and, without even looking, fired over his shoulder.

Lausard spurred over to despatch the man but he was too late. More by luck than judgement, the lead ball caught Milliere in the face, punctured his cheek and shattered several teeth. The officer jerked back in the saddle, his horse rearing wildly, losing its balance and hurling him to the ground as it teetered for interminable seconds on its hind legs before toppling back. Milliere could not avoid its falling bulk. The horse crashed down onto him, whinnied loudly, then struggled to its feet, kicking out wildly. One hoof connected with the officer's temple. The sickening sound of cracking bone was clearly audible. Lausard leapt from his own saddle and ran to the officer's aid. Rocheteau also saw what was happening and spurred across. Three more Prussian cuirassiers, intent on escape, found they had no choice but to ride over the dismounted trio. Rocheteau dragged his carbine free and shot down the leading horse, its rider cartwheeling across the bloodied dirt. Lausard, cradling Milliere's head on his lap, struck out with his sword and caught another of the horses across the muzzle. The wound was deep and the horse veered off to one side, colliding with another fleeing Prussian. Milliere's eyes were half open but there was no recognition in them. He looked blankly at

Lausard, his mouth hanging open like that of a freshly caught fish. The sergeant was certain which of the injuries was the most serious. Although the pistol shot had left a hole the size of a thumb nail in the officer's cheek, it was the kick to the head that could prove to be fatal. Blood was streaming down Milliere's face. When he tried to speak, more of the crimson fluid ran from his mouth and he could manage only a hoarse, gurgling whisper.

'Get help,' roared Lausard, still crouching with the officer.

Rocheteau swung himself into the saddle. Several of the other dragoons were around them now, looking down at the stricken officer. Exhausted, they were content to leave the pursuit of the Prussian heavy cavalry to their comrades, who were driving the white-clad riders back beyond the blazing remains of Schleiz itself.

'Bring a surgeon, quickly,' the sergeant shouted. 'Put a gun to his head if you have to but get him here as quickly as you can.

'Hold on, Captain,' Lausard said, gripping the officer's hand.

The pressure exerted in return began to fade rapidly.

All around, the fighting continued but, for Lausard, everything had been condensed into the tableau before him. He saw only the bloodied face of Milliere. Heard only his incoherent babbling.

'Hold on,' he repeated.

Thirteen

Napoleon warmed himself beside the large camp fire that burned before his tent and glanced at the aide-de-camp standing before him. Despite the chill of the night, the officer was sweating profusely, his face grimed by dust and dirt from his ride. The Emperor himself reached for the jug of claret on the table outside his tent and poured the ADC a measure of the liquor which he accepted gratefully. Other officers and higher ranking figures moved back and forth around the Corsican, either engaged in their own private tasks or anxious to hear what their commander had to say. Marshal Berthier sat at his portable desk, quill poised in his hand. Ever ready to jot down any instructions the Emperor might care to give. Marshal Bessiéres and General Savary, both still clad in their full dress uniforms, also stood beside the fire. Bessiéres was chewing on a chicken leg, wiping the grease from his chin with the back of one hand. The Emperor and his entourage were protected by a unit of Imperial Guard grenadiers, formed into a square around the group. Beyond them, their companions sat around camp fires in relative silence. Sentries patrolled the perimeters of the bivouac, ever vigilant, squinting into the darkness as they strode purposefully back and forth, their tall bearskins nodding as they walked.

'According to this,' said the Corsican, holding up the communication he'd received from the ADC, 'Soult has occupied Hof without opposition. He is camped between Plauen and Hof.' The Emperor put a hand on the shoulder of the aide. 'Take a fresh horse and ride back to the Marshal. Give him these orders.' The Corsican turned towards Berthier. 'This is what appears to me most clear: it seems that the Prussians intended to attack; that their left was intended to debouch by Jena, Saalfeld and Coburg; that Prince Hohenlohe had his headquarters at Jena and Prince Louis at Saalfeld. The other column has issued by Meiningen on Fulda so that I am led to believe you have nothing in front of you, perhaps not ten thousand men as far as Dresden. The news that one thousand men have retired from Plauen on Gera leaves me no doubt that Gera is the point of union of the enemy's army. I doubt if they can unite before I arrive there.' Napoleon paused, gazing momentarily into the leaping flames of the fire. 'You will advance on Gera through Weida.'

Berthier finished writing, folded the parchment and handed it to the aide.

'Go quickly and may God protect you,' said the Corsican.

The aide saluted and disappeared into the gloom. Moments later, the sound of horses' hooves echoed through the night as he sped off.

'What of the other corps?' Napoleon enquired.

'Marshal Lannes is bivouacked around Grafenthal, sire,' Berthier informed him. 'He has light cavalry on the road to Saalfeld. Marshal Augereau is at Coburg.'

'Close enough to support Lannes?' the Corsican wanted to know.

'Not as yet, sire,' the Chief of Staff answered.

'And Bernadotte?'

'He is camped around Schleiz and Saalburg. Marshal Davout has reached Lobenstein. He has dragoons and heavy cavalry close behind him. The Guard cavalry are also in that vicinity. Marshal Ney is at Münchberg. The Bavarians at Bayreuth.'

'And the Prussians?'

'Their *exact* positions are still unknown, sire,' Savary said, almost apologetically.

Napoleon stalked back and forth, head lowered.

'Why is this so?' he demanded.

'Intelligence reports have not revealed their whereabouts,' Savary offered.

'So, I am forced to make my plans in the manner of a blind man, unable to see my opponent,' snapped the Corsican. 'Have there been no reports from any of Murat's patrols? He has half of Germany swarming with light cavalry. How can they fail to find an entire army?'

'The Prussians seem to be spread out over a large area, sire,' Berthier interjected. 'Were they concentrated then it would be a small matter to locate them.'

The Corsican sighed then nodded almost imperceptibly.

'Instruct Ney to advance towards the area around Schleiz,' he said, quietly. 'The Bavarians will take his place in line behind Soult. Lefebvre, with the Guard, is to march directly to the village of Schleiz itself. The cavalry of d'Hautpol, Nansouty, Klein and Grouchy are also to make their way there, as are the artillery and the engineers. Bernadotte and Murat will proceed at once to Auma to intercept any enemy troops attempting to concentrate there and along that route. Marshal Lannes will attack Saalfeld itself, supported by the corps of Augereau who will join him by forced marches. Tell Lannes to expect a major battle.'

Berthier finished writing and looked at the Corsican, as if waiting for more instructions.

The Emperor was gazing into the flames once more.

Aides were called to take the orders. The night was filled again with the rattle of many harnesses.

'Still the Prussians are reluctant to show where their true strength lies,' the Corsican murmured. 'Let us see how they react to these manoeuvres. In time we will find them and when we do, we will destroy them.'

'He is lucky to be alive,' Rocheteau murmured as he sipped at his broth, using a piece of stale bread to mop up the dark liquid.

'How bad were the injuries?' Bonet asked.

Lausard shrugged.

'Four broken ribs, a bullet wound to the face and a cracked skull,' the sergeant announced. 'He's in a field hospital a mile south of Schleiz.'

'The captain is as lucky as you, Sonnier,' chuckled Rochteau.

'Any man who survives a firing squad as Sonnier did

is not lucky,' Delacor added. 'He is in league with the Devil.'

A number of the other dragoons laughed.

'How long before the captain can return to duty?' Tabor wanted to know.

'They'll send him back to France now, you half-wit,' Delacor snapped.

'I just thank God he's alive,' Moreau murmured.

'And what of us?' Rocheteau wanted to know. 'Who is to be our commander now? Lieutenant Royere?'

'He is a very able man,' Lausard intoned. 'But Captain Milliere must be replaced by one of equal rank.'

'They could promote the lieutenant,' offered Roussard.

'They could promote *me*,' Giresse grinned. 'You'd all follow me, wouldn't you?'

'I wouldn't follow you to a river if I was dying of thirst,' Rocheteau chuckled, and the other dragoons joined in.

'I would lead you to the finest women in Europe and order them to ravish you,' Giresse teased.

'Then *I* would follow you,' Delacor interjected.

'Joubert would lead us on a hunt for food,' Rocheteau said. 'Tigana and Karim would find us the finest horses.'

'And Giresse would steal them,' laughed Carbonne. 'Just like he used to.'

'Rostov would lead us all back to Russia,' Charvet intoned.

'Moreau would lead us all to the nearest church and turn us into priests,' Delacor said, disdainfully.

'A regiment of priests,' Rocheteau mused. 'Now that

really would be worth seeing. Even though I doubt if any of us would qualify would we, Moreau?' He slapped his companion on the shoulder.

The other men laughed heartily.

'What about you, Alain?' Bonet wanted to know. 'Would you accept the task if it was offered to you?'

'To lead this squadron?' Lausard mused. 'The chain of command rarely passes from captain down to sergeant, my friend. Like Roussard, I would favour the promotion of Lieutenant Royere. He has the respect of the squadron. He is a brave and sensible man. The two qualities, however, do not always walk hand in hand.'

'But if you *could* lead it?' Bonet persisted.

'I have no desire to do so. I am content to allow others to make their mistakes. If an order is given I will obey it. As long as it is not *too* ridiculous.' He smiled. 'But I would not want to give that order myself.' He took the bottle of wine from Rostov and drank deeply as he watched the flames of the camp fire.

All around, hundreds of other pyres lit the blackness with their orange and yellow hue as men from many different units huddled around them, anxious to stay warm. Sentries patrolled the outer perimeters of the camp. Close to the dragoons, their horses were tethered and many men were attending to their own mounts, Gaston among them. Lausard could see the young trumpeter busily brushing the mane of the grey that he rode. Close by, Sonnier stood chatting to him, his carbine sloped over his shoulder. All over the camp men were eating, talking, playing cards, drinking or trying to sleep as best they could on the hard ground. Lausard himself had his head propped against his saddle, his green cape around his shoulders, his shabracque over his legs like an embroidered blanket. Some light infantrymen were quietly singing a tune the sergeant recognised as 'Let us watch o'er the safety of the Empire'. Lausard could hear Tabor humming close by. Bonet joined in a moment later, as did Charvet. Lausard found the melody pleasant and, as he sat warming himself by the fire with his belly full of broth and wine and his ears filled with the pleasing sound, he felt a fleeting sense of serenity he had not experienced for some time. He allowed himself this brief luxury for a moment longer then got to his feet.

'Another walk in the darkness?' Rocheteau asked.

Lausard nodded and headed away from his companions, past other troops, some of whom glanced in his direction as he passed. Most, however, were too concerned with keeping warm and paid little heed as the sergeant moved among them. The gentle slope upon which the bulk of the French troops were camped was sparsely wooded. The trees had been stripped of their lower branches to build the many bivouac fires that now burned and Lausard had little doubt that any Prussian troops within a mile or two would have little problem spotting the flames. Away to the right was the Saale river and Lausard knew that the town of Saalfeld itself, some three miles to the north, had but one bridge across the mighty river. French light cavalry, he knew, were already positioned ahead, reporting back constantly on the positions of the waiting Prussians. The sergeant had little doubt that the enemy would attempt to maintain control of the bridge over the Saale and this would prompt the battle he expected and, in many ways, hoped for. Even through the darkness, Lausard could see the single main road that led to Saalfeld snaking through the narrow valley ahead like a tongue hanging from the mouth of a parched man. He had little doubt that, come the morning, the French would continue to advance along that road. What lay in store for them he could not begin to imagine. A battle for sure but with what outcome? Like the majority of the men in the French army, Lausard had little doubt that this war, like the others before it, would end in victory for himself and his countrymen. But the wounds he had seen sustained by Captain Milliere had reinforced Lausard's belief that many more of his companions would eventually meet the same fate. Or perhaps one even worse. Who would fall the following day? Rocheteau? Karim? Gaston? Even he, himself? The thought did not trouble him unduly. He had seen enough of death to respect it but not to fear it.

He walked further up the slope, nodding at a sentry as he passed. The infantryman returned the gesture, muttered something about it being a cold night, then returned to his robotic movements back and forth, barely able to grip his Charleville his hands were so chilled. Like that of Lausard and most of the French army, the infantryman's uniform was filthy, held together only, it seemed, by the dirt and the dozens of patches sewn onto it. The cuffs were frayed beyond repair. The man had only one gaiter. His shoes were scuffed so badly that one was almost worn through on the toes. Rags, stained with boot polish, were wound around both his feet. *La*

Grande Armée, mused Lausard somewhat sardonically.

His thoughts were interrupted by the sound of horses' hooves approaching rapidly from the north. He saw three riders and recognised one of them immediately as Marshal Lannes. The young commander was dressed in his full dress uniform and the gold lace on his jacket sparkled in the firelight. Alongside him, two aides guided their horses along the single main road, one of them glancing over his shoulder as if fearing pursuit. Lausard squinted into the gloom but saw no enemy pursuers. He saluted as Lannes and his companions slowed their mounts and the Marshal returned the gesture, dismounting and making for the nearest camp fire. The troops gathered around it immediately stood up and saluted but Lannes motioned for them to remain seated. He pulled a piece of chicken from the bird that was roasting on a bayonet spit over the fire and chewed it hungrily. One of the voltigeurs present offered him a bottle of brandy and the Marshal readily accepted, drinking deeply before handing the bottle back to the infantryman.

'Try to get some sleep,' said the Marshal. 'I fear I will have work for you all come the morning.' He swung himself back into the saddle and raised his plumed bicorn into the air. '*Vive l'Empereur,*' he called and the men returned the salute. Lausard watched as the Marshal and his aides rode off, back down the slope into the heart of the French camp.

Lausard waited a moment longer, gazing out over the valley then, he too turned and wandered back towards where he knew his companions still remained huddled around their fire. As he picked his way back down the

slope, now stepping over many sleeping men of all ranks
and units, he looked up at the sky and saw that it was
relatively clear. There were the odd banks of cloud but,
for the most part, the heavens were uncluttered and the
silver pinpricks of stars glinted against the blue-grey
backdrop of the firmanent. It looked to Lausard as if
someone had fired cannister into a piece of thick velvet.
He saw some horse artillery lying beneath an ammunition caisson, wrapped in their cloaks. Another man was
asleep on the actual carriage of the gun itself and Lausard
was amazed that he did not topple off onto the cold
ground. During a campaign, it was remarkable the variety
of places men sought, and found, to snatch a few hours
much needed rest. The sergeant himself wondered if the
hour was late enough for he himself to find refuge in
the oblivion of slumber. It never came easily to him but
the day had been a tiring one and he hoped that he
might not find it too difficult to drift off into the all-
embracing arms of sleep. He knew that Joubert would
already be dead to the world. The big man never had
any problems succumbing, irrespective of where he was.
Lausard had seen him sleep in the middle of insect-
infested vineyards and marshes in Italy, on the dew-
soaked sand of Egypt, in the freezing passes of the Alps
and the bone-numbing plains of Moravia. Some men,
the sergeant had discovered, seemed able to sleep as soon
as their heads were laid down, others found it virtually
impossible, even in the most comfortable of surroundings. Fear was as likely to keep a man awake as discomfort. Many men found it impossible to sleep before a
battle, their heads filled with the possible horrors of the

coming day. Would they live or die? If they *were* to die, how would that death come? Then those same men slept like new-born babies when the battle was over. So grateful to be alive that they found slumber with ease. Until the next confrontation.

Lausard was one of the unlucky ones. But it wasn't always the terrain or the conditions that caused his wakefulness. Over the years he had resisted sleep because of the dreams it brought. He had no wish to re-live his worst nightmares trapped within the confines of unconsciousness. He had no desire to witness the death of his family replayed countless times inside his head. For that was the dream that came to him when he did find rest. At first it had been unbearable but, as the years had passed, the images had not come with such frequency or clarity. Lausard sometimes wondered if they would recede completely one day, but he doubted it. In many ways he did not *want* those foul pictures to leave him. He feared if they did he would forget his guilt.

As he drew closer to the area where he knew his companions to be he passed a number of men from the second squadron. Corporal Charnier stood and shook his hand and Lausard embraced his companion warmly.

'Still alive?' he said, smiling. 'Perhaps the Devil does not want you with him just yet.'

'And you, my friend,' Charnier grinned. 'If you are still alive then at least I know that God retains a sense of humour.'

The men nearby laughed.

'What news of Captain Milliere?' Charnier said, finally.

'Spared for now, like us all.'

'Have you met his replacement yet?'

Lausard looked puzzled.

'He arrived here from Grouchy's division,' Charnier continued, hooking a thumb over his shoulder. 'You should have been here to greet him, Alain. He's with *your* boys now.'

Lausard looked in the direction of the fires that marked the bivouac of his squadron. In the dull orange glow of the flames he could see that many of the dragoons were on their feet.

'I'd better go and meet this man,' he murmured then turned to face the corporal once more. 'You I will see again soon enough. In hell probably.'

He shook hands with Charnier once more then moved off in the direction of his companions. As he drew nearer he saw most of them gathered around the figures of Lieutenant Royere and another officer whom he did not recognise. The man was tall and lean with wide eyes, a bushy moustache and thick sideburns. There was a deep scar running from the corner of his left eye, across his cheek as far as his chin. Unlike the other men, his brass helmet was not protected by an oilskin cover; it sported instead its tall red plume, as though he wished to be noticed. Lausard wondered if he would discard the decoration when the time came for battle. He was holding a bottle of brandy in his hand, and Lausard noticed that many of the other dragoons also brandished them.

'A gift,' Rocheteau said, holding up the bottle as Lausard approached. 'From the captain.'

The newcomer turned towards Lausard.

'Sergeant Lausard,' said Lieutenant Royere. 'This is Captain Barthez, he—'

The other officer cut him short.

'Captain Maximillian Barthez,' said the man in clipped tones. 'I am your new commander.' He extended his right hand and gripped Lausard's in a powerful grip.

The sergeant saluted.

'As you can see, I have already met your comrades,' Barthez told him. 'I thought it only fair that they should meet the man who will be giving them orders for the forseeable future. I also wanted to show you and your men that I am no different from the rest of you apart from my rank. Look upon me as you would look upon the rest of these fine men. All I ask of you is that you obey the orders I give you.'

'I am a soldier, sir,' Lausard told the officer. 'What else would you have me do?'

Barthez smiled crookedly. 'Sit down,' he urged, motioning to all the men around him. 'All of you. I wish to speak with you. There are certain things that must be said.'

Erebus trotted over, sniffed at the newcomer, then lay down close to Gaston who was warming himself beside the fire. The dog lay contentedly beside the trumpeter, who stroked its thick black fur.

'I have no desire to know you as men,' Barthez said, flatly. 'And I do not mean those words to sound harsh. You all know, as well as I, that by this time tomorrow night we may all be dead. If I know nothing about you, I will not mourn you. I will regret your passing but I will be unaffected by it. It does a soldier no good to form anything but passing friendships in the midst of war.'

'But we have all fought together for more than ten years now, sir,' Lausard said. 'Do you expect us to disregard that time? To abandon the comradeship that has developed between us?'

'That is not what I said, Sergeant,' Barthez intoned, stroking gently at the scar on his cheek. 'But when a man cares too much for the well-being of his companions, it can affect his abilities to fight should he lose one of them. If I were to die tomorrow you would not grieve for me as you would for one of your comrades because you know nothing about me. You do not know me as a man and there is no *need* for you to. All you need know is that I command. That I expect you to follow me. If I order you to charge, you obey.'

The other dragoons sat around the camp fire, some with their gaze fixed on the officer, others merely watching the flickering flames.

'You said you were a man like us, sir,' Lausard reminded Barthez. 'Yet your views are very different.'

'I am like you in as much as I am a simple man. A common man, if you will. I was once a private, as you were. A simple trooper. A product of the Revolution.' He smiled. 'Are we not all children of that struggle, just as our Emperor is? He is the shining light. The example to us all.'

Lausard didn't speak.

'Fifteen years ago, I could not have attained the rank of captain,' Barthez continued. 'Not while those Bourbon leeches sat on the throne of France. Men were appointed to positions of authority because of their backgrounds, not their abilities. The command of a regiment could be *purchased* rather than earned. Generals were made at the whim of some over-fed "pekinese". The Emperor made it possible for men such as you and I to rise above our origins. My father was a saddle maker. He earned next to nothing. My mother raised me and my four brothers. We had little to eat. We dressed in rags. As I am sure did you and many of your men. Two of my brothers died before they were ten. Another on the day of his fifteenth birthday. Smallpox. Hunger. Disease spread by rats. Typhus took my parents and my other brother. I alone survived. I learned from an early age that I should rely on no one but myself. It has been a valuable lesson. I joined the army when I was fourteen. I have made my way through my own efforts and I will continue to do so.'

'It would appear that you and Lieutenant Royere share the same kind of idealism, Captain,' Lausard commented.

'What I speak of is more than that,' Barthez snapped. 'The ideals of the Revolution became a reality for me. I wish sometimes that my family could see how I escaped the environment that killed them. They would be proud of me. Of my ambition. Of my achievements.'

'I am sorry for your loss,' said the sergeant. 'But then we have all suffered in similar ways. There is not a man in this squadron or, indeed, in this entire army who has not been stricken as you have, Captain.'

'Do not pity me, Sergeant,' Barthez murmured. 'I lost my family but I gained a position in the army, in life. I will continue to strive for advancement. No matter what the cost.'

'And where will your quest end, Captain?' Lausard wanted to know. 'When you are a colonel? A general? A Marshal?'

'Perhaps,' Barthez mused. 'But in the meantime there is something I want and nothing – I repeat, nothing – will prevent me from attaining it. I want the *Légion d'Honneur*. And I *will* have it. No matter what it takes.'

Fourteen

⇒►◆◄⇐

Despite the thick smoke drifting across the battlefield, Lausard could see rank after rank of French infantry advancing towards the town of Saalfeld. Most had appeared from the heavily wooded ridge to the left of where the dragoons were positioned. In the centre of the Prussian line, the village of Beulitz had already been overrun and Lausard had seen the enemy troops fall back in considerable disarray. It had taken the French infantry just over two hours to dislodge the stubborn Germans but there had been a sense of inevitability about the outcome of the struggle and now the lines of foot soldiers were moving towards their next objective. With their eagles fluttering above them, the lines and columns moved inexorably forwards like a blue tide. Ahead of them, swarms of skirmishers used the narrow defiles and thickly wooded terrain as cover, keeping up a constant fire against the dark-uniformed Prussian and white-coated Saxon troops who faced them. Nearby, a battery of French four-pounders poured roundshot into the town of Saalfeld itself, much of which had already been demolished by the solid balls. Others were ablaze, the smoke belching from them mingling with that from hundreds of muskets and dozens of cannon. Millions of tiny cinders twisted and whirled in the air so it appeared that a cloud of minute black flies was weaving to and fro across the field, driven by the swells of warm and cold air. Hundreds of burning cartridge papers dotted the ground, glowing like furious fireflies. The constant crackling of musket fire was punctuated and occasionally eclipsed by the roar of cannon from both sides. They were sights and sounds that had become very familiar to the sergeant and his companions during their time in the army, but ones that still never failed to cause Lausard's heart to beat that little bit faster. He wasn't sure how much of that was the prospect of facing death or the sheer exuberance of seeing the fine fighting machine that was *La Grande Armée* in full flow. He glanced across at the guidon of his own regiment and felt a swell of pride that raised the hairs on the back of his neck.

Captain Barthez was walking his horse agitatedly back and forth before the waiting dragoons, occasionally glancing through his telescope towards the fighting.

'Our new captain is impatient,' said Rocheteau, nodding towards the officer.

'He wants his medal,' Lausard mused, sardonically. 'He won't get it sitting watching the infantry do all the fighting.'

'He seems a very honest man,' Bonet interjected. 'He made no attempt to hide his ambitions from us.'

'I agree,' Lausard said, patting his horse's neck. 'But I am more concerned with his temperament than his honesty. If he is so desperate to win the *Légion d'Honneur*, to what lengths will he go? He himself admitted he would stop at nothing to attain it. Personally, I do not wish to become a casualty on the road to Captain Barthez' ambition.'

'What do you mean, Alain?' Rocheteau asked, warily.

'Ambition is like an unbroken horse,' the sergeant muttered. 'If it is harnessed correctly it can be magnificent. If handled unwisely it can damage both those who seek to control it *and* anyone associated with them.'

'You're speaking in riddles,' Delacor said, dismissively. 'What difference does it make to us if this new captain wants some bauble to pin on his chest? Let him have his medal.'

'And how does one win such a decoration?' snapped Lausard. 'By proving one's bravery, correct?'

Delacor nodded slowly.

'To Barthez, bravery may well be charging a battery of guns or trying to break a square of infantry,' the sergeant continued.

'Nothing we haven't done before,' Rocheteau reminded him.

'When the need has arisen, I grant you that.' Lausard looked across once more at the officer who was still squinting through his telescope. 'But we have performed these acts out of necessity, not desire for recognition.' There was a tone of mistrust in the sergeant's voice.

Away to the right, Lausard heard the movement of many horses but he kept his gaze fixed on Barthez. The captain turned in his saddle and saw several squadrons of French hussars moving forward at a canter, across the uneven ground towards the village of Woelsdorf. Their trumpeters sounded the notes of the advance and Lausard could see a frown beginning to crease the features of the dragoon officer. He snapped his reins and urged his horse across to where the green-clad troops sat patiently waiting, watching as the hussars advanced, supported by a column of infantry.

'Are we to sit here all day long?' Barthez hissed. 'We are better qualified to aid in the taking of a village than light cavalry.'

Lausard didn't answer. He was more concerned with watching the hussars who had now broken into a gallop and were bearing down on a number of units of Saxon troops arrayed before the village, who seemed unsure whether or not to form a square or simply run. They chose the latter, and Lausard watched as the light cavalry crashed into them, riding men down, sabring the fleeing Germans. He was still gazing at the carnage when there were several loud explosions from the high ground above the village. A Saxon battery, its green-coated gunners working tirelessly at their pieces, opened a steady fire against the advancing French. Roundshot landed amongst cavalry and infantry alike, bringing down men and horses in bloodied heaps. The cannonballs that didn't strike a soft target first time either ricochetted or buried themselves in the earth, sending up geysers of dirt and dust high into the already smoke-filled air. Dozens of men at a time were felled by the accurate fire. Lausard saw an eagle-bearer decapitated by one roundshot, his headless body striding on robotically for a few more steps before crumpling to the ground.

Other eager hands snatched up the precious flag and bore it on into the battle. The Saxon gunners continued to fire.

'Trumpeter,' Barthez roared. 'Sound the advance.'

Gaston hesitated for a moment.

'Do it,' the captain bellowed.

Lausard glanced to one side and saw the look on Rocheteau's face. The corporal shook his head almost imperceptibly.

'We will advance upon that battery,' Barthez said, pointing towards the Saxons, high up on the hillside.

'We have received no orders to advance, Captain,' Lieutenant Royere reminded him.

'Must you be told *everything*, Lieutenant?' Barthez snapped. 'The decision to advance is mine. That battery is a danger to our troops in front of the village. It must be eliminated. I require your support with the second squadron.'

Royere saluted and rode off to head the other unit of dragoons.

'Draw swords,' Barthez shouted, his voice drowned by the metallic hiss of hundreds of three-foot-long blades being pulled from their scabbards. 'Advance.'

As one, the dragoons moved off. At a walk to begin with, horses neighing loudly as if in expectation. Gradually they increased their pace. Lausard could see the hussars more clearly now as the dragoons passed close by. Prussian infantry had joined the battle and the light cavalry were hacking away at them too, some even glancing at their green-clad countrymen as the dragoons swept past the melee and towards the slope of the hill upon which the Saxon battery was sited.

The incline was steep. Lausard was forced to put spurs to his horse to get it up the first slope. The ground levelled out slightly then rose even more steeply. The sound of the Saxon guns was deafening now and the sergeant realised that they could be no more than three hundred yards away from the yawning barrels of the four-pounders. The gunners had noticed the advance and Lausard saw several of the NCOs re-adjusting the elevation of their barrels. He saw the crews loading cannister. Moreau crossed himself. Rocheteau gritted his teeth, preparing for the gales of shot that would soon be tearing into the dragoons. Ahead, his sword brandished above his head, Barthez rode on, occasionally rising in his stirrups, sometimes glancing over his shoulder as if doubting that his men had followed him. Lausard gripped his own sword more tightly, knowing, as did his companions, that the first volley of fire was about to meet them. He could see the Saxon gunners holding their glowing portfires in their hands, awaiting the order to fire. The dragoons thundered on as best they could, slowed by the increasingly precipitous slope. They were now less than two hundred yards away. The dragoons could even hear orders being shouted as the gunners prepared themselves. Several horses stumbled on the approaches, some throwing riders from their saddles, others causing the lines to break and halt momentarily.

'Hold the line,' roared Barthez. He pointed his sword at the battery. 'Charge.'

No sooner had the word left his mouth than all four

of the Saxon guns opened fire simultaneously. There was a thunderous roar as the cannon erupted and many of the dragoons flinched involuntarily as fire and smoke belched from the barrels. The cannisters erupted and spewed their deadly load of two-ounce lead balls, twenty-seven from each barrel, at the onrushing horsemen. Shot tore into the dragoons. Lausard ducked slightly over the neck of his horse and, all around him, he heard the screams of men and horses as the cannister fire tore bloody swathes through the ranks. Horses crashed to the ground, some of them holed in three or four places by the lethal shot. The sergeant felt something hot and wet splash his face, and realised it was blood spouting from a wounded horse and its rider. The man had been hit in the stomach by a ball and was doubled over in his saddle, trying to hold his intestines in. He finally fell backwards off the horse, next to another man who had been hit in the chest.

A ball took the end of Rocheteau's scabbard off. Another shattered the stock of Carbonne's carbine. Lausard glanced behind him and saw the bodies of men and horses scattered about – some lying still in spreading pools of blood, others wounded and seeking help. Riderless horses dashed back and forth, some in front of the charging dragoons, causing further havoc. But the sergeant realised that the uneven ground they were ascending had actually worked to their advantage. Unable to retain rigid formation, the dragoons had not suffered as badly as they might have done from the burst of cannister. Had they been more tightly packed then the effects would have been critical. But the undulating terrain and the precipitous climb had broken up their formation and left many gaps. Despite the damage wrought by the cannister, Lausard was relieved it was not worse. With the charging dragoons now less than one hundred yards from the guns, he and his companions realised the Saxons would have no chance of reloading. The sergeant gritted his teeth and urged his horse on, seeing two of the crews struggling to ram fresh rounds into the barrels. The other men simply fled.

Delacor slipped the axe from his portmanteau and hefted it before him. He caught one of the Saxons between the shoulder blades with it, tugging the weapon free as he rode on.

Karim swung his scimitar above his head as he bore down on a gunner with a rammer. The Saxon tried to use the long wooden implement as a weapon but the Circassian avoided the clumsy swipe and struck the artilleryman a savage backhand blow that carved open his shoulder.

Lausard swung his own sword down onto the head of another gunner, slicing the man's black-plumed bicorn in two and splitting his skull.

Rocheteau simply rode his horse into another of the Saxons, allowing the animal's churning hooves to crush the man. As he tried to rise, the corporal skewered him through the throat.

Barthez was like a man possessed, hacking to his left and right. He pulled a pistol from his holsters and shot down a fleeing Saxon. Another of the men had hauled himself onto one of the horses that dragged the ammunition caisson. He drew his own sword as Barthez hurtled towards him but he was too slow. He had barely removed the weapon from its scabbard before the dragoon captain drove his own blade into the man's chest with such force that several inches of steel erupted from his back. Barthez then used his bloodied sword to cut the traces on the shaft and jabbed his sword into each horse in turn. The animals darted off in all directions, some crashing into the fleeing gunners. Sonnier brought his horse to a halt, pulled his carbine free and swung it up to his shoulder. He shot down one of the gunners, reloaded with incredible speed and brought down another. Lausard reined in his own mount, peering back and forth through the dense smoke. One of the Saxon gunners was approaching Barthez, his arms raised in surrender, his face white beneath the smudges of gunpowder.

The captain rode towards the man who was shouting something in German and stretching his arms even higher into the air.

Barthez cut the man down, hacking through his face with a powerful stroke.

'What are you doing?' Lausard shouted, guiding his horse towards the officer. 'That man wanted to surrender. By the rules of war you should have allowed him to.'

'Don't lecture me on the rules of war,' snarled Barthez. 'There is only one rule that matters. Kill the enemy.'

'Sergeant Lausard is right, Captain,' Royere added, joining them. 'You should have allowed him to surrender.' The lieutenant looked down at the motionless form of the Saxon gunner, the huge gash across his face having practically split his head open from forehead to chin.

'Look around you,' Barthez rasped, pointing back through the drifting smoke. 'Look at your fallen comrades. That man helped to destroy them.' He hawked loudly and spat on the body of the Saxon.

Royere was about to speak again but then thought better of it. He noticed that the attention of the captain had been drawn towards the town of Saalfeld itself. From their position, high up on the ridge, the dragoons could see down into the town even though it was still shrouded by thick sulphurous smoke. The dark swelling surge of the Saale river cut through the town and the single bridge that spanned it was already clogged with Prussian and Saxon troops, desperate to reach the relative safety of the far bank. Lausard could see French infantry fighting their way through the narrow streets, brushing aside with ease what remaining resistance they encountered. The thoroughfares were littered with dead and dying. Smoke continued to pour from the buildings, great tongues of flame occasionally rising through the choking pall.

'Form column,' roared Barthez and the trumpeters blasted out the familiar notes that informed the dragoons of the manoeuvre required.

Lausard and Royere exchanged a silent glance then the horsemen were moving again, this time down the slopes, many of the mounts struggling to maintain their footing. Their momentum carried them on at a speed guaranteed to exhaust already weary animals and Lausard tried to rein in his own bay in a vain effort to spare it such furious exertion. Joubert dug his knees hard into his own horse and, for precious seconds, he felt he was going to overbalance as the dragoons hurtled down the slope. Charvet too struggled to retain control of his mount. The valley floor seemed to be rushing up towards them with incredible speed and Lausard wondered if the entire squadron would simply plough into the ground when they finally reached the relative safety of the bottom of the ridge. Close behind him a horse slipped, hurling its rider from the saddle. The animal rolled help-lessly, crashing into others. Whinnies of pain and surprise rose into the air, mingling with the thundering of hooves and the jingling of so many harnesses. The curses of riders were also clearly audible despite the cacophony. And now another sound began to fill Lausard's ears too. The crackle of muskets. The thunder of cannon and the shouts and screams of fighting men. The stench of gunpowder became more powerful as the dragoons finally hurtled headlong into the valley. Lausard felt a choking blanket of warm air wrap itself around him. It was difficult to breathe in the fumes but he took deep lungfuls of the polluted air and rode on, steadying his horse as best he could, as he and the other men spilled down the slopes, crashing into some French hussars and infantry. The foot soldiers scattered to avoid the horse-men, some shaking their fists angrily at the dragoons.

Barthez led them on, towards the pandemonium of the town. From the hillside, Lausard had thought how narrow the streets looked, far too constricted to allow easy passage for cavalry, but Barthez simply rode on, his horse's hooves clattering on the cobbles. Others followed. Lausard saw the guidon of his regiment being held aloft, carried through the streets of Saalfeld, and he followed it as a moth would follow a candle flame.

'This is madness,' gasped Karim, his horse neighing loudly as it almost slipped in a puddle of blood which stained the cobbles.

Infantry in the streets stepped back into buildings to avoid the dragoons as they swept through. Those unable to find shelter were simply ridden down, no matter what uniform they wore. One grenadier, his head heavily bandaged, raised his Charleville to his shoulder as if to fire at the horsemen. Lausard saw him mouthing something but could not hear the words. A wounded man, lying in the street, tried to drag himself clear of the onrushing hooves but it was no use. Lausard managed to guide his horse around the injured private but several of the horses following trampled him. And, all the time, ahead of the main body of dragoons, Barthez rode furiously towards the bridge across the Saale, his bloodied sword still held above his head, his eyes blazing madly.

A number of Saxon troops turned and formed a ragged line, muskets levelled at the onrushing dragoons. Barthez seemed not to notice and merely spurred his horse towards them even more furiously.

'With me,' he bellowed.

Rocheteau and Lausard galloped across a smoke-filled square until they were almost level with the officer. Several dozen of their companions followed, aware that the Saxons were preparing to fire.

The volley, when it came, was piecemeal. Two or three muskets spewed out their load, then one more. There was no concentrated fire and for that Lausard was grateful. One bullet struck his left stirrup and sang off the steel. Another clipped the ear of Rocheteau's mount and the horse whinnied in pain. Barthez rode into the line, hacking madly to his left and right. The white uniforms of the Saxon troops were quickly stained crimson as they fell around him. Most were content to flee across the bridge, some even jumping into the swiftly flowing water in an effort to escape this madman. Lausard held up his own sword as if to halt his companions and he pulled his own carbine from its boot and shot down one of the enemy troops. Firing from the saddle, the other dragoons did likewise, firing and reloading with great speed and skill. Even more acrid smoke began to cloud the area around the approaches to the bridge. Lausard tore a ball from the cartridge with his teeth, poured powder down the muzzle and spat the lead projectile after it. He rammed down the ball and wadding then swung the Charleville up to his shoulder and fired, repeating the action several times until the muzzle was hot against his lips and tongue and the grains of powder stung his mouth. Sonnier kept up a regular fire, picking off half a dozen of the fleeing enemy troops even though the thick smoke made it like firing through noxious fog.

To the left and right of him, Lausard could see French infantry forming up into lines, pouring volleys of musket fire into the retreating Saxons. After three or four such fusillades, they began to advance across the bridge, stepping over bodies, careful not to slip in the blood that had pooled on the cobbles. All around, discarded weapons, packs, cartridge cases and headgear further testified to the speed of the Prussian retreat.

'See them run?' Barthez said, triumphantly, his breath coming in gasps. 'They have no heart. On another day we will catch them and destroy them.' He looked at Lausard with wide eyes and a wide grin. The sergeant glanced back impassively.

All around them, the rattle of muskets and the roar of cannon continued.

Lausard thought the silence that pervaded the column as it moved along the road was somewhat unusual. Although talking in ranks was largely frowned upon, it was common practice for troops to mutter among themselves as they marched, especially after a battle, but Lausard had noticed that his companions all seemed strangely subdued, despite the relatively light casualties the French had suffered at Saalfeld two days earlier. Even Erebus, trotting along beside the horses, didn't seem willing to give voice to a bark or growl. The big black dog loped along, tongue lolling from one side of his mouth, occasionally dodging between the legs of the horses as they advanced. To Lausard, the campaign seemed to be progressing with little trouble. The resistance they had encountered so far was minimal and, judging by the Prussian army's conduct in the confrontations to date, Lausard had little fear for when the two main armies finally clashed. Others, it seemed, did not share his optimism. The French troops moved efficiently through undulating countryside, dense with trees, scouts occasionally galloping ahead to check any potentially hazardous thoroughfares, but it scarcely seemed necessary. Marshal Murat's light cavalry were always ahead of the main French columns, scouring the Saxon terrain for any sign of enemy troops. So far they had found none. The sergeant glanced around him at the faces of his companions. Most were set in resigned expressions and, without exception, the men looked weary. A number, including himself, hadn't shaved for two or three days and, as he rode, he scratched at one cheek, feeling the bristles there. His long brown hair needed washing too. He felt a flea on the nape of his neck and plucked it free, squashing it between his thumb and forefinger. He wondered how many more of the parasites were already nesting in his ragged, filthy clothes. He had taken a fur-lined cloak from a dead Prussian officer at Saalfeld and it was wrapped around his shoulders like a shawl in an effort to keep out the chill wind that swept the valleys and ridges along which the French travelled. Rocheteau sported the greatcoat of a Saxon officer. He had taken a gold gorgette from the throat of the same dead man. It now rested in his portmanteau with the rest of his acquisitions: several plugs of tobacco, half a bottle of schnapps and some pieces of stale bread. Pickings had been similarly slim for the other members of the squadron. Some food and drink but that had been the sum total of their plunder. Tabor had even shared some salt beef he'd taken from a Prussian corporal with Erebus, and the dog had accepted the offering with relish.

Lausard glanced towards the head of the dragoon column where Captain Barthez rode alone. The sergeant was certain it was this officer's presence that had succeeded in quieting his normally talkative companions. A number of horses had been destroyed following the squadron's furious charges at Saalfeld and some of the men were now riding remounts taken either from dead Prussian cavalrymen or from their own incapacitated countrymen. Some had even been given light cavalry mounts, and the animals laboured under the amount of equipment they were forced to carry. Lausard had seen many go lame or throw shoes in the past two days and the farriers had been kept busy trying to tend to so many deficient horses. They had passed a group of five mounts further back down the road, all being shoed with the aid of a mobile forge that was even being used to make plates for the stricken animals. Lausard had seen the farriers stripped to the waist as they worked despite the chill in the air. He accepted the bottle of wine Rocheteau handed to him and drank deeply before returning it.

'I hear the Prussians lost one of their generals at Saalfeld,' the corporal mused. 'Prince Louis Ferdinand was killed.'

'Quartermaster Guindet of the tenth hussars killed him,' Bonet added. 'I was speaking to one of their men about it the other day. Prince Louis was wounded several times; Guindet called on him to surrender but he refused. Guindet had no choice but to kill him.'

'I understand Prince Louis was a very able man,' Lausard said. 'He will be a great loss to the Prussians, fortunately. Though I am beginning to wonder if we are ever going to encounter their main army.'

'Good,' said Roussard. 'The longer we avoid them, the longer we stay alive.'

'Prince Louis was lucky Roboly did not reach him first,' Bonet offered. 'He is also a trooper in the tenth. They say he has incredible power in his sword arm due to the fact that he was born in Constantinople.'

'Explain the logic in that, schoolmaster?' Rocheteau wanted to know.

'They say he has a little bit of Turk in the wrist.'

The other men laughed.

'Like you, Karim,' Giresse interjected. 'I have seen *you* part men's heads from their bodies with that crooked blade of yours.'

Karim smiled.

'It is the blade that does the damage,' he offered. 'In the right hands, any blade will cut. My arm is guided by Allah, all Praise to Him.'

'It's a pity someone doesn't guide a sword into *that* bastard's back,' Delacor grunted, nodding in the direction of Captain Barthez. 'He'll get us all killed before the week is out. Him and his glory hunting. Perhaps the next time we go into battle, one of us should shoot him. No one would ever know where the bullet came from.'

'There would be so many suspects the war would be over before we had all been spoken to,' Lausard mused.

The men laughed once more.

Barthez turned and glanced in their direction. The laughter faded immediately.

The column moved on.

Fifteen

——◆◆◆——

As General Caulaincourt approached the Imperial tent
he was astounded by the number of aides standing
outside the entrance to the imposing makeshift dwelling.
Grenadiers of the Guard stood on either side of the
entrance, muskets at the port position. At the foremost
two corners of the tent and also above the entrance fluttered Imperial eagles. Men were coming and going
constantly from the tent, and Caulaincourt was forced
to wait as first one, then another, were either ordered
in or dismissed. He slid past the flap and saw Napoleon
sitting on a rickety chair, one foot propped up on
Berthier's mobile desk while the Chief of Staff himself
scribbled away furiously each time the Emperor spoke.
The Corsican ran a hand through his short cropped hair
and kept his eyes fixed on each report, scanning them
with incredible speed, yet taking in every word and
inwardly digesting it. As he finished, he placed each one
on another desk beside him, sometimes muttering something to Berthier but, for the most part, he seemed
content to keep whatever information the despatches
contained to himself.

An ADC dressed in a red dolman jacket and pelisse, both stained with gunpowder and mud, stood stiffly to attention before the Emperor. Caulaincourt could see that the man's red boots were in serious need of a polish. Part of his sabertache had been dented by a bullet and he had a small bandage wrapped around his left thigh. From the brilliance of the uniform he wore, Caulaincourt guessed that the aide had come bearing news from Marshal Murat. The cavalry commander's own flamboyance was reflected in the resplendent uniforms worn by his staff and this red-clad figure was no exception. It appeared that every part of the uniform, from the pelisse to the tassles on the man's boots, was trimmed with gold lace. He saluted as he saw the Master of the Horse enter the tent. The movement made the scabbard of his sword rattle against his leg and Napoleon glanced up. He nodded at Caulaincourt then brandished the despatch he'd been reading in the general's direction.

'Reports from the direction of Gera,' the Emperor said. 'Still no sign of the Prussian main force. They must be located further north or west, not northeast as I originally anticipated.' He looked up at the aide. 'You may go.'

The man saluted and left the tent.

'No sign of the enemy on the river Elster,' Napoleon continued. 'Nor as far as the approaches to Leipzig. Lannes reports that they have not crossed to the east bank of the Saale either.'

'They mean to avoid us for as long as possible, sire,' Caulaincourt offered.

'And when will they give battle, my friend? When they reach the very outskirts of Berlin itself?' The Corsican got to his feet and crossed to one of the many maps spread out on the floor of the makeshift dwelling. 'They are retiring without protecting their communications with Leipzig. That leads me to one conclusion: that their main force is located further to the west.'

'Closer to the Russians,' Berthier interjected.

'There is not enough time for the Russians to come to their aid,' snapped Napoleon. 'Frederick William would not sacrifice his capital for the sake of unifying with an ally who could not possibly arrive in time to be of any use to him. I feel increasingly sure that they will offer battle in the vicinity of Erfurt.' He tapped his forefinger gently against his chin, his brow furrowing slightly. 'However, there is still room for doubt. Certain measures must be taken to guard against any unforeseen manoeuvres on their part. Instruct Soult to remain in the vicinity of Gera to watch for any signs of activity to the north or east. I am completely enveloping the enemy but I have to take measures against what he might attempt to do.' He continued to gaze fixedly at the map. 'Auma will be designated the new centre of operations. Tell General Villemanzy to bring all the corn and bread which is at present on the road, to form a magazine at Auma. I also wish for a hospital to be established there. Davout's corps is to press on to Naumburg. Bernadotte to move from Gera to Zeitz and from there to Kosen. They will then be in a position to support Lannes and Augereau who are to cross the Saale at Jena and Kahla.' He wandered around the map while Berthier scribbled away frantically. 'As far as I can ascertain, the Prussians have two alternatives open to them. They can either accept battle before Erfurt, in which case the V, VI and VII corps will hold them frontally while the I and III move down from the north against their left and rear.'

'Or they could try to run, sire,' Caulaincourt interjected.

Napoleon nodded.

'Towards Halle, where their reserves are located,' he conceded. 'From there to Magdeburg and the right bank of the Elbe. It would offer them comparative safety.'

'How do you counter that possibility, sire?' Berthier wanted to know.

'I will lead the main body of the army through Jena. Davout and Bernadotte will intercept them before they reach the Elbe. They would be forced to accept battle in such a situation. Whatever the case, I do not expect a battle before the sixteenth. Four days from now.' He exhaled deeply and returned to his chair. Caulaincourt passed him a glass of wine and the Emperor accepted it gratefully. 'In the meantime, Berthier, we have other business to attend to.'

The Chief of Staff looked ˙quizzical.

'On the first of this month, the King of Prussia demanded that we leave his country,' Napoleon reminded his Chief of Staff. 'He issued France with an ultimatum and was most insistent that it receive a reply. I think the time has come to respond to that communication.'

'I would have thought the presence of our troops on

his soil and the destruction and capture of so much of his territory and his army would have been answer enough, sire,' Berthier smiled.

Napoleon nodded.

'He had the effrontery to present me with an ultimatum, Berthier,' said the Corsican, quietly. 'It would be remiss of me not to reply in words as well as actions.' The Emperor took a sip of his wine then cleared his throat. 'My honourable brother,' he began as Berthier wrote. 'In response to the demands you made upon myself and my country I trust you will study your present situation and reconsider your ill-advised presumptions. Should you do so you may still be in a position to maintain some semblance of dignity. The armies you send against me will be crushed. Have no doubt of that. If you wish to spare your soldiers unnecessary suffering then all you need do is agree to my proposals for peace.'

'He will never do so, sire,' Caulaincourt offered. 'No king with any semblance of self-respect would bow to fresh demands at this stage of proceedings.'

'Then let it not be said that I did not offer an olive branch when all *I* was offered was a bayonet,' snapped Napoleon.

Caulaincourt held the Corsican's gaze for a moment longer, then turned and poured himself a glass of burgundy.

'The terms that will bring about a mutually advantageous peace are the very same as those I first outlined to you at the end of last year,' the Emperor continued. 'You will find their edicts contained within the Treaty of Schönbrunn. Should you choose to ignore these terms then let history record that it was Prussia and not France who initiated war. Your brother, Napoleon, Emperor of France.' The Corsican reached for his snuff and took a pinch. 'Send in General Rapp. He can carry my answer to the King.'

Caulaincourt nodded and returned a moment later with General Jean Rapp, who saluted and stood to attention before the Emperor.

'I thought to send you on an errand, my friend,' Napoleon grinned. 'But, as I think about it, I would not demean you with such a worthless task. Perhaps de Montesquiou might be better suited to deliver this message.'

'With respect, sire, he is merely an orderly officer, an aide-de-camp of Marshal Davout,' Caulaincourt offered. 'Surely General Rapp would be the more honourable choice to present such a document to the King. To send someone other than a member of your own headquarters staff would be an insult.'

'And what did Fredrick William offer me other than an insult, Caulaincourt? He issued an ultimatum. There can be no graver insult from one monarch to another. If I send Rapp, the King may well believe I am concerned for my own position. His very seniority invests this errand with more gravity than it merits. Send de Montesquiou.'

'In the meantime, sire, do we wait for the Prussians to attack us?' Rapp wanted to know.

'We have no need to wait. They are still running. We will hunt them down until they can run no further. When they turn and face us, we will destroy them.'

* * *

Lausard sniffed the bread before he pushed it into his pocket. It smelled fresh enough. The other men were not so fussy. Joubert tore off a large piece and stuffed it into his mouth as he waited in line to receive his ration of biscuits and sausage.

'Don't be asking me for any of my food when we get back on the road,' said Delacor, watching the big man chewing hungrily. 'If you eat all yours now, fat man, you can starve for all I care.'

'One ounce of bread, one pound of meat, two ounces of corn,' said the man standing beside the open wagon. There were two dozen similar transports beside the road, French troops gathered around each in untidy lines, waiting for their own rations. Men dressed in civilian clothes moved over and around the wagons like bees in a hive, each with a designated task. Civilian drivers sat astride the teams of horses that pulled the wagons, all of which were laden with provisions. The man scratched at his cheek and looked on disinterestedly as the dragoons received their quota. His hair was cut short and his skin swarthy. 'That's the limit. It's the same for every man.'

'And what profit are you bastards making out of this?' snapped Delacor.

'Just take what you are entitled to and go,' insisted the man, looking away from Delacor.

'You work for the Breidt company don't you?' Bonet said.

'Who the hell are they?' Rocheteau wanted to know.

'Civilian contractors hired by Bonaparte to act as commissaries,' Lausard interjected. 'They never carry more than a week's supplies. Isn't that so?'

The man nodded.

'What's wrong with us finding our own food like we usually do?' Rocheteau complained.

'The enemy must be near,' Lausard told him. 'You know we only ever see these civilians when foraging is dangerous, impossible or likely to give away our position.'

'And where did *you* get all this food?' Charvet asked the man.

'From the locals,' he told the dragoon.

'We could have got it ourselves,' Rostov offered.

'Look, this is none of my business. I just work for the company,' said the man, wearily.

'And when all this is over you will go home,' Roussard rasped. 'You will not have to risk your life in battle, unlike us.'

'I suffer the same hardships as you,' the commissar protested. 'If the Prussians attack I have as much chance of getting *killed* as you.'

Roussard was unimpressed. He took his rations and moved on.

One by one the dragoons returned to their horses, stored their supplies as best they could and swung themselves back into their saddles. Captain Barthez was sitting on a low rise watching his men, occasionally glancing up the road towards the hilly terrain that marked the approaches to the next town.

'Where the hell are we anyway?' Delacor wanted to know.

'About five miles south of a town called Jena,' Bonet told him.

'We know where *we* are. Where are the Prussians?' Giresse mused.

'God knows,' Tigana added. 'And if He does then He has no intention of telling us.'

Some of the other men laughed.

'Marshal Murat has most of his light cavalry searching for them and still we are none the wiser,' offered Carbonne.

'Those "pekinese" couldn't find horse shit in a stable,' sneered Delacor. 'They should send *us* ahead to find those sausage eaters.'

'So we could all get killed more quickly?' intoned Roussard.

'Ask your God to tell us where our enemies are, your holiness,' Rocheteau said.

Moreau crossed himself.

Lausard tore off a piece of bread and threw it to Erebus, who caught the doughy lump in his jaws and chewed it hungrily. The sergeant glanced up once more at the lone figure of Captain Barthez.

'They may be closer than we realise,' he murmured, his eyes never leaving the officer.

'The sooner we get to grips with them the sooner we can finish this business and get home,' Giresse said.

'Like we did after Austerlitz?' Rocheteau grunted. 'I'm beginning to wonder if we're *ever* going to see France again.'

'I know one man who won't be too anxious to return,' noted Lausard. 'Not until he has what he came here for.'

'Barthez,' Rocheteau said, flatly.

The sergeant nodded. 'Until he has his medal he will

not rest. He will not want this war to end.'

'There'll be other wars for him,' Rocheteau said, quietly.

'And for us,' echoed Giresse.

'Why does he want it so badly?' Bonet mused. 'It won't change him as a man. It won't make him any better than he is now.'

'It will change how others perceive him,' said Lausard. 'With the *Légion d'Honneur* pinned to his chest all who look at him will be forced to admit his bravery.'

'He'll strut all around Paris with it, the arrogant bastard,' sneered Delacor.

'I don't think so,' Lausard murmured. 'He doesn't strike me as that kind of man. It isn't arrogance that drives him and he seeks to attain the medal by the only method he knows. By using his courage.'

'You sound as if you admire him, Alain,' Rocheteau interjected.

'I respect his motives but not necessarily his methods,' the sergeant admitted. 'What is so wrong with seeking advancement?'

'Nothing,' Rocheteau conceded. 'But you were the one who said he was dangerous.'

'I said I feared his recklessness. That does not prevent me from respecting what he has done during his time in the army. He has risen from the rank of private to that of captain. He is to be admired for that. The only thing that concerns me is how many men alongside him died to ensure his promotions.'

'And how many of *us* will have to die to get him his stinking medal?' Delacor hissed.

'I could steal one for him if he wanted it so badly,' Rocheteau chuckled.

'I fear our new captain has no use for second-hand plaudits, my friend,' the sergeant smiled. 'He will not be satisfied until Bonaparte himself has pinned that medal upon his chest.'

'Let us hope we are alive to see it,' Roussard offered.

Joubert chewed on a piece of sausage and glanced at the officer riding ahead of them.

'If he gets his medal perhaps he'll get promoted too, and then who will replace him?' asked the big man.

'Another glory hunter?' mused Charvet.

'Perhaps Lieutenant Royere will finally be promoted,' wondered Rocheteau.

'Captain Milliere might return,' Gaston said, hopefully.

'I wonder how he is?' Bonet murmured. 'He was hurt badly.'

'Men have suffered worse wounds and survived, schoolmaster,' Delacor retorted.

'I prayed to God to spare him,' Moreau intoned, crossing himself.

'As I did to Allah, all Praise to Him,' Karim added.

'It will be doctors who help him, if they can,' snapped Delacor. 'Not your gods. Yours or anyone else's.'

'Captain Milliere is not our concern for the time being,' Lausard explained. 'We should be more interested in what Barthez has in mind.'

'We will know soon enough,' Rocheteau offered, 'if we ever run into the Prussians.'

Lausard didn't answer. His gaze was still firmly fixed

on the officer who rode at the head of the column.

'I thought an order had been issued instructing that we were to rest today,' Giresse offered. 'Not just us but the entire army.'

'I heard that too,' Bonet added. 'A corporal of engineers told me that the Emperor himself wished that the army should rest, round up stragglers and take on provisions.'

'You had best tell our captain then,' Lausard noted. 'The order seems to have slipped past him. I fear a respite is the last thing *he* wants at the moment.'

'I'm surprised he hasn't ordered us to charge towards Jena on the chance we run into some Prussians,' Delacor grunted. 'That way he might get his medal more quickly.'

'No one knows if there are Prussians in Jena,' Bonet reminded his companion. 'Or anywhere else in the vicinity for that matter. If there were, surely we or the light cavalry would have run across them before now, wouldn't we?' He looked towards Lausard as if for confirmation but received only an almost imperceptible nod of the head by way of an answer.

'Perhaps they are gathering their forces for one big battle,' Charvet offered. 'The question is, when will it come?'

'Rest assured,' said Lausard. 'We will be among the first to know when it *does* finally happen. And, if our new captain has his way, we will be the first to join it.'

As the Imperial post-chaise moved along through the Saxon countryside, Napoleon glanced at the words he had written the previous night, rereading them, wondering if there were points he should add or change.

My eternal love Josephine,

I am today at Gera, dearest love, and everything is going very well. The campaign proceeds according to my hopes despite the fact that my enemies seem even more anxious to avoid confrontation. My health remains excellent, and I have put on some weight since my departure. Yet I travel from 20 to 25 leagues each day on horseback, in my carriage, etc.

I retire to rest at eight o'clock and rise at midnight. I sometimes imagine that you will not yet have retired to bed. My thoughts, as ever, are with you. My heart, for all time, remains in your hands.

I remain, as always, your loving husband.

It was signed with his usual sweeping signature.

For long moments he studied the letter then finally folded it and tucked it into the pocket of his tunic.

'I sometimes think that the wives of soldiers suffer greater torments than the men who stride across battlefields and expose themselves to all manner of death,' the Corsican said, reflectively.

Berthier, as usual positioned at the portable desk inside the carriage, nodded sagely. 'I agree with you, sire,' he said. 'War makes great demands upon the wives of soldiers.'

Napoleon gazed out of the side window of the carriage as it rumbled along, momentarily lost in his own thoughts. His ruminations were interrupted by a number of raised voices, clearly audible even above the thunder of horses' hooves and the rumble of the post-chaise. The vehicle came slowly to a halt and General Caulaincourt pushed open the door nearest to him to find two aides sitting there on heavily lathered horses. Both men and animals looked exhausted and one of the men was gasping for breath. Caulaincourt took the pieces of paper they brought and handed them to the Emperor who swiftly read them.

'Augereau reports from Kahla that enemy troops are moving towards Erfurt,' the Corsican said, still scanning the despatch. 'Troops originally based at Jena.'

'That would concur with the information we received from Marshal Murat concerning the presence of the King and Queen of Prussia in Erfurt three days ago,' offered Caulaincourt.

'And, most damning of all,' Napoleon added, 'Davout has learned from deserters and civilians not only that Frederick William and his Queen were indeed in that town on the eleventh but that no enemy troops are to be found between Naumburg and Leipzig. I was correct in my assumption that the Prussians plan to give battle in front of Erfurt. They must be assembling there as we speak.' He smiled and dropped the despatches. 'At last, the veil is lifted,' said the Corsican, excitedly. 'Instruct Murat to move as quickly as possible to support Bernadotte's corps as it marches on Dornburg. Tell him I believe that the enemy will either attempt to attack Marshal Lannes at Jena or that he will retreat. If he attacks Lannes then Murat's presence at Dornburg will enable him to support Lannes. Tell him also that, from two this afternoon, I shall be at Jena.'

Berthier's quill moved with its customary speed as he scribbled down his commander's instructions.

'I also desire the light cavalry and the first corps to fill the gap between Davout and Lannes along the Saale,' Napoleon continued. 'Ney is to march for Roda. Order the heavy cavalry from Auma to Gera and also St Hilaire's division. The remainder of Soult's command is to move northwest to Kostritz in order to cover the area near Leipzig. Augereau is to move the VIII corps with the utmost haste from Kahla to Jena.'

'There is still no word from Marshal Lannes, sire,' Berthier reminded the Corsican. 'And he is closer to the enemy than anyone at this present time.'

Napoleon nodded and stepped down from the coach followed by Caulaincourt and the Chief of Staff.

'It is time for us to take to the saddle, gentlemen,' he said. 'We will ride to Jena. If Lannes cannot get word to me on the enemy situation then I will see it for myself.'

Lausard glanced around at the empty buildings that lined the streets of Jena but could see no movement from within. The town had not been fortified by his country-men and none of its previous inhabitants were in evidence either. The conglomeration of buildings was like a ghost town. The hooves of the dragoons' horses echoed eerily through the stillness of the deserted streets. On all sides, the town was surrounded by dense woods and steep slopes, which crowded in on the area as if attempting to sweep it from the map. The dark, silver-grey tongue of the River Saale was clearly visible off to the northeast. It curved its way through the countryside before cutting through Jena itself. The men heard it rushing beneath the bridge as they crossed.

'Where the hell has everyone gone?' Rocheteau wanted to know.

Lausard merely shook his head, unable to supply the corporal with an answer.

'If the houses are empty there'll be rich pickings inside,' Delacor grinned.

Lausard cocked one ear as he heard some distant crackling that sounded only too familiar. He was certain it was musket fire.

'Forget about plunder,' said the sergeant. 'We have more important things to contend with.'

'You forget, Alain, we are thieves,' chuckled Rocheteau. 'Old habits die hard.'

The other men laughed.

But now, more of them began to notice the distant popping of muskets. Moreau crossed himself.

Captain Barthez turned to look at the leading troopers in the squadron, his eyes narrowed slightly. The men saw him turn his mount and canter back towards them.

'No glory in an empty town,' Lausard murmured as the officer approached.

'It seems as if the battle is close,' said the officer as he reined in his mount.

'It sounds like skirmishers, sir,' Lausard answered. 'Little more.'

'Rumours have been coming back from the leading troops that the Prussian army is near,' said the officer. 'It would appear that is so.'

'So you will have the battle you wanted then, sir,' Lausard observed.

Barthez eyed the sergeant warily for a moment then smiled. 'We are all soldiers, Sergeant Lausard,' he said. 'What man does not yearn for glory? If he is truthful.'

'I would settle for victory, sir.'

'Victory *is* glory. How a man acquits himself before the enemy is of equal importance.'

'I am not sure the Emperor would agree with you, sir. I think he would appreciate a victory, no matter how it is won. Rather that than a defeat embellished by the bravado of overzealous fools.'

Barthez held the sergeant's gaze a moment longer, the smile still hovering at the corners of his mouth.

'Select six of your best men,' the captain instructed. 'You will accompany me forward.'

'Have orders been given that we are to advance?' Lausard enquired.

'I did not attain this rank by waiting around for instructions like some green recruit. I use my initiative where I feel it is needed.' He turned his horse. 'Six men,' he called and guided his mount, at a canter, through the deserted streets of Jena.

Lausard watched the officer then jabbed a finger at the first six men he saw. Lieutenant Royere also joined the small unit of dragoons as they followed Barthez across the single bridge that spanned the Saale, hooves echoing loudly in the stillness of the deserted town. As they left Jena itself behind, Lausard could see even more clearly how thickly wooded the hills and countryside around it were. The road cut through low ridges and, every so often, a towering knoll would thrust upwards into view. The sergeant saw a windmill atop the first of these imposing natural obstacles. There were already a number of blue-jacketed French troops swarming around the building. Others were making their way tortuously up the steep slopes towards the summit.

'Ahead is the Schneke pass,' Bonet observed, glancing at the map he'd pulled from his portmanteau. 'It leads through to a village called Cospeda.'

'What of the terrain beyond?' Barthez wanted to know.

'There is a plateau, sir,' the former schoolmaster said. 'It appears to be comparatively open ground overlooked by many heights. That is the tallest of them.' He pointed to a particularly imposing and precipitous mound. 'It is marked on the map as the Landgrafenberg. The peak is called the Windknollen and is calculated to be over three hundred and sixty metres high. It appears that there are French troops upon it already.'

The other dragoons looked up and saw many of their countrymen swarming over the summit and slopes of the knoll. Lausard could see several eagles fluttering high above, the steadily growing wind causing them to flap against their staffs.

'It doesn't sound like good ground for cavalry, sir,' Lausard observed. 'Perhaps there is no glory to be had on this field after all.'

Barthez was not slow to catch the disdain in Lausard's voice. '*Every* battle gives an opportunity for glory, Sergeant,' he snapped. 'No matter how big or how small that conflict may be. Besides, if we cannot fight the enemy on horseback we will do so on foot.'

The dragoons took the narrow road that led past the foot of the Landgrafenberg, through some dense woods and out onto the plain beyond. Lausard could see more French troops moving in open order across the ground, using the gulleys and dips in the terrain as cover. As far as he could make out, the vast majority of them were voltigeurs. Barthez reined in his mount and pulled his telescope from his pocket. He squinted through the eyeglass, surveying the landscape ahead. The steady popping of musket fire continued. Thin whisps of smoke, driven by the breeze, drifted across the open ground.

The captain handed the telescope to Lausard, who also inspected the terrain ahead.

'What do you see, Sergeant?' Barthez wanted to know.

'Very little, Captain,' Lausard told him, flatly.

'Then look more closely,' snapped the officer. 'Shall I tell you what *I* see? I see my destiny.'

'Perhaps you have better eyesight than I, sir,' said Lausard, handing the telescope back to his superior.

Barthez was smiling.

'Rider coming in.'

The shout echoed even above the pounding hooves of Napoleon's hastily moving escort and headquarters staff. The Emperor himself glanced in the direction of the shout and saw a blue-clad ADC thundering along the road towards the mass of guard chausseurs that formed a protective screen before the Corsican and those close to him. As the aide drew nearer, the chausseurs parted to allow him through. The man tugged hard on his reins to halt his lathered horse and saluted the

Emperor, handing a piece of paper to Berthier who, in turn, passed it to the Corsican.

'From Lannes,' he said, finally, his eyes still scanning the message. 'Word at last.'

'What news, sire?' Caulaincourt enquired.

'He reports between twelve and fifteen thousand Prussian troops in position to the north of Jena,' Napoleon mused. 'Possibly another twenty to twenty-five thousand between Jena and Weimar. Patrols have been sent out to confirm this. Lannes intends to hold his position outside Jena.'

'Are the Prussians finally going to fight, sire?' Berthier asked.

'I can see no other reason why they would have concentrated so many men in such an area. It would appear that they are tired of running. It seems certain they are preparing to attack Lannes in force either tonight or tomorrow morning.' He looked at Berthier, his eyes blazing. The Chief of Staff recognised that look so well and felt the hairs rise on the back of his neck. 'The time is upon us at last, gentlemen. Send orders to Davout. Tell him if he hears the sound of firing from the south that he is to manoeuvre to the west from Naumburg this very evening with the object of falling upon the enemy's left. Bernadotte is to continue towards Dornburg but to move across the Saale immediately to Lannes' aid if he is attacked. If they hear no cannon fire then both corps are to wait until they are issued orders tomorrow.'

'What of Marshal Murat's cavalry, sire?' Berthier enquired.

'They are to continue towards Dornburg. Both Soult and Ney are to rapid march for Jena. Issue the same instructions to Lefebvre and the Guard infantry. They are to join me at Marshal Lannes' forward headquarters with all haste.' The Corsican looked around at his staff. 'The Prussian fox has finally shown itself. Let us conclude this hunt before it has time to escape us again.'

Sixteen

The wind gusting around Napoleon and his staff was so strong that, on more than one occasion, the Emperor was forced to grip his hat in one hand to prevent it flying from his head. The Corsican held the bicorn firmly and squinted at the terrain before him, his eyes watering slightly as the chill wind buffeted him. Maps that had been laid out on the ground were held down by large rocks, or, in one case, held in place by the boots of staff officers. Marshal Jean Lannes took off his plumed bicorn and gestured with it in the direction of the array of villages so easily visible from so precipitous a position. Arranged between and around these villages were three vast lines of dark-coated Prussian troops.

'It looks as though your initial estimate was correct, my friend,' said Napoleon, gazing at the awesome array of enemy troops stretching before him. 'There most certainly appear to be around forty thousand men facing us.'

'While our present strength is less than twenty-two thousand,' mused Savary. 'Even the arrival of the Guard will increase it only by four or five thousand.'

'The Prussian strategy seems obvious, sire,' Lannes offered. 'They seem intent on driving us back across the Saale.'

Napoleon nodded almost imperceptibly.

'I am surprised that they have not already pressed their advantage,' he said. 'We must be thankful, for the time being, that they have not. If an attack *does* come then this position must be held until the arrival of the IV, VI and VII corps. Our strength will be increased to over ninety thousand by their presence.'

'But none of those units can possibly hope to reach here before midday tomorrow, sire,' Savary interjected.

'And we are desperately short of artillery, sire,' Lannes added. 'I have just fourteen guns to protect this position.'

'But protect it you will,' the Corsican said, still surveying the uneven, wooded ground stretching away in front of him.

'I will hold it until the last man if that is what you command, your Highness,' Lannes said.

Napoleon slapped him heartily on the shoulder. 'The first and most important task is to gather what artillery we have here,' he jabbed a finger at the ground beneath his feet.

'The only route is a narrow track, sire,' Lannes informed his superior. 'It was pointed out to me by a Saxon priest when I first entered Jena.'

Napoleon looked quizzically at his companion.

'A Saxon priest with a grudge against the Prussians,' Lannes continued. 'It seems we have allies in the most unusual places, sire. The problem is that the track is not easily traversed. It will make transportation of both men and equipment very difficult.'

'Regardless of the difficulty of the task, it must be accomplished as soon as possible. We moved cannon across the Alps; are we to be defeated by a mere dirt road?' He turned back to face the Prussian masses. 'Their main strength seems to be to the west,' the Emperor noted. 'Around the villages of Isserstedt, Kotschau, Kappellendorf and Gröss Romstedt. There is good cover for all of their positions too.' He took a telescope from Berthier and scanned the entire scene slowly from right to left, his lips moving soundlessly as he digested every detail of the terrain and the array of troops before him. 'Three lines of villages,' he murmured. 'All will have to be carried if victory is to be assured.'

'Rödigen, Closewitz, Lützeroda and Copseda, sire,' Berthier said, also training his own glass on the conglomeration of buildings.

'My men pushed their advanced guard back into Lützeroda and Cospeda earlier today, sire,' Lannes told the Corsican, 'without too much trouble.'

Some of the other officers present laughed.

'There appears to be a ravine leading from the outskirts of Closewitz down towards the Saale itself,' Caulaincourt offered, pointing in the direction of the village. 'Some two hundred yards to the right of the Apolda road.'

'The ground beyond slopes upwards, sire,' Savary said, glancing at one of the wind-blown maps. 'It is known as the Dornberg. At its highest point it is even more elevated than where *we* now stand.'

'And beyond that?' the Emperor wanted to know.

'The wood and village of Isserstedt,' Savary informed him. 'From there the terrain is little more than flat, open fields.'

'They would be growing potatoes and turnips at this time of the year,' Lannes murmured.

Napoleon turned and looked quizzically at the young Marshal. 'I realise that your father was a farmer, my friend,' he smiled. 'But I have interest in something other than agriculture at the moment.'

The assembled staff laughed loudly, Lannes among them.

'What of the second line of villages?' the Corsican asked, swinging his telescope back towards the enemy positions.

'Nerkewitz, Krippendorf, Vierzehnheiligen and Isserstedt,' Savary called, raising his voice as a particularly vehement gust of wind wailed around the tip of the knoll. 'Two or three kilometres behind those lie Klein Romstedt, Gröss Romstedt and Kotschau.'

'Villages, woods and valleys,' mused the Emperor. 'Difficult terrain in which to move troops quickly. I think it is time I inspected it more closely.' He snapped his telescope shut and pushed it into his pocket. As a staff officer held his horse's bridle, the Corsican hauled himself into the saddle of his white, Arab stallion. The other assembled officers did likewise.

'It is almost five, sire,' Berthier noted. 'It will be dark soon.'

'Then let us see the ground upon which we will fight while we still have the chance, gentlemen,' Napoleon said. 'Or, if the Prussians decide to attack before dawn, perhaps we should pick out the places we would like to be buried.'

Rocheteau tossed the rabbit to Gaston, watching as the young trumpeter caught the dead animal. 'Skin that,' the corporal grinned.

Gaston pulled a knife from his belt and set to work, expertly stripping the fur from the creature. Erebus watched hungrily and the young trumpeter cut off a paw and threw it to the black dog.

'What's the point?' Delacor growled. 'We have nothing to cook it on anyway. Hasn't the order been given that no fires are to be lit?'

'We are too close to the enemy,' Bonet told him. 'The Emperor does not want to give away our positions.'

'I know why the order was given, schoolmaster,' Delacor snapped. 'But that doesn't make it any easier to eat raw rabbit, does it?'

'We've eaten much worse over the years,' Lausard reminded him. 'If you do not want your share I'm sure that Joubert would be more than happy to eat it for you.'

The big man rubbed his mountainous belly and it rumbled protestingly.

Lausard returned to the task in hand. He was using a flat stone to sharpen his sword. When he was satisfied he gently ran the pad of one thumb over the razor-like edge. Karim, who was also busy attending to his own scimitar, handed the sergeant an oily rag, and Lausard carefully wiped the length of steel before sliding it back into its scabbard. That particular task completed, he began checking the firing mechanism of his carbine. Reaching into his cartouche, he pulled out a fresh flint and set about replacing it. Like his companions, he carried two or three spares. Good quality flints would last from thirty to fifty rounds. All came from the little village of Meusnes in central France. They were commonly believed to be the best flints in the world for their purpose. Napoleon guarded their mining and construction jealously and had banned their export, but usually after a battle most men, given the time, would collect as many as possible from the dead. Lausard had often seen Sonnier checking the flints in discarded muskets, examining each with an expert eye. When Lausard had finished replacing the flint, he set to work cleaning the touchhole of his carbine, using the *epinglette* provided, pushing the heavy needle in and out of the hole to dislodge any stray particles of gunpowder or grit that might have clogged the mechanism. All around him, his companions were engaged in similar tasks, readying themselves for the battle they suspected would come the following day. Bayonets were sharpened, cartridges checked and counted, swords oiled. Rostov was using his screwdriver to secure the trigger guard of his carbine which had worked itself loose.

'Why do we have to hunt in these fields and woods for food when the town is full of supplies?' Tigana wanted to know.

'Perhaps when the Guard have been allowed their fill we will be permitted to sift through their leftovers,' sneered Delacor.

'The Guard passed through Jena some time ago,'

Lausard said, getting to his feet. He stroked Erebus' head as the dog nuzzled against him.

'Then there will be *nothing* left for us,' Delacor groaned. 'They'll have stripped the place clean.'

'Not staying to share in the banquet, Alain?' Rocheteau grinned as Gaston finished skinning the rabbit.

Lausard shook his head.

'I understand Bonaparte has work for us,' he said. 'I suggest that none of you gets too comfortable.'

'Not much chance of that,' Roussard grunted, pulling his cape more tightly around him. 'No food and freezing cold. At least if we were working we'd be warm.'

'What kind of work, Alain?' Giresse wanted to know.

'The artillery commander who was taking guns to the summit of the Landgrafenberg took the wrong track,' Lausard announced. 'The guns, wagons, limbers and caissons are backed up as far as Jena. Some say there are over a hundred of them unable to go forward or backward. Bonaparte has sent for tools from the engineers. The path to the summit has to be opened.'

'You are quite right, Sergeant.'

The voice came from the darkness beyond the ring of men but Lausard recognised it immediately as belonging to Captain Barthez.

'The work is being carried out battalion by battalion. I have volunteered our squadron to be the next to help,' the officer announced. 'All of you, on your feet, follow me.'

A chorus of groans and mutterings greeted Barthez' words but, moments later, the dragoons were trudging across the night-shrouded terrain in the direction of a number of lanterns. They cast a meagre yellow light but, in that sickly luminescence, Lausard could see men toiling away with picks and shovels, some stripped to the waist despite the chill of the night. He could also see another, more familiar figure.

Napoleon was standing on a large rock, a lantern in his hand, alternately watching the furious industry of the infantry or wandering back and forth urging the drivers of the teams of horses dragging the guns to pull their precious cargo up the steadily widening track. Other infantrymen wandered around carrying lighted torches, raising them high in the air to give the men digging some much needed light. Lausard picked up a shovel and set to work. The infantryman beside him looked on gratefully and both men began digging at a particularly large boulder that was close to the side of the dirt track. Lausard put his spade beneath it and levered it free. Rocheteau and Tabor joined him, the big man shifting huge shovelfuls of earth with each movement. He muttered to himself as he struck something hard just below the surface. A few more spadefuls of dirt revealed it was another large rock. Tabor bent down, curled his arms around it and heaved. Veins throbbed at his temples and in his neck but the rock gradually came free. He tossed it aside contemptuously and continued digging, discarding his shovel for a pick. He shattered several smaller rocks to splinters with powerful blows of the tool.

'Good man,' called Napoleon, walking towards him. 'That's the way, my fine fellow.'

Tabor drew himself to attention before the Emperor, who smiled at him and tapped him warmly on one huge arm.

'Well done, all of you,' he said, striding back and forth among the dragoons.

Lausard glanced at the Corsican, the constant crash and clang of metal against stone ringing in his ears. Horses, waiting to haul the four- and eight-pounders up the sharp incline, whinnied impatiently in the darkness. The night smelled of sweat, damp earth and horse droppings. Lausard continued to dig, aware that Napoleon was only ever a few yards from him. The sergeant could feel sweat running in rivulets down his face. His hands were sore from the friction of the wooden shaft of the tool against his palms but he, like his companions, kept up their labours with unceasing vigour. Lausard marvelled again at the almost hypnotic power the Corsican seemed to exert over those who followed him. The work was carried out in virtual silence and with incredible enthusiasm by men who, like himself, wanted only to sleep, eat or sit around a camp fire and warm themselves against the freezing night. But, with their Emperor near, men seemed to forget everything. His very presence seemed to negate the need for food, drink, warmth or rest. He brought them more than that. He gave them something they could never hope to buy, steal or forage. He brought them love. Lausard knew that was what many felt for the small man in the greatcoat moving purposefully back and forth in the darkness, a lantern gripped in his fist. Every man in the French army would happily give his life for this Corsican. Not because he was ruler of their homeland but because he understood them and cared for them. He realised the hardships they suffered. They would perform any task for this man because that feeling was reciprocated. If Napoleon gave love then it was returned to him a thousand-fold by those in his army. It was a commodity worth more than countless riches and as valuable on a battlefield as twenty thousand men. Lausard paused momentarily to wipe perspiration from his face then he continued hacking away at the ground on either side of the narrow track.

He felt a hand on his shoulder and turned to see Napoleon standing there. The Emperor nodded and smiled as Lausard prepared to continue and, despite himself, the sergeant felt the hairs on the back of his neck rise. He dug with even greater ferocity, as if that touch had imbued him with some kind of power. A power he could never hope to explain. Close by, Rostov and Carbonne were using axes to hack away at the thickly planted trees that grew so densely beside the rough pathway. Moreau was using a pick too. As were Sonnier and Gaston. A little further up the slope, Lieutenant Royere was also digging furiously. He was helping Charvet and Giresse to pull a stubborn tree stump free of the earth using ropes that they'd lashed to the thick, tentacle-like roots. The three men hauled furiously, finally joined by Captain Barthez himself. All of them gripped the ropes, tugging madly until the recalcitrant stump began to rise from the dark earth. Tabor moved to the other side and put his considerable bulk behind it, gritting his teeth as the object finally came free. The men smiled triumphantly and Napoleon was among them, slapping them on the back and congratulating them. Lausard saw the Corsican hurry down the middle of the dirt track towards the waiting teams of horses. Twelve black beasts, as dark as the night itself, were lashed to the first of the guns, waiting to haul it up to its position at the peak of the Landgrafenberg. Erebus barked triumphantly as Napoleon waved the team forward and the gun trundled up the track. The Corsican looked on delightedly and moved back to the side of the track.

Already, infantry were moving in amongst the dragoons, taking the tools from them, relieving them of their back-breaking labour.

'My squadron will continue, sire,' Barthez said as Napoleon passed him.

'They have done enough, Captain,' said the Corsican. 'And there will be a different task for them come the dawn. You may go back into Jena and collect supplies. Once you have done that, fires may be lit to cook by. One for every hundred men. I do not want to advertise our strength to the enemy until I have to.'

Lausard wiped the sweat from his face once again and smiled as he handed his shovel to an infantry corporal.

'It suits you,' he said.

The corporal muttered something under his breath and set to work.

Lausard and the dragoons made their way back down the slope, past the line of vehicles that were still waiting to ascend the summit. The night enveloped them once more, like a black shroud.

* * *

French infantry moved relentlessly over the bridge that spanned the Saale river, their muskets across their shoulders as they marched. Lausard saw a never-ending stream of them as he and his companions wandered back into Jena itself. The sound of hundreds of tramping feet, the rattle of metal-rimmed cannon wheels on the cobbles, the jingle of harnesses, the clatter of hooves and the occasional whinnying of horses filled the air. But for all that, the column moved in virtual silence. Lausard could see the endless parade stretching away into the night and could only guess at how many men were contained within it. The sergeant walked slowly alongside the column, the scabbard of his sword dragging occasionally on the cobbles. Up ahead of him, several of his men were inside one of the many empty houses, searching for food, drink or anything of value. Further down the street, he could make out the figures of Rocheteau and Delacor moving towards one of the town's larger inns. They disappeared inside. As Lausard walked, he sniffed the air and an unmistakeable smell filled his nostrils. He glanced at Karim, who was alongside him.

The Circassian nodded. 'Smoke,' he said, quietly.

'Perhaps the battle has begun but no one has informed us,' Lausard grinned.

'There,' said Karim, nodding in the direction of the next street. A dull yellow glow was beginning to spread across the black sky. It spread steadily. Lausard could hear raised voices.

'It seems we are not the only ones in search of plunder,' Karim mused.

As if to reinforce his opinion, he and Lausard saw several French infantrymen come scuttling into view. One was carrying a lighted torch. The others were struggling with pieces of meat and loaves of bread. One was even dragging several coats behind him. Another had cutlery spilling from his pockets. Lausard could hear it bouncing on the cobbles as the man ran.

'We are an army of thieves,' Lausard murmured.

'I told you the stinking Guard would strip this place clean, didn't I?'

He turned to see Delacor emerging from the inn holding two bottles of wine.

'Rocheteau and I searched the cellars,' Delacor continued. 'Those bastards took everything they could carry. Wine. Brandy. Schnapps. There are a few broken bottles but that's all.'

'The houses are the same, Alain,' Rocheteau added. 'Everything of any value has been taken. Probably either stolen by the Guard or carried away by the locals when they fled.'

Lausard wandered on down the street, past the constantly moving column of troops and equipment, some of whom cast curious glances at the dragoons. The sergeant stepped inside a house and looked around at the contents. The inhabitants had been simple people. There was a table and four chairs in the centre of the room. Some coal had spilled across the floor from the open fireplace. He wandered into the kitchen and found a half-empty sack of potatoes. Karim gathered some of them up and swung them over his shoulder. There were two or three iron pots beside the fire. He took those too.

Lausard left the Circassian downstairs and wandered up the rickety steps to the first floor of the small building. It was identical, both inside and out, to almost every other dwelling in Jena. Simple houses built by simple people who had lived uncomplicated lives until the spectre of war had been cast across first their country and now the very place they called home. The sergeant could imagine the blind panic that had seized these people when they heard of the approach of the French army. He could visualise how they had grabbed what little they possessed and fled, as families, from the oncoming enemy troops. The reputation of the French army as frenzied foragers was well known and it was deserving of fear. Lausard moved into the first bedroom and found a large bed, stripped of blankets. It was the same in the other room. Except here he found something lying close to the window, virtually hidden by an overturned stool. Lausard bent and picked up the object. It was a small doll, fashioned from wood and straw. The face had been roughly painted into a wide smile, he guessed by the man who was master of this family. By a father who had seen fit to rescue his family from the savagery of their invaders. Men like himself and his companions. He turned and caught a glimpse of his reflection in the mirror that hung on the wall. For long moments, Lausard stared at the unshaven, dirt-grimed visage that looked back at him. Unwashed hair framed his gaunt features. Steel-grey eyes peered almost accusingly at a face he barely recognised. It was the face of an invader. A thief. With one swift movement, Lausard drew his sword and struck the mirror from the wall. It shattered into a dozen pieces.

From below he heard Karim's voice. 'Alain, are you all right?'

'There's nothing here worth taking,' he called, then he gently laid the doll on the bed and regarded it silently for a moment. He turned and headed for the stairs, crushing a piece of broken mirror beneath his boot.

The Prussian camp fires looked like a thousand grounded stars stretched across the black backdrop of the terrain below the Landgrafenberg. Napoleon regarded them slowly, first through his telescope and then with the naked eye. The wind, which had been biting around the precipitous knoll all day, had grown steadily colder as the night had progressed, and the Emperor shivered slightly as he scanned the positions of his enemy. The breeze hissed and wailed in his ears like the cries of a banshee. The Corsican clasped his hands behind his back and wandered back and forth for a few yards, his eyes never leaving the myriad array of fires that signalled the presence of so many Prussian and Saxon troops. It appeared that his most pressing concern had been nullified. The Prussians showed no inclination to attack at present and, for that, the Corsican was grateful. Behind him, traversing the newly widened road constantly on their way to the summit of the Landgrafenberg, French troops were crowding into position on the plateau in readiness for the combat to come. More than thirty cannon had already been hauled up the precipitous slope and more were to follow. The troops were packed so tightly that there was barely an arm's length between them. Men slept sitting up, back pressed against a comrade, huddling around the few fires of their own they had been permitted to build. An unearthly silence pervaded the French positions, one that the Corsican knew would be eclipsed tomorrow by the roar of guns and the rattle of musket fire. Napoleon finally turned away from the sight before him and wandered back to his own bivouac fire to warm himself against the icy chill.

Grenadiers of the Guard, formed into a huge square, their massive bearskin headdresses nodding in the breeze, stood sentinel around their commander. Inside the formation, staff officers, Generals and Marshals busied themselves with minor tasks, stood talking of tactics and the coming battle. Some spoke of their homes, their wives, their families and their hopes for the impending conflict. Rank was immaterial on the night before a battle. Those who carried the batons of Marshals felt the same icy fingers of anxiety as any humble private or drummer boy. Death, they knew only too well, was no respecter of how much gold lace was sewn onto a uniform. Most warmed themselves around the roaring fire. Others drank and ate from the offerings on the small table that had been set up close by. Napoleon himself accepted a glass of burgundy from General Savary and raised it in salute. The other officers mimicked the gesture and joined their leader as he drank.

'All the troops available to me should be in position by dawn,' the Emperor announced. 'Once they are, we will begin the attack.'

'Would it not be best to wait until the army was at full strength, sire?' enquired Berthier.

'If I do that I lose more than half a day. I also give

the Prussians the initiative. Either to attack or to withdraw. We have pursued them long enough. I will not allow them to escape again.'

'Surely, sire, if they were going to attack they would have done so by now,' Lannes offered. 'They must be aware of our position and our numbers.'

'They are cautious,' Napoleon mused. 'Don't forget, they are an army commanded by old men. Willingness to take risks comes with the onset of age. Caution is a creeping sickness to men like Brunswick and Hohenlohe. They may be the descendants of Frederick the Great but they share none of his abilities.' He drained what was left in his glass. 'Lannes, you will attack at six a.m. Secure a line from Lützeroda to Closewitz. As each corps arrives it will perform the duty I ascribe to it. I will issue my orders for the morrow soon. You will all know your tasks, gentlemen. I know I can trust you to carry them out.' He looked around at the faces of the men who surrounded him. 'Now, I suggest you all get some sleep if you can. The morning promises to bring with it some considerable exertions.'

Almost as one, the group of officers saluted then disappeared in various different directions to rejoin their units. As Lannes turned away, the Corsican caught him by the arm as if to delay him.

'Your part in this campaign so far, as in every campaign in which you have served, has been considerable,' Napoleon said. 'Tomorrow I ask you to continue with your work.'

'Do you doubt for one second that I would, your Highness?' Lannes asked.

'A commander of an army has to trust those who fight with him. I trust all of my Marshals. None of you achieved your positions because of your breeding but because of your abilities. However, I would like to think that you are as much a friend to me as a commander.'

'I am your servant, sire. I am *honoured* to be a friend.'

'Any honour you attain is born of your valour. I am sorry I must call upon you to open the battle tomorrow. It will be a bloody task.'

'I am *thankful* you chose me, sire.'

Napoleon smiled and gripped the Marshal's shoulder.

Lannes saluted again then wandered off into the darkness towards the makeshift road leading to the plateau of the Landgrafenberg, where still more troops were arriving in a silent, steady stream.

'Do you wish to issue your orders now, sire?' Berthier asked, seating himself at the table and spreading out several sheets of paper upon it. 'I am ready.'

'As you always are,' the Corsican grinned. 'Very well, let us begin.'

Lausard looked up at the cloudless sky and pulled the blanket more tightly around him. There was already a light frost covering the iron-hard ground and the sergeant could feel it despite the layers of clothing and protection he wore. Horses tethered nearby also shivered in the chill, their breath clouding around them. Tigana passed among them, rubbing the necks of some, ensuring that as many as possible were covered by their green shabracques. The saddle cloths offered little in the way of warmth but then, in temperatures such as the men and beasts were being asked to endure, every little helped. Erebus lay curled up close to Gaston, who was sleeping with his head propped against his saddle, both dog and trumpeter seeking warmth from the other. Joubert, with his customary ability to sleep irrespective of the place or the time, was snoring loudly. Rostov too was sleeping, as were most of the men around Lausard, some more lightly than others. Sonnier was wrapped in his cloak and several sheets that he'd taken from a house in Jena. Only his head protruded from the linen cocoon.

'We needed some cloud cover,' said a voice nearby. 'That would have kept the frost at bay.'

Lausard turned to see Captain Barthez walking towards him, his own long green cape wrapped tightly around him.

The sergeant nodded. 'It is too late now,' he murmured.

Barthez sat down beside Lausard on the cold ground and glanced in the direction of the Landgrafenberg, where French troops continued to arrive steadily.

'How many men do you think will be involved in the battle tomorrow?' the officer remarked.

'Numbers are not important are they, sir? A man can die fighting one opponent as easily as he can fighting a dozen.'

'I heard that there could be up to eighty thousand Prussians opposing us. It will be a hard battle.'

'More opportunity for glory?' Lausard asked, raising one eyebrow, quizzically.

'Perhaps. Why do you find that so curious, Sergeant?

My desire to win the *Légion d'Honneur* seems to surprise you. Why do you find it so hard to understand my motives? You, as much as any man in this unit, should appreciate my position. You are a man from a similar background to myself. You have attained your own rank through your own efforts. Why is my quest for this medal such a puzzle to you? Would you not accept it with all your heart if it were offered to *you*?'

'Medals are mere decoration, Captain. I do not feel I need to display one to know my own worth. A man is generally what he feels himself to be. And perhaps our backgrounds are not as similar as you may suppose.' Lausard knew that he could not tell this son of a saddle maker that, fifteen years earlier, they would have been at completely opposite ends of the social ladder. At least until the Revolution had not only torn that ladder down but smashed its rungs and burned it. While Barthez and his family were fighting disease and poverty, Lausard and *his* had been enjoying the fruits of a more privileged lifestyle. One that had been brought to an abrupt and bloody halt by the blade of the guillotine.

'I hear you were a thief,' Barthez said, scornfully. 'You and most of your companions. Thieves. Forgers. Rapists. Horse-thieves. All criminals. Do not presume to imagine yourself better than I, Sergeant.'

'I can assure you I am under no such illusion, sir,' Lausard told him. 'What I was in the past is no longer important. I am not the man I was then.'

'Nor I.'

'The gold on your uniform has not changed you as a man. The addition of the *Légion d'Honneur* will not transform you either. You are the son of a saddle maker and that is what you will always be, no matter how many decorations you wear. No matter what rank you achieve. We are commanded by Marshals who come from even more humble stock than yourself, Captain. Marshal Murat's father was an innkeeper. Marshal Ney is the son of a cooper. Lannes and Mortier both the offspring of farmers. Strip away all their gold lace, fortunes and feathered hats, they are still the same men they always were.'

'But remember, Sergeant, that in civilian as well as in military life, the distinction is made between people. If your uniform was stripped away would it not leave merely a thief?'

Lausard smiled thinly. 'Possibly,' he mused.

The two men locked stares.

'Why is it so important to you?' Lausard enquired. 'Tell me, Captain, why? It is just a decoration. A piece of enamel tied to a length of washed silk. It's worthless.'

'It's not worthless to me. It represents my transition from the life I once knew. It forces people to accept me for who I am now. It is a beacon. A testament to my bravery. To the kind of man I am, and no one will be able to ignore it.'

'I wish you good luck in your hunt, Captain. I'm surprised the medal has eluded you for *this* long. How many men would you sacrifice to attain it?'

'Lives are not important in matters such as this. Do you think the Emperor stops to consider how many men he will lose before each campaign? No. He makes plans and he carries them out, without the hindrance of conscience, remorse or delusions of morality. A man in his position cannot afford such emotions. I have learned from him. I will not rest until I have achieved my objective.'

'No matter what the cost in lives?'

'I am willing to risk my own life as readily as any of those whom I command. I would never ask men under me to perform a task I would not be willing to do myself.'

'And if that task involves the deaths of many, would you still go through with it?'

'If I had to, yes.'

'I wish you well in your quest, Captain. I hope I am alive to see you wear the medal you desire so badly.'

Barthez got to his feet and rubbed his hands together.

'Come nightfall tomorrow, you too may be wearing a medal, Sergeant,' the officer observed.

'We will see, Captain,' Lausard murmured. 'When the battle comes, I will have more on my mind than decorations and glory.'

'Such as?'

'Survival.'

Barthez wandered off, pulling his cloak around him once more. Lausard watched as the officer was swallowed up by the darkness. In the gloom, hidden by the impenetrable night, the ever present sound of marching feet could still be heard as French troops continued to arrive. Lausard glanced at his watch. It was just after two a.m. Dawn would be upon them in less than four hours.

Napoleon felt the hand on his shoulder and awoke immediately. He snapped his head around to find Berthier and Lannes standing close by him. It was the tall Chief of Staff who had woken him. The Corsican rubbed both hands hurriedly over his face then blinked hard, instantly alert.

'There has been a development, sire,' Berthier told him.

'Have the Prussians run from us again?' the Corsican smiled.

'We have received a communication from Marshal Davout in the vicinity of Auerstadt, fifteen kilometres to the west, sire,' the Chief of Staff said. 'He reports large-scale enemy activity to the front of his positions.'

'A flank guard,' said the Corsican waving his hand dismissively in the air. 'Nothing more.'

'Davout stresses that there are considerable numbers of men facing him, sire. It would appear that the Prussians are preparing to attack him.'

'They may have divided their forces, sire,' Lannes added.

'Why would Brunswick do that?' Napoleon snapped. 'He is not likely to divide his army when they are faced by our own main force here. He may be cautious but he is not a fool.'

'For the duration of this campaign, sire, we have known little of the Prussian troop movements and dispositions,' Lannes insisted. 'That is still the case. We have no idea *exactly* how many men are arrayed against us.'

'The full might of the Prussian army is encamped little more than a mile from where we now stand,' Napoleon insisted. 'I have no doubt of that.'

'We have nothing to support that supposition, sire,'

Lannes persisted. 'We are still as ignorant of the full Prussian dispositions as we were when we emerged from the Thüringer Wald a week ago.'

'What if Lannes is right, sire?' Berthier added. 'If Brunswick *has* divided his force, we have no way of knowing how strong the army before us is. Nor how powerful the forces arrayed against Marshal Davout are.'

'We are facing the main Prussian army,' the Corsican insisted. 'I am certain of it. Davout will be more than capable of brushing aside whatever stands before him, marching on Apolda and cutting off the enemy line of retreat. He commands upwards of twenty-nine thousand men and forty-six guns. Bernadotte, who commands a further twenty-one thousand men and fifty guns, is close enough to move to his aid if necessary.'

'What if you are wrong, sire?' Lannes wanted to know. 'If we have been unable to pinpoint exact Prussian troop movements then would it not be safe to assume that *they* have had similar problems locating and identifying our *own* formations? You say that Davout is facing just a flank guard at Auerstadt. Could that not be the same case with us here? Might we be bringing our main force to bear on an enemy who could be swept aside with just one or two corps? There is no way of knowing how many men either ourselves or Davout are faced with.'

'Your concerns are unfounded, Lannes,' Napoleon retorted. 'The battle will take place *here*.' He jabbed a finger at the ground beneath his feet. 'That is why I intend to mass one hundred and forty-five thousand men and one hundred and sixty guns here. We will destroy the troops before us. By tomorrow night, the Prussian army will cease to exist.'

Lannes sucked in a weary breath.

'I hope to God you are right, sire,' he muttered. 'For our own sakes *and* for those of Marshal Davout and his men.'

'What message should I send back to Davout, sire?' Berthier wanted to know.

'Tell him to dispose of any enemy troops who oppose him as quickly as possible,' snapped Napoleon, 'so that his march towards Apolda is not delayed. He should be able to join us as we celebrate our victory.'

Berthier hesitated a moment and glanced at Lannes who merely shook his head.

Napoleon looked at each man in turn.

'Send the message,' he hissed. 'And here, we attack in four hours.'

Seventeen

Alain Lausard awoke in fog so thick he could barely see a hand in front of him. As he drew in a deep breath, the white blanket of cold air seemed to gush down his throat into his lungs. The fog was undisturbed by any light breeze. It merely hung over the landscape as densely as if someone had packed cotton wool around the sergeant and the thousands of other French troops currently being dragged from their slumbers by the onset of dawn. At least Lausard assumed it was dawn. Daylight was scarcely perceptible through it. So thick was the mist it was impossible to see the sky. It was as if the clouds had simply drifted down from the heavens during the night and come to rest on the frost-covered ground. All around him he heard slow, cautious movement. All completed in virtual silence, adding to the unreality of the entire tableau. The sergeant got to his feet and bumped into Rocheteau. Nearby he heard Erebus yelp as another of the other unsighted dragoons trod on one of his paws. Men picked up their equipment and tried to move into position, despite the fact that their vision was so severely hampered by the dense fog. And yet someone, somewhere, was able to move. Lausard heard the tramping of many feet and he looked up to his right, in the direction of the Landgrafenberg, although it was impossible to see what was happening on the precipitous knoll. To his left, also, there was considerable movement, and he was sure that infantry were moving forward, despite the fact they were marching blindly across potentially treacherous terrain towards an enemy who may well be less than two hundred yards from them.

Still the unearthly silence pervaded the area around the dragoons. Lausard waved a hand before his face, as if to clear some of the fog away, but, unlike smoke, it merely dissipated momentarily then drifted across his line of vision once more. He and the other dragoons groped their way towards their waiting horses and swung themselves into their saddles. Once more, Lausard was struck by the all-pervading silence that surrounded them. A yard or two ahead of him he heard horses' hooves as an animal was walked back and forth in front of the waiting cavalry. Although he couldn't see, the sergeant was sure that the mount belonged to Captain Barthez. The dragoons were so tightly grouped that Lausard's boots were rubbing against those of the men on both his left and right. He looked in both directions and managed to make out the features of Rocheteau and Bonet. As they exhaled, their breath clouded in the air, adding to the already impenetrable blanket of fog. Lausard wondered how it would be possible to fight a battle in such conditions but realised that, as the day wore on, the fog would lift. How rapidly that happened was another matter.

Horses pawed the ground in nervous anticipation. From behind him, Lausard could hear whispered prayers and realised that Moreau was responsible for the words. Other men seemed paralysed by the silence, reluctant to break it, many wondering exactly how close to the enemy they actually were. For all they knew, Prussian guns could be massed only yards from them. In such appalling visibility anything was possible. Lausard wondered if enemy troops were, at this moment, moving silently and stealthily towards them, bayonets levelled, muskets ready to pour volleys into them. Erebus even abandoned his usual prowling and crouched beneath Gaston's horse whimpering quietly.

Lausard pulled his watch from his pocket and squinted at it. Just after six a.m. Even if the sun rose, it would not burn off the fog for another two or three hours at least. The dragoons were crushed together in silence, blind to what lay before them, helplessly awaiting the intervention of the elements to clear a path for them. Lausard heard the rumble of a cannon limber and, somewhere off to the left, a heavy gun was dragged past. He hoped the gunners lined the barrel up in the right direction. In these terrible conditions, the chance of being shot at by one's own side was a distinct possibility. Lausard had seen it happen during clear visibility. What could happen within this apparent vacuum of silence and fog he hardly dared imagine. All around, other units moved into position with similar difficulty, but all with the kind of iron discipline that had made *La Grande Armée* such a formidable fighting machine. Infantry, cavalry and artillery were all packed together in the ravines and gulleys that scarred the terrain, all invisible to each other. All hidden by the ever present clouds of fog. Lausard felt his heart begin to thud more rapidly against his ribs. To the front of the dragoons, he heard that single horse continue to wander back and forth interminably. He checked his watch again and waited.

Napoleon Bonaparte angrily snapped his telescope shut and gazed out into the thick fog.

'Has Lannes begun his attack yet?' the Corsican wanted to know. 'I can see nothing from here.'

'The fog will not rise for another few hours yet, sire,' Berthier said. 'But, as far as we can tell, Marshal Lannes' corps is advancing on Closewitz as you ordered.'

'How long before the Prussians realise they are being attacked?' General Rapp mused, also squinting myopically through the fog.

'If they are still in their positions,' Berthier murmured.

'They will not have withdrawn,' Napoleon declared. 'We would have known if they had left their positions during the night before this fog descended.'

'There was heavy fog before the battle of Austerlitz,' Savary reminded his companions. 'Let us hope today's outcome is the same.'

'The fog was not as bad as this before Austerlitz,' Berthier offered. 'We are like blind men in its grip.'

Ahead of the huddle of officers and their Emperor, French infantry were marching down the Landgrafenberg in formations so tightly packed that some men in the centre of columns were physically lifted off their feet. The packs of those in the leading ranks were inches from the faces of their companions behind them. Many men marched with their gaze directed towards the ground, ensuring they didn't slip on the icy, rutted terrain. The entire massed phalanx moved down the slopes and onto the plateau that led towards the villages of Cospeda and Lützeroda, neither of which was visible to them.

'Forty thousand men advancing like ghosts,' Napoleon smiled. 'Silent and undetected.'

'Should I order the artillery to open fire yet, sire?' Berthier wanted to know.

'Not yet,' the Corsican told him. 'They will know when that time has come.'

Rapp blew on his cold hands. Savary looked around into the mist. It was General Bessiéres who gave voice to the thought they all had.

'When will this accursed fog lift?' he rasped.

The loud blast of a single cannon opening fire was unmistakeable and Lausard looked in the direction of the sound. He guessed it was some five or six hundred yards away. The sound reverberated through the unearthly stillness of the fog shrouded morning, ringing in the ears of every man on the battlefield. It was soon followed by another, then another. Within a matter of minutes, the blasts had joined to form salvos. Lausard could hear shouts and sometimes screams until the steady thunder of cannon began to obliterate every other noise. Thick sulphurous smoke began to belch from the mouth of both French and Prussian guns, the noxious fumes combining with the fog to create an even more impenetrable veil. Moreau crossed himself once more.

Now Lausard heard the more strident crackling of musket fire coming from the same direction. He could hear orders being shouted. In the stillness, every syllable seemed to carry more acutely.

'It begins,' Bonet whispered.

'The Prussians are closer than we thought,' murmured the sergeant, gazing blindly in the direction of the firing. 'Our forward units must have been camped close to them last night and not even known it.'

'They'll know it *now*,' Rocheteau observed as the cannon fire intensified.

Some horses whinnied anxiously as the sound of the guns grew ever louder and Lausard was certain that the French artillery were now replying. Matching each burst of cannister or roundshot with their own lethal projectiles.

'Trumpeter.' The voice was unmistakeably that of Captain Barthez, and it ripped through the fog like a knife through linen. 'Sound the advance.'

Gaston did as he was instructed and the keening notes of the advance began to swirl around in the clogged air.

'What the hell is he doing?' Rocheteau rasped. 'We can't even see each *other* in this, let alone the enemy.'

The dragoons moved forward at the walk, the horses picking their way over the uneven ground. Lausard glanced down at the terrain and thought how unsuitable it was for cavalry. It would be so easy for any number of the mounts to turn hooves or even break legs in the dense fog and on such a treacherous surface. His own bay snorted and tossed its head skittishly as it advanced and on more than one occasion he was forced to dig his knees into its flanks to keep it steady. The animals were as unsettled as their riders by the fact that they couldn't see what lay ahead of them. Swords clanked against the boots of other men. Stirrups clashed with a series of metallic clangs and the horses were continually bumping into each other, so compressed were they.

Lausard was aware of the leading ranks mounting a ridge. The climb was made even more dangerous by the frosted ground but the horses kept their footing and continued onwards until the terrain thankfully levelled out somewhat. To his relief, Lausard felt sure that the fog was beginning to lift. He could still see only the figure of Captain Barthez riding two or three feet ahead but it was something. However, other than that, the entire battlefield remained shrouded in all directions. So thick was the fog that even the muzzle flashes of cannon were not yet visible and Lausard could tell from their deafening roars that they were close. He heard three or four withering volleys of musket fire, which swiftly degenerated into sporadic popping and crackling, only for another more thunderous fusillade to rip through the morning air again. The smell of human and horse sweat was pungent in his nostrils. It mingled with the stink of horse droppings, oiled swords, gunpowder and polished leather – smells that were now only too familiar to him, ones he associated with an advance. For the horses, anything other than a steady walk was impossible, and also suicidal, in the fog.

To the right there were several loud explosions and Lausard realised that a French battery had opened up.

They were close. Not only was the concussion blast from their barrels detectable but also the stench of the choking smoke that poured from the bronze cylinders as they spewed out their deadly loads. He heard the gunners relocating the cannon and, moments later, another salvo of shot erupted from the battery. Still the world was condensed into three or four feet of fog-shrouded ground, and it was as if the sounds of battle were happening elsewhere. As if the dragoons were in some kind of clouded, protective bubble. Lausard knew that this illusion would be shattered at any moment. He had no idea how close they were to the Prussians but he gripped his reins more tightly and felt his heart thumping hard. A horse to his right stumbled and almost toppled over but its rider kept it under control. The men around him also righted their mounts and the line stayed as straight as possible considering the conditions.

Lausard heard the roar of the Prussian guns seconds before the first salvo of roundshot came scything through the advancing dragoons.

The solid six-pound balls roared out of the fog and struck men and horses. They sent them spinning as if they were toy soldiers struck by a petulant child. Blood erupted into the air as several men were simply blasted to pieces by the shot. A horse, its head torn off at the shoulder, stumbled on a few more paces, its rider's lower torso still upright in the saddle, then pitched forward onto the frosty ground.

'Dismount, fight on foot,' roared Barthez.

He had barely given the order when a blast of musket fire caught the dragoons in the flank. Several more men and horses went down in bloodied heaps.

Erebus began barking wildly, dashing back and forth in the fog.

Lausard had no idea if the musket fire was coming from Prussian or French guns and he doubted if those firing had much idea who they were shooting at either. But the source of the bullets wasn't important. All that mattered was that the dragoons were within range and taking casualties. The sergeant pulled his carbine free and swung it up to his shoulder, preparing to fire back in the direction from which the musket volley had come, unsure whether or not he was firing into the enemy formations or into those of his fellow countrymen. In the fog it was impossible to tell.

Ahead there was a thunderous explosion. A huge mushroom-shaped plume of fire rose into the air, searing through the fog, ripping aside the blinding veil and threatening to incinerate the sky. For fleeting seconds, the dazzling light and savage heat illuminated everything within a hundred yards. The sudden onslaught of images registered in Lausard's mind like the afterburn of some exploding supernova. For what seemed like little more than a heartbeat he saw French troops formed into long lines pouring musket fire into their white-uniformed Saxon enemies from point-blank range while, in the gaps between them, four- and eight-pounders did likewise. From the other side, Prussian six-pounders blasted back with similar ferocity. Men and horses went down in bloodied piles. There were already hundreds of men lying dead or dying on the bone-hard ground.

Elsewhere, the wounded of both sides were trying to

drag themselves away from the scene of slaughter, uncertain in the fog of where they were going. He saw a man with his right arm torn off at the shoulder staggering aimlessly back and forth, using his left to balance and plead for help from those raging all around him. Another man, his uniform so drenched with blood it was impossible to see whether he was friend or foe, sat helplessly on the bloodied ground, both legs having been blasted off just below the knees. Bodies holed by bullets, punctured by cannister or simply obliterated by roundshot lay scattered around like reeking lumps of meat in some vile slaughterhouse.

In that brief moment of illumination, Lausard and many others also got their first fleeting glimpse of the battlefield upon which they fought. In places, French troops were swarming through the streets of Closewitz. Saxon infantry stood their ground as long as possible but the ferocity of the French attack was overwhelming. Lausard could see enemy cavalry off to the left. Several batteries of Prussian artillery, some on a low ridge near to Closewitz, were working furiously at their pieces, keeping up a steady fire into their invisible enemies.

Barthez also saw the batteries.

As some men reeled back from the massive explosion, others took the chance to assess their position as best they could. Rocheteau was also gazing around. Erebus barked madly in the direction of the spiralling pillar of fire and smoke. Gaston, still in the saddle, pulled hard on his reins as his horse reared. Joubert, too, also struggled to keep control of his mount. The animal was bleeding from a bad wound on its left flank and the pain, combined with the sudden eruption of noise and light, had sent it wild. Rostov rushed across and caught the bridle of the animal, slapping its neck hard to calm it. Charvet was shielding his eyes from the fire. Moreau crossed himself.

'Mount up,' roared Barthez, swinging himself into the saddle. 'To horse. Now.'

The initial blast had faded and everything had been swallowed once again by the enveloping fog. Lausard cursed the gossamer veil as he hauled himself into the saddle. Tabor's horse bumped into his and the big man raised a hand as if in apology.

'Draw swords,' bellowed Barthez. 'Prepare to advance.'

'What the hell is he doing?' Rocheteau snarled.

'At the trot,' the officer shouted and trumpets echoed the order, notes rising through the fog.

Lausard said nothing, he merely allowed his right hand to drop to the hilt of his sword and then, with one expert movement, he pulled the three-foot length of razor-sharp steel from its scabbard. All around him, the other dragoons also complied with the order, many of them still unsure of exactly where they were and how close both their comrades and the enemy were. Lausard caught a brief glimpse of Lieutenant Royere, his face splashed with blood, riding fast across the front of the rapidly forming line of horsemen. The guidon of the regiment also fluttered into view before being swallowed by the fog again.

All around him, Lausard was aware of horses crashing

into each other as the dragoons attempted some semblance of order in the appalling conditions. Visibility was still down to three or four feet and many of the horses were as anxious as their riders about advancing at speed across ground they could not see. Cannon and musket fire continued unabated but it was now joined by the jingling of harnesses and the rumble of hooves as the green-clad cavalrymen gradually picked up speed.

There was a deafening roar from in front of them and Lausard involuntarily ducked over the neck of his horse as a volley of roundshot came hurtling out of the fog from the Prussian six-pounders. He actually heard the air part as one of the solid balls tore past him. It killed and wounded half a dozen horses as it ploughed through the dragoons' ranks. Lausard saw a man to his right flung from the saddle as if yanked by invisible strings. His brass helmet spun from his head, seemed to hover in the foggy air for a second then fell to earth. Curses and screams of pain merged in equal volume as the dragoons swept on, still gathering pace.

Lausard and his companions heard the notes of the trumpet signal the charge and the sergeant put spurs to his bay, urging it on to the six hundred paces a minute required for that furious action. He felt the wind and the fog rushing past him. The stench of blood and smoke filled his nostrils. The familiar surge of adrenaline swept through him. Like so many of his companions he opened his mouth to roar his intent. The horses also felt the fury of their riders and drove onwards over the uneven ground, through the fog and smoke.

It took less than thirty seconds before the horsemen

crashed into the first of the Prussian guns. Lausard hacked to his left and right, cutting down two men. Others turned and fled, only too happy to abandon their equipment to the rampaging French horsemen who seemed to have appeared from nowhere. Karim swung his scimitar at a fleeing gunner and laid open his back with a single stroke of the wickedly curved blade. Rocheteau rode down another man then struck at his companion with his sword, cutting the Prussian across the head. The impact, as his weapon struck solid bone, sent a shudder the full length of his arm. The man's bicorn, neatly sliced in two by the blow, fell to the ground beside him.

Lausard wheeled his horse, almost colliding with Carbonne who was in the second rank. Along the ragged lines, the dragoons seemed as concerned with avoiding accidental contact with their companions as they did about finishing off the Prussian gunners. Once again, the impenetrable fog seemed to close around them. The sergeant could hear the sound of swords crashing against other weapons or cutting into flesh but he could still see little of what was happening around him. All he knew was that their charge had carried them beyond the village. The sound of fighting had now spread in all directions and cannon fire was becoming both incessant and more concentrated on both sides. He tugged on his reins, his bloodied sword still gripped in his fist, his breath coming in gasps. Visibility was still down to a couple of yards. Lausard was beginning to wonder if the fog was ever going to lift.

* * *

Napoleon glanced at his watch and saw that it was just after ten a.m. Muttering under his breath, he turned towards General Savary.

'Your watch,' the Corsican snapped, as if reluctant to trust his own timepiece. 'Let me see it.'

Savary obliged and Napoleon nodded curtly. There was barely a minute between them.

'Everything appears to be going as you planned, sire,' Savary offered. 'What are you concerned about?'

'Marshal Lannes has taken Vierzehnheiligen, sire,' Berthier said. 'Marshal Soult's men have cleared Closewitz. The villages of Cospeda and Isserstedt are under attack. The plateau before us is clear of enemy troops. You have the ground you need to deploy the remainder of the army as it arrives.'

Napoleon nodded slowly and peered through his telescope, grateful that the fog was finally beginning to thin. However, it was still hanging over several areas of the battlefield in thick banks, mingling with the smoke from so many cannons and muskets.

'Where are Soult's men now?' the Emperor demanded, without taking his ever roving gaze from the constant movement of troops before him.

'Current reports indicate that they are in the Zwaten woods, sire,' Berthier said, glancing at a crumpled piece of paper before him. 'There is a strong Prussian force opposing them. Other than that, the enemy appear to be falling back from all sectors of the field.'

The Corsican nodded slowly.

All around him, aides were constantly arriving with reports or leaving with orders for his commanders. Men stood by with fresh horses for the messengers. Medical staff also waited to see if the aides themselves needed any attention. More than one had already arrived during the course of the morning with a wound or two. Berthier sat at his makeshift desk scribbling away frantically whenever the Emperor dictated an instruction. It was then passed to a waiting aide and the man hurtled off to hand that message to the appropriate source. The summit of the Landgrafenberg was a constant hive of activity. Strutting around from map to map, apparently oblivious to the frenzied action taking place all about him, Napoleon constantly checked and rechecked the positions of those troops he could see himself through his telescope. He was the first to spot the dark mass of a Prussian column moving towards the village of Vierzehnheiligen.

'Cavalry, artillery *and* infantry,' the Emperor remarked, directing the attention of his staff to the steadily advancing enemy horde. 'They are forming up for a reason.'

'They fear for the safety of their flank, sire,' General Rapp offered, looking through his own telescope.

'There are Saxon troops in support,' murmured Savary, noting the profusion of white-uniformed infantry among the advancing enemy soldiers.

'They appear to be taking up position in the interval between the left of Lannes' men and the right of Augereau's,' Napoleon observed. 'The fog is still sufficiently thick to cover them from those closest to them.'

'Perhaps our enemies have chosen to attack at last, sire,' Rapp said.

'It is a large concentration of troops,' Napoleon muttered. 'It appears more like some kind of blocking manoeuvre and yet we have no troops in that part of the field at the moment.'

There was a sudden eruption of fire from several Prussian batteries arranged on a low rise close to the village. Napoleon saw the smoke belch from the barrels then roll across the already shrouded landscape in a choking blanket.

'Sire, look,' said Savary, pointing towards several units of blue-clad troops moving in the direction of the Prussian guns.

As two regiments of French light cavalry and five battalions of infantry swept towards the Prussian battery, Napoleon clenched his teeth angrily.

'Ney,' he murmured, lowering his telescope, momentarily. 'What is he doing? He had orders to wait until his corps had reached full strength before committing them to the battle.' The Corsican raised the glass to his eye and swept it back and forth over the mass of advancing troops. The one he sought was clearly visible. Clad in his full-dress Marshal's uniform, his feather-trimmed bicorn held in one hand, his shock of red hair like a beacon in the gloom, Marshal Michel Ney spurred his horse forward, waving his men onwards to meet the Prussian column.

'It can be little more than an advance guard,' Berthier commented. 'Four thousand men at most. The bulk of his command is still back in Jena itself.'

Napoleon dragged his own bicorn from his head and hurled it furiously to the ground at his feet.

'That damned Gascon,' he shouted. 'Can he not control his impetuousness for even a moment? He had no orders to attack. Why has he done so? His impatience may cost us dearly.'

'He is outnumbered two to one,' Savary observed.

'Ney is a brave man but sometimes I wish he would temper that bravery with a little common sense,' rasped Napoleon. 'His eagerness to join the battle has exposed his men to unnecessary danger and might well force me to rethink my own dispositions. He will have to be supported if he is to stand against such a powerful enemy force.'

Berthier snapped his fingers and gestured to one of the waiting ADCs, whose uniform was already grimed with mud and smoke. The man hurried over, pulling his horse by the reins. The Chief of Staff looked at his superior, as if waiting for the order he thought would be inevitable. The aide coughed, clearing his throat of the acrid smoke that clogged it, then patted his horse's neck, steadying the animal as it too patiently waited.

From his vantage point, the Corsican could see Ney's men advancing. Entire files of them were brought down by the concentrated fire of the Prussian cannon but they continued with their movement, led by the red-headed Marshal himself. The battle was short and decisive. They swept through the Prussian battery and Napoleon saw several eagles waving triumphantly on the low ridge that the gunners had occupied. Most of the enemy artillerymen were now fleeing wildly towards their oncoming comrades. The bodies of dead and dying French troops littered the ground despite their triumph.

'They have taken the battery, sire,' Savary mused.

'At what cost?' Napoleon snarled. 'Look.'

Even as he spoke, Prussian cavalry were already thundering towards Ney's exhausted men.

Eighteen

❖

The ground was shaking. Despite the almost constant roar of cannon and musket fire, Lausard could still hear the sound of pounding hooves and, beneath his feet, he felt the ground vibrate to their fearsome rhythm too. Shouts and the neighing of horses filled the air, adding to the cacophony already deafening him. Like his companions, he had seen the French infantry take the Prussian battery nearby, despite heavy losses. Many of those men were now being helped from the battlefield by companions. Others were left to lie where they'd fallen. He had seen the unmistakeable figure of Marshal Ney riding among the foot soldiers, directing their attack. Now that same commander was attempting to rally the infantry as the Prussian cavalry launched its attack. The sergeant swung himself into his saddle and looked in the direction of the ever growing noise. Through the last vestiges of the fog and the rolling smoke, Lausard saw row upon row of big men on big horses hurtling across the open ground. Prussian cuirassiers, their swords held high above their heads, bore down on the French infantry and hussars away to the right. Behind them raced Prussian dragoons, clad in light blue tunics, swords also drawn as they swept towards their enemies. A battery of French horse artillery galloped up, swiftly unlimbered their four-pounders, and Lausard saw the gunners hurrying to load their pieces with cannister as the Prussian cavalry drew ever nearer. The infantry were already forming into squares, aware of the danger the enemy horsemen posed.

'Form up and meet the charge,' roared Captain Barthez, appearing close to Lausard, his sword already drawn.

'More glory?' sneered Rocheteau, his face stained with blood and smoke. His breath was coming in gasps and there was black powder smeared around his mouth. He tried to swallow but it felt as if his throat had been filled with chalk. The grains of gunpowder stung his tongue and he coughed and spat.

Moreau, bleeding from a cut on his left arm, crossed himself.

Karim brandished his scimitar before him and reached out to steady Carbonne as the big man swayed uncertainly in the saddle. The former executioner was bleeding from a deep gash on his right temple, the blood cutting a crimson path through the grime on his cheek.

Lieutenant Royere, part of his collar missing, his surtout torn and bloodied around the chest, rode across to join Barthez.

'Are you all right, Lieutenant?' Lausard called.

'It's not my blood, Sergeant,' the officer called back, wiping sweat from his face with the back of one hand.

'They're heavy cavalry,' grunted Rostov, clutching at his right ear. 'They'll ride us down.' Blood was seeping through his fingers and, when he withdrew his hand, Lausard saw that the tip of the Russian's ear had been torn off by a fragment of metal or a bullet. Another two inches to the right would have meant certain death.

'It's not us they're after,' Lausard told him. 'It's the infantry.'

'Form line and fire from the saddle,' bellowed Barthez.

With the precision borne of so many hours spent in both battlefields and drill, the dragoons pulled their carbines free and loaded them, swinging the Charlevilles up to their shoulders, keeping their horses steady with their knees. Through the rolling smoke and fog, Lausard and his companions could see that the onrushing Prussian cavalry were already less than six or seven hundred yards away. The slight slope down which they galloped added to their already considerable momentum.

'Prepare to fire,' Barthez shouted.

The horse artillery nearby opened up and some of the dragoons' mounts reared slightly. Yet more smoke belched across the line of waiting French cavalry, momentarily obscuring the waves of Prussian horsemen.

Lausard saw entire ranks veer off towards the French infantry, who had now formed a square and were sending volleys of musket fire into the white-clad ranks. Men toppled from their saddles, horses cartwheeled hurling men to the ground. Those following stumbled over their fallen comrades but the surge seemed to have lost none of its momentum.

The remaining cuirassiers were now within four hundred yards.

Lausard pulled the carbine more tightly into his

shoulder, readying himself for the recoil when he fired.

Three hundred yards.

'Hold steady,' shouted Lieutenant Royere, his sword in one hand, a pistol in the other.

Two hundred yards.

'Wait for my command,' Barthez shouted, his voice barely audible above the combined din of cannon and musket fire, thundering hooves and the shouts and screams of the onrushing Prussian cavalry.

One hundred yards.

The leading ranks lowered their swords and accelerated into the charge.

Lausard kept his eye fixed on the figure of a cuirassier captain who was leading one Prussian squadron. The gold lace on his tunic made him an obvious target as he led his men towards the stationary line of dragoons, a number of whom were now actually looking in the direction of Barthez waiting for the order to fire.

'Hold steady,' the officer ordered, his words barely recognisable over the battlefield cacophony. The thundering hooves, the cannon fire. The rattle of muskets. Screams and oaths of men locked in mortal combat.

'Fire,' whispered Rocheteau, through clenched teeth.

The thundering Prussian cuirassiers were no more than fifty yards away now. Another few seconds and they would smash into the line of dragoons like a hammer into glass.

Lausard was breathing hard, his nostrils clogged with the stench of the battlefield, his eyes already stinging from the flecks of gunpowder and the millions of tiny cinders drifting around in the air.

Twenty yards.

'FIRE!'

The order was received and executed with something close to relief.

All along the line, muskets spewed forth their deadly load as one. A great hail of bullets tore into the charging Prussian heavy cavalry. Huge clouds of sulphurous smoke rolled across that section of the battlefield and, for fleeting seconds, the dragoons found themselves plunged back into the same kind of blindness that they had been forced to endure from the fog earlier that morning. Lausard heard screams from both men and horses and there were loud crashes as animals and riders alike went down in sprawling heaps, the ranks behind crashing into their fallen comrades. From such point-blank range it was impossible to miss. Almost every lead ball found a target and the effect was devastating. Lausard and all the others reloaded as quickly as possible, the sergeant feeling the heat from the barrel against his lips as he spat a fresh ball down the muzzle.

Then came the impact as those cuirassiers who had survived the initial withering volley came hurtling into the dragoons, swords swinging left and right. Lausard parried a cut with the butt of his musket then swung the Charleville like a club, catching his opponent in the face, pulping his nose and sending him toppling from the saddle. A riderless horse slammed into Lausard's own mount, almost knocking the animal over and, before the sergeant could recover his composure, he saw another Prussian trooper bearing down upon him. This time he couldn't avoid the cut. The sword caught him across the left arm, tore open his jacket and gouged into his flesh. Lausard hissed in pain and swung his musket up, firing into the Prussian's chest from such close range the muzzle was touching the man's body when it was discharged. The sergeant pushed the empty weapon back into the boot on his saddle and quickly drew his sword in time to meet another cuirassier. The trooper had been wounded in the chest and there was little power in his thrust. Lausard easily deflected it then buried his own sword a good ten inches into the man's stomach.

All around him, similar individual battles raged. Karim struck at another Prussian with such force and skill that he practically carved the man's head off with his scimitar. Delacor, the reins gripped in his teeth, swung the axe with one hand and his sword with the other. He buried the sharpened hatchet blade in the chest of one enemy then caught another in the side with his sword. Both fell from their saddles, fatally injured. He was about to swing the axe against another foe when a sword pierced his back, puncturing the flesh and erupting from the other side just below his ribcage. Delacor shouted in pain and slumped forward in the saddle, aware that his opponent was preparing to skewer him once more. Rocheteau rode his horse straight at the Prussian cuirassier, knocked both animal and rider off balance and pressed his advantage, driving his own sword into the chest of the Prussian. He grabbed Delacor's hand and the wounded man nodded sharply, glancing down at the wound in his side. It was painful but, thankfully, seemed to have missed any vital organs. The two men exchanged a brief glance then Rocheteau found himself confronted by two more of the Prussians. He pulled a pistol from his holster and shot one, the other he fended off with his sword, finally delivering a shattering backhand blow that smashed the cuirassier's forearm. As the man shrieked in pain, Rocheteau stabbed him twice in the chest.

Lausard, seemingly oblivious to the wound in his arm, fought like a man possessed in the closely packed melee. He saw Lieutenant Royere cut across the face. Witnessed Tabor, bleeding from a wound on the forehead, fighting on foot against two Prussian cuirassiers. The big man was standing beside the carcass of his dead horse, striking to left and right with his sword. He caught one of the Prussians across the thigh, hacking so deep the blade severed the man's femoral artery. Blood erupted into the air, some of it spattering Tabor, who simply ducked beneath a wild sword cut and grabbed at his assailant. He hauled him bodily from the saddle, crushing him close in a bear-like grip which forced the air from the Prussian's lungs. Tabor dropped the man, grabbed him by the head and twisted sharply. The Prussian's neck snapped like a twig.

Roussard and Charvet fought side by side, both of them drenched with blood.

Sonnier shot down a cuirassier officer then shouted in pain himself as a bullet struck him in the shoulder, just missing his collar bone. It ploughed through flesh and exploded from his back carrying small fragments of pulverised muscle and uniform with it.

Gaston, his knee a crimson mess, felt his horse buckle beneath him as it was hit by several pistol bullets. The young trumpeter was thrown clear as the animal hit the ground and he struggled upright, trying to keep his weight on his good leg. Lausard spurred towards him, catching the reins of a riderless horse as he did. He guided the big black mount towards Gaston, who hurriedly swung himself into the saddle.

Bodies of men and horses littered the ground in all directions. Riderless horses dashed backwards and forwards through the choking banks of rolling smoke, sometimes crashing into fighting men, sometimes seeking escape from the hell of the battle. And, constantly, the roar of cannon and the crackle of muskets continued. Lausard could barely breathe. Sweat was pouring down his face, and his arms felt as if someone had attached lead weights to them but he kept fighting, knowing that he, like his companions, must find reserves of strength they didn't know they had if they were to survive. Everywhere he looked the dragoons were outnumbered by their adversaries. Every yard of earth was a killing ground as men hacked, stabbed, shot and battered each other to death. The stench of blood was as strong as that of smoke now. The red fluid spouted into the air as each new casualty was felled. Lausard had no idea how long the fighting had been going on. Time lost its meaning in situations like this. All he knew was that unless the dragoons were either withdrawn or reinforced, they faced annihilation.

Away to his right, the French infantry squares stood firm as Prussian cavalry swirled around them like the sea breaking on rocks. Every so often, a volley of fire would illuminate the smoke-shrouded battlefield, the blaze of light burning its image on Lausard's retina. He coughed and spat mucus and powder grains.

Close by, the sergeant saw the guidon of the regiment appear through the smoke like some kind of multi-coloured phantom. Seconds later, the man carrying it was struck from his saddle by a Prussian cuirassier. The standard fell to the ground and Lausard spurred towards it. Captain Barthez arrived a fraction of a second before him. The officer drove his sword into the Prussian then leapt from his horse and retrieved the guidon, brandishing it before him. Lausard rode alongside him, shooting another onrushing Prussian from the saddle with his pistol.

'We will have to pull back, Captain,' the sergeant shouted.

Barthez merely shook his head.

The officer's uniform was soaked with blood, some of it his own. There were several sword cuts across the chest and shoulders but none of them was deep enough to have caused any debilitating damage. He gripped the staff of the guidon in one bloodied fist and brandished it before him.

'What use is your medal to you if you are dead?' roared Lausard, angrily.

Barthez met his gaze for fleeting seconds then rode on, slashing frenziedly to his right and left, the guidon flying proudly above his head.

From somewhere behind him, Lausard heard a steadily growing rumble that he recognised as horses' hooves. One single thought entered his mind and stuck there. Were he and his companions surrounded? He squinted through the smoke but could see nothing. The

sound of approaching hooves grew louder. Lausard
sucked in a tainted breath, the hot air burning his lungs.
He turned his horse this way and that, preparing to meet
this second attack but also conscious of the Prussian
cuirassiers who were still milling about amongst the
dragoons. Bodies from men on both sides lay all over
the ground. Dead and dying horses also added to the
confusion. Riderless mounts dashed wildly in and out
of smoke banks, men who had lost their horses staggered helplessly among those who still fought from the
saddle. A number of dragoons, including Sonnier, had
dismounted and were using some piled up horse
carcasses as cover while they kept up a sustained fire
against the enemy heavy cavalry, picking off the white-
clad riders with their carbines. Sonnier kept up his
robotic firing for so long that the Charleville finally
became too hot in his hand. There was always the danger
of the powder exploding due to the heat. He dropped
the weapon and retrieved another from the saddle of a
fallen horse. He checked the flint then loaded with his
customary speed and efficiency and continued firing.

Volleys of fire were still erupting from the squares of
French infantry as the Prussian cavalry swept helplessly
around them. Sometimes they would hack impotently at
the foot soldiers with their swords but they dared not
take their mounts too close for fear of being shot from
the saddle or run through by the *chevaux de frise* of bayonets which extended from all four sides of the squares.

Lausard looked around and saw hundreds of blue-
jacketed cavalrymen sweeping forward from behind him.
He recognised them immediately. The Horse Grenadiers

of the Imperial Guard, their tall bearskins nodding, smashed into the already disorganised Prussian heavy cavalry with the force of a sledgehammer. The exhausted dragoons looked on as their companions drove the enemy back.

'About time those "big boots" got involved,' gasped Rocheteau, wiping his face with the back of his hand.

Close behind the Horse Grenadiers came several ranks of fast-moving chausseurs, resplendent in their lace-trimmed, green dolman jackets and red pelisses. Holding their sabres high in the air, they too crashed into the already reeling mass of Prussian heavy cavalry. The world seemed to degenerate into the sound of steel on steel, the neighing of horses and the shouts and curses of men as they fought. Lausard blinked hard, trying to clear his vision which had been clouded both by smoke and by sweat. All around him his companions gratefully allowed the guard cavalry passage through them, too exhausted even to follow up the destruction of the Prussian cuirassiers. Lausard noticed that there was hardly a man among them who did not bear a wound of some kind. At first glance none seemed unduly serious but, he knew too well, only time would tell. The pain from his own arm was tolerable and he was able to grip his sword in that hand without too much discomfort.

'Where's that bastard Barthez?' gasped Delacor, wincing as he pressed a hand against the wound in his side. 'Chasing the Prussians back to Berlin on his own?'

'Let's hope so,' Giresse panted.

'Form line,' called Lieutenant Royere, blinking blood from one eye.

'What now, Lieutenant?' Lausard demanded. 'What orders has he given you?'

'Just those, Sergeant,' the officer said, trying to swallow.

'Most of these men are wounded or dead, *you* know that,' the sergeant hissed. 'What the hell does Barthez hope to do with us now?'

'I have no idea, my friend,' Royere admitted. 'Like you, I follow orders.'

'No matter how ridiculous?' rasped Rocheteau.

'What choice have we?' snapped Royere. 'Any of us?'

Lausard held the officer's gaze for a moment.

'None,' said the NCO. 'And before this day is over, not one of us may be alive to care.'

Napoleon Bonaparte gripped the reins of his horse and guided the magnificent white animal slowly back and forth before the massed ranks of the Imperial Guard infantry. Aides and officers gathered in a large group close to the Emperor, who was glancing ahead at the panoramic view of the battlefield. He had moved down from the precipitous summit of the Landgrafenberg more than an hour ago, surrounded by the Guard and accompanied by his staff. The impenetrable fog of early morning had now been replaced by weak sunlight and the Emperor looked up briefly in the direction of the burnished orb. To his right and left, batteries of artillery were pouring a steady fire in the direction of the Prussians. Several units of horse artillery galloped past on their way to support French units that were advancing on every sector of the battlefield. Napoleon pulled his watch from his pocket and saw that it was almost one p.m.

'We have close to one hundred thousand men on the field, sire,' Berthier told him. 'Over fifty thousand engaged and almost as many in reserve. The day has proceeded as you envisaged.'

'Despite the impetuosity of some of my commanders,' Napoleon observed, looking across the smoke-clouded landscape. 'Ney is fortunate that his behaviour did not cause us more of a problem.'

'The moment is passed, sire,' General Savary offered. 'Marshal Ney is now engaged in a frontal attack on the remains of the Prussian army together with the corps commanded by Marshal Lannes.'

'Word is that the enemy are collapsing on all sectors of the battlefield, sire,' Berthier added.

'It would appear that your time is close, Murat,' said the Corsican, glancing at his brother-in-law.

Marshal Joachim Murat nodded and smiled, brushing some dust from the sleeve of his heavily embroidered, fur-trimmed coat. The cavalry commander brandished his riding whip before him.

'Give me the word and I will chase the Prussians to the gates of Berlin itself,' he said, triumphantly.

'I wonder what Frederick the Great would think of his descendants,' mused Napoleon. 'Brushed aside so easily. Out-fought, out-manoeuvred. Left to the mercy of incompetents.'

'Frederick himself would not have stood against our might today,' Murat grinned.

Some of the other officers laughed.

Napoleon turned and looked at the ranks of Guard grenadiers, standing immobile, awaiting his order. Any of them would have gladly given their lives for the Corsican and he knew it.

'I have no need of their bravery today,' he said to Marshal Lefebvre.

The older man nodded and smiled.

'They will not thank you for leaving them idle, sire,' he grinned.

'Forward.'

The shout came from behind the Emperor and he turned irritably in its direction. Murat and Lefebvre also jerked their heads around in the direction of the sound.

'Forward,' came the call once more.

'What is that?' asked Napoleon, his eyes scanning the ranks of elite troops. 'Only a beardless youth would presume to judge in advance what I should do. Let him wait until he has commanded in thirty pitched battles before he dares to give me advice.'

'They are eager to partake in the victory, sire,' Murat observed. 'What do fighting men exist for but to fight?'

'There will be other days,' Napoleon said, quietly. 'For now they will stand and wait.'

'Be grateful for their love, sire,' Murat intoned. 'Men would die for such devotion.'

'I have earned that love,' the Corsican said, flatly, 'by giving them more victories than they can count. Let them heed my words. I will not risk their lives when it is unnecessary.'

Berthier turned his horse as an aide, his blue shabracque singed by fire and his face blackened by smoke, guided his mount towards the group of officers. The Chief of Staff took the piece of paper the aide handed him and scanned it.

'The Prussians are retiring, sire,' said Berthier, a slight smile on his face. 'Towards Weimar in the west and Apolda in the north. They're not retreating, they're running.'

Napoleon nodded.

'Straight into the arms of Davout and Bernadotte,' he mused. Then, to Berthier, 'Order all units not so engaged to pursue.' He turned his attention to Murat. 'Take your horsemen and ride them down,' he said. 'All of them.'

The fire from the Prussian cannon had all but ceased. Lausard could see many of the gunners scurrying away from their pieces, anxious to join the thousands of their companions already fleeing the battlefield. As the dragoons advanced at a walk, columns of French infantry to either side of them, they passed the pitiful remnants of their defeated enemy. Scattered reminders of the magnitude of their victory – muskets, packs, canteens, headgear, uniforms and even shoes and boots – lay discarded. The equipment had been flung away in panic, abandoned as surely as the thousands of wounded that were strewn across the terrain. Mounds of dead horses dragged together to form some kind of fleshy barricade were surrounded by Prussian corpses. Lausard saw several wounded Prussian and Saxon troops crawling around looking for water, drinking from the hundreds of discarded bottles on the field. Some were mortally wounded and had little chance of surviving the night without adequate medical attention. Some would be dealt with after the French wounded had been attended to but Lausard knew that a large proportion of those scattered all around him would never see the dawn.

Around him he glanced at his own companions. Many of them bore wounds of varying severity and Lausard looked angrily in the direction of Captain Barthez, wondering how many of those injuries could have been prevented. Without the officer's suicidal orders, most of those now bloodied would probably have escaped unscathed, himself included. Beside the narrow road along which one of the infantry columns marched, Prussian standards lay in the dirt, hurled aside by their bearers with as much disregard for their importance as the muskets and packs they'd also divested themselves of. Prussian martial pride, it seemed, had been as effortlessly destroyed as their fighting force, mused Lausard. Every so often an infantryman would stoop to retrieve one of the trophies and, as each did, a cheer arose from his companions. Lausard had already counted twelve of the enemy colours. He had no doubt that many more would come into French possession before darkness fell. Ahead of him, Lieutenant Royere and Captain Barthez rode alongside the trooper who bore the regimental guidon of the dragoons. The flag was tattered and smoke-stained but it still flew proudly and Lausard, despite himself, felt a surge of pride as he saw it flapping in the breeze. The bronze eagle at the top of the staff seemed to eye those around it with indifference.

There was a slight rise ahead, and beyond it Lausard could hear shouts. Some sounded like orders. The French continued their orderly advance, driving their defeated foe before them with ease. Every so often, the front rank of blue-clad infantry would halt and fire a volley into the backs of their fleeing enemy. More bodies fell to the ground to join the hundreds that already littered it. It was as they reached the crest of the slope that the sergeant and the other French troops saw what awaited them. Standing solid amidst the frantically fleeing enemy troops was a square of white-clad Saxon infantry. Formed in the regulation three rows, the square was like an island of order in the sea of fugitives sweeping past it on all sides. At the sight of the square, Barthez rose in his stirrups then turned to Royere, a grin on his face.

'A sitting target, Lieutenant,' the captain exclaimed almost gleefully. 'Form the men for attack.'

'Would it not be more prudent to allow the infantry . . . ' Royere began.

'To hell with the infantry,' snarled Barthez, cutting him short. 'I gave you an order.' He looked over his shoulder. 'Trumpeter.'

Gaston spurred the few yards to the head of the column, wincing as his injured knee scraped against his saddle. There was already blood there, some of it having trickled down the stirrup leather. Lausard also joined the trumpeter.

'We will disperse that square of enemy troops,' Barthez announced.

'They are in good order, Captain,' Lausard noted. 'There appear to be no gaps in their formation.'

'There will be once they have felt the force of our charge,' Barthez snapped.

'Attacking that square is a needless exercise, Captain,' Royere protested. 'The infantry are better equipped to deal with it. You know that.'

'I am well aware of the capabilities of cavalry and infantry, Lieutenant.'

'Then you will also be aware of the damage they will cause amongst us,' snapped Royere.

'I am aware that *your* insubordination may lead you to face a firing squad,' snarled the captain, angrily.

'I agree with Lieutenant Royere, Captain,' Lausard added. 'Attacking an infantry square without the support of horse artillery is madness.'

'War itself is madness, is it not?' said Barthez, flatly. 'Will you obey my order or not?'

The three men faced each other for interminable seconds.

'Damn you to hell, Captain,' said Royere, finally. As he spoke he drew his sword. 'Damn your orders. Damn your rank and damn your ambition.'

Barthez also drew his sword.

'Will you charge or will I have you shot on the spot for disobeying an order?' the captain wanted to know.

'Lead us, Captain,' said Lausard. 'Perhaps you will find what you seek in the blood of those you intend to sacrifice. But I swear this now, if the Prussians do not kill you, then *I* will.'

'Get back in line,' Barthez said, smiling crookedly. 'Trumpeter, order the advance.'

The high, keening notes rose into the smoke-filled air and the dragoons formed up into tightly packed ranks.

'Draw swords,' shouted Barthez, and the sound of

hundreds of lengths of steel being drawn from scabbards filled the ears of all those within a hundred yards. Horses pawed the ground expectantly. Riders sucked in deep breaths of resignation and anxiety. Moreau crossed himself. Lausard sat bolt upright on his horse, his gaze trained on Barthez. On both sides, the infantry were forming lines too, their mounted officers looking on in bewilderment as the dragoons began to move forward at a walk. Shouts of encouragement mingled with cries of amazement, as the foot soldiers looked on in disbelief. To Lausard it seemed as if the watching infantry were as incredulous at the spectacle unfolding before them as he and his own companions were at what they were about to participate in. Barthez lifted his sword into the air and waved it twice in the direction of the Saxon infantry. Lausard could already see the white-coated men steadying themselves. The late afternoon sunlight glinted on their bayonets. The wickedly sharp points were like a steel hedge, tightly packed and apparently impenetrable.

'Is this how he purchases his medal?' rasped Rocheteau as the dragoons increased their speed. 'With the lives of those he commands?'

'It is a currency he is rich in,' Lausard answered, wearily.

The dragoons coaxed their mounts into the trot, then the canter. Lausard could see the Saxon grenadiers gripping their muskets more tightly as they prepared for the onslaught of the dragoons. He could see several officers stalking back and forth inside the formidable formation, one of them mounted on a grey horse. All of the commissioned men were shouting orders, occasionally pushing some of their more reluctant troops into position in the walls of the square like a child would push a building block. Lausard kept his eye on the officer on the grey who had wheeled his animal towards the side of the square the dragoons would reach first. The silver and crimson waist sash and sword knot and gold gorget he sported marked him out as a man of more senior rank. It would be he who gave the order to his men to fire when Lausard and his companions were close enough. The sergeant fixed his gaze on that older man and ducked low over the neck of his horse as the dragoons thundered down the slight incline towards the square.

'Charge,' screamed Barthez and the shrill blasts from the trumpets echoed his command. The dragoons accelerated, their horses' hooves pounding the ground, throwing up clods of earth as they bore down on the waiting square. Men in the ranks around and behind Lausard also roared oaths and curses. The sergeant himself gave vent to a bellow of fury but his eyes were now turned in the direction of Barthez. The wind rushed past him. Particles of earth struck his flesh as they were flung skyward by the churning hooves of the horses. He could smell the acrid stench of gunpowder. The Prussian fugitives who were still swarming away from the oncoming French seemed to quicken their pace as the dragoons on that part of the battlefield charged. Fleeing men screamed in terror but all Lausard seemed able to concentrate on, as his horse bore him nearer to the immobile square, was the figure of the Saxon officer who had now halted his own mount and was waiting for the dragoons to come within suitable range. Lausard felt as if he could see every single detail of the older man's features. As usual during a charge, he experienced that same savage, almost disconcerting clarity the closer he drew to the enemy and also to possible death. Lausard could actually see the Saxon officer's lips forming the words as he shouted instructions. When the dragoons were less than fifty yards from the gleaming bayonets, he would give the order to fire.

Behind the charging dragoons, two lines of French infantry were also advancing, muskets levelled. Every single horseman who hurtled towards the square knew that the infantry should have made the first assault. Bonet glanced over his shoulder but saw only the contorted faces of his companions. Rocheteau roared his defiance. Charvet pointed his sword towards the waiting wall of white-uniformed enemy troops. Moreau whispered a prayer. He was not alone.

At thirty yards, the mounted officer opened his mouth. Lausard saw him shout something to a subordinate then he bellowed the order to fire.

One side of the square erupted as hundreds of Saxon muskets were discharged. Smoke momentarily hid them from view as it belched from their muzzles. Lead balls cut into the dragoons like a scythe into corn. Lausard heard one sing past his ear. It caught a man in the rank behind and sent him crashing from his saddle. Rocheteau grunted in pain as another of the deadly projectiles tore open his upper arm, ripping away part of his tunic. Men and horses went down in heaps. Lausard tried to avoid one falling horse but his own bay stumbled on the blood-slicked ground as it tried to hurdle a bullet-riddled carcass. The stricken animal hit the ground with a bone-jarring thud, catapulting Lausard from the saddle. He managed to avoid the heavy beast as it rolled helplessly over, neighing in terror. He grabbed at its reins as it rose, hauling himself back into the saddle as successive ranks of dragoons swept around him, some colliding in the process. Lausard's horse was bleeding heavily from a wound in its neck but the animal hurtled on, galloping past other fallen animals and men. Lausard could see that the leading ranks of his companions had already reached the gleaming hedge of bayonets. They swept helplessly around the square, slashing at the infantry. He saw one man lean too far out of his saddle as he hacked at the Saxon troops. Three bayonets were immediately thrust upwards, two of them puncturing his chest. As he fell to the ground another of the enemy infantry skewered him through the throat.

Lausard pulled a pistol from its holster and fired at the men in the square nearest to him. One fell but another merely stepped forward from the rank behind to take his place. Yelling furiously, Tigana hurled his sword, the blade spinning end over end before burying itself in the chest of another Saxon with a dull thud. The man reeled backwards, blood spouting from the wound but, as with the other casualties, he was merely replaced by a companion. Those wounded were pulled back into the centre of the square for what treatment was available. Lausard could see two or three men busily bandaging the worst cases. Another volley of fire from the opposite side of the square tore into the dragoons and dozens more hit the ground. Smoke had now almost completely enveloped the formation and the muzzle flashes cut through the sulphurous fumes like lanterns in fog. The musket fire seemed to roll around the square, each side firing in turn, wreaking havoc among the dragoons as they swirled helplessly around the stoic Saxons. Lausard spurred his horse towards Barthez and grabbed at the officer's arm.

'Call off the attack,' he roared, trying to make himself heard above the deafening sounds of battle.

Barthez angrily shook loose and fired his pistol into the tightly packed white ranks.

'They will break,' the officer snarled.

'They will *not*,' Lausard bellowed back.

Another volley of fire drowned his furious protests.

A bullet struck him in the shoulder, another tore off the cuff of his right boot. Two more hit his horse. The animal reared and sent Lausard crashing to the ground. He struggled to his feet and saw Lieutenant Royere lying a few yards from him, pinned beneath the bloodied carcass of his own mount. Lausard hurried across to him and tried his best to move the dead horse but it wouldn't budge. The sergeant could see that Royere had also been hit. One bullet had punctured his cheek. Another had cut through the flesh of his arm just above his elbow, narrowly missing the bone. His face was a mask of blood as he tried to drag himself free of the bulk of his dead horse.

'Tabor,' shouted Lausard, and the big man leapt from the saddle and used his incredible strength to drag the dead horse off Royere's leg. The lieutenant, aided by Lausard, managed to free himself, and both men sought refuge behind a rampart of dead animals and men. Bullets from the Saxon square struck the carcasses, spilling fresh blood onto ground that was already soaked with the crimson fluid. Lausard and the officer lay breathlessly exchanging a silent glance. Royere merely shook his head.

'Alain, look,' shouted Rocheteau, reining in his mount beside the two men. He was gesturing towards the lines of French infantry now hurtling towards the Saxon square. A battery of four-pounders was galloping up in support and the gunners were already hurrying to un-limber the pieces.

The Saxon square, with remarkable skill and precision, began to move. Like some vast amoebic mass, the soldiers who formed its four sides moved effortlessly across the landscape, retaining their formation despite the now waning efforts of the dragoons and the newly found attentions of the French infantry. A shell burst high in the air and Lausard looked up towards the ridge beyond, where half a dozen Prussian mortars had been set up to cover the retreat as best they could. Several more incendiary missiles came arcing towards the French, some exploding in mid-air and raining lumps of hot metal onto those below, others hitting the ground then detonating. Under cover of the barrage, the Saxon infantry retired in relatively good order. The French artillery, now prepared, directed their fire towards the howitzers on the ridge, and Lausard watched as several geysers of earth sprayed upwards when the roundshot struck the ground.

'Re-form,' roared Barthez, galloping amongst his bloodied and dazed men, his sword held above his head.

Dragoons without horses grabbed at the harnesses of riderless mounts. Many men, wounded in the saddle, attempted to follow the officer's instruction. Others were merely wandering around the battlefield in bewilderment. Lausard saw one man staggering blindly towards the approaching infantry holding his dented brass helmet in one hand and his broken sword in the other. He had been shot in the stomach and face. Blood was pouring into his eyes from another wound on his forehead. Injured horses raised their heads as if soliciting help. In many places, their riders lay close beside them or, in some cases, across their carcasses. The guidon bearer had also been wounded by a bayonet cut that had gashed his left thigh. He rode back and forth, slumped forward in his saddle, barely able to hold the guidon he was so weak from loss of blood. But, despite their injuries, men found the will to re-mount and to form ragged lines behind Barthez as he swept back and forth waving his sword in the direction of the fleeing Prussians.

'He's insane,' snarled Rocheteau, glaring at the officer.

Lausard didn't answer. He merely hauled himself into the saddle of a riderless horse, steadying the frightened animal with a pat to its neck.

'Form your men and follow me,' Barthez said, glancing down at the bloodied form of Lieutenant Royere.

'He can't continue,' snapped Lausard, angrily. 'Even *you* must be able to see that, Captain.'

'Then you can command the second squadron, Sergeant,' Barthez said, grinning. 'Form them into line for the advance.'

'No,' Lausard said, flatly.

'Do it now,' rasped Barthez.

'You heard what I said, Captain. I will not do it.'

'I am giving you a direct order, Sergeant.'

'And I am giving you my *response* to that order, sir. I will not lead more men to their deaths at your whim.'

'The Prussians are retreating,' Barthez said. 'It is our duty to pursue them. It is *your* duty to obey the orders of a superior officer. Now form the second squadron into line.'

Lausard shook his head.

Barthez reached for one of his pistols and aimed it at the sergeant.

'I will shoot you on the spot if you do not obey,' he hissed.

'Do as you will,' Lausard said, his gaze never leaving that of the officer. 'But I will not be responsible for the death of one more man just so that you can pursue your quest for some worthless medal.'

Barthez raised the pistol so that it was pointed at the sergeant's head.

'Squeeze the trigger, Captain,' Lausard told him, defiantly.

'If you shoot you will be the next to die.'

Barthez turned in the saddle and saw that Sonnier had his carbine trained on him.

'You have just one shot, Captain,' Rocheteau added, brandishing his bloodied sword. 'I will gut you like a fish before you can fire another.'

'You will all be court martialled for this,' said Barthez, evenly. 'I will see you all in front of a firing squad. How dare you disobey a direct order?'

'It is no order, sir, it is a death sentence,' Lausard snarled. 'I will have no part of it. If you want your medal then there are the enemy.' He nodded in the direction of the fleeing Prussian and Saxon hordes, now little more than a terrified rabble.

For interminable seconds the entire scene was frozen, as if suspended in time. The deafening rumble of horses' hooves seemed to shake all of the men from their trance-like state.

Tabor was the first to see the source of the awesome sound.

Thousands of French cavalry, led by yelling squadrons of cuirassiers, their breast-plates glinting in the late afternoon sun, were thundering down an incline away to the right. Followed by more dragoons and the multi-coloured hordes of hussars, they swept along the narrow defiles and body-strewn terrain in pursuit of the fleeing enemy troops. At their head, Tabor saw the resplendent figure of Marshal Murat waving not a sabre but a riding crop above his head as he led his horsemen in a furious pursuit of the devastated enemy.

Lausard did not allow his gaze to deviate from Barthez for one second.

'If you want glory, Captain,' he said, flatly, 'then join them. Do not expect us to be at your side. You have already caused the deaths of too many.'

'I told you I would see you court martialled for your insubordination,' Barthez insisted. 'And I swear that I will.'

He turned his mount, looked back at Lausard then rode across to the guidon bearer. The sergeant watched as he snatched the flag from the wounded man's hand, gripped it in his own fist then galloped off after the fleeing enemy troops. Some of the terrified Prussians were stopping to fire, as if that token gesture would somehow stem the furious tide of French horsemen, groups of them gathering together in a vain attempt to protect themselves from the attacking cavalry. It was towards one of these groups that Barthez spurred. He rode his horse into the closest of the Prussians, cut down another with a powerful sword stroke and kicked out with one foot at a corporal who rolled over, dropped his musket then leapt to his feet and ran off. The guidon of the dragoon regiment fluttered in the air as the officer carved a path through the fugitives, even using the staff of the flag itself as a weapon as he struck madly to his left and right. As more and more smoke rolled across the battlefield, only the tip of the regimental eagle was visible, and Lausard narrowed his eyes in an attempt to see through the noxious veil. A breeze blew and parted the smoke momentarily. Barthez was still cutting his way through the terrified Prussians.

'He's determined to get that stinking medal, isn't he?' Delacor grunted.

Lausard didn't answer, his eyes were fixed on two Saxon infantrymen who were advancing towards Barthez, their bayonets glinting. The officer hadn't seen them, and Lausard knew that shouting a warning would be useless in the cacophony of sound that was battle. The sergeant suddenly put spurs to his horse.

'Alain, what are you doing?' shouted Rocheteau.

'He will lose the eagle,' Lausard roared back.

'Let him,' snarled Delacor, grabbing at the sergeant's arm but Lausard shook him loose.

'It may not mean anything to *him* but it should to *us*,' rasped Lausard.

He thundered off towards Barthez, who was still unaware of the Saxon troops behind him.

Karim and Roussard rode to join Lausard, who almost collided with several French cuirassiers.

Barthez tugged hard on the reins of his horse and turned the animal but it was too late. He managed to deflect one bayonet thrust but the second caught him in the thigh. The long triangular blade practically pinned him to his saddle and the other Saxon struck upwards, driving his own blade into the officer's stomach then up into the chest.

Barthez shouted in pain and anger and cut one of the men across the head. He dropped the guidon and Lausard saw a retreating Prussian corporal snatch it up.

The bayonet in the officer's leg snapped and he managed to pull it free, blood jetting from his thigh. A bullet caught him in the chest, another in the side of the face. He fell from the saddle, unable to defend himself as another Saxon infantryman stabbed him twice in the chest with his bayonet. The dragoon officer's horse bolted, itself bleeding from a dozen wounds.

Lausard rode past the figure of Barthez and crashed his horse into one of the Saxons. Karim swung his scimitar at another and caught the man across the back. Roussard despatched another man with a blow to the head. The remaining infantry ran but it was the Prussian corporal upon whom Lausard fixed his gaze. The man was struggling to run with the captured French guidon in his hand and Lausard reached him easily. He caught him across the shoulder with a backhand stroke and the man went down, sprawling face first in the mud. Lausard jumped from his horse and snatched up the guidon before swinging himself back into the saddle and brandishing the flag triumphantly above his head.

'Well done.'

The words were roared from close to him.

'Good man,' shouted Marshal Joachim Murat, grinning at Lausard. 'Return to your regiment or join us in our hunt. You have earned that choice by your bravery.' The cavalry commander looked up at the guidon then smiled broadly at Lausard himself before galloping off with a group of French cuirassiers.

Karim, his scimitar dripping with blood, joined Lausard, both of them gasping for breath. On all sides, French cavalry continued to thunder past, only too eager to pursue and ride down their defeated enemy. The late afternoon sun was a burnished orb high in the smoke-clouded sky. Another two hours and night would begin to creep across the land.

Lausard flicked his reins and guided his horse back in the direction of the Landgrafenberg. Behind him, the chorus of shouts and screams continued.

Nineteen

❖

Napoleon Bonaparte rode slightly ahead of his staff as he crossed the battlefield, his expression inscrutable. He felt the joy that came with any victory, especially one as complete as that he had enjoyed in the preceding hours. But, as ever, mingled with that elation was the distress at seeing so many of his men lying dead on the field of victory. He had heard his name shouted by his victorious regiments. He had seen captured Prussian standards waved at him from both sides of the narrow road he now moved along. Troops had lifted their headgear onto the ends of their bayonets and swords to salute him. Captured Prussian cannon and prisoners had been lined up for him to peer at as he made his way back towards Jena itself. Yet, despite these scenes of triumph, the Corsican had been most struck by the suffering of his own wounded. He had paused to supervise their evacuation in a huge convoy of flat, open wagons, particularly those who had fallen in and around the villages of Cospeda and Closewitz. A huge field hospital had been set up to the south of Jena, and that was where the wagons would deposit the unfortunates who had survived the conflict but who were now at the mercy of infection, fever, gangrene and the unavoidable savagery of the surgeons and their amputation tools.

Parties of sappers were already busily digging the mass graves that would be the final resting places for Prussian, Saxon and French dead. As Napoleon passed one of these details, the men stopped their task, stood to attention beside a pile of bodies that reached their waists and shouted, '*Vive l'Empereur.*' The Corsican raised his hat in salute. Also scattered over the field were the carcasses of thousands of dead and wounded horses, and the early evening air was filled with the sound of gunshots as farriers put wounded animals out of their misery. Other groups of sappers, equipped with hooks and chains to drag the dead animals, collected the corpses and buried them in even larger holes in the already pock-marked ground. Those dead animals not too badly bullet blasted or smashed by cannon fire were cut up for food, although the Emperor doubted the meat would be necessary. The fleeing Prussians had abandoned everything including their rations and their baggage and supply trains. The victory had been as complete and as comprehensive as Napoleon had demanded. The air smelled of smoke and blood. It was a familiar odour to the Emperor and his staff, made all the more pungent by the crispness of the approaching night. He rode past the Landgrafenberg and on towards Jena itself. As he entered the town he saw that it was also full of wounded. Even those sitting in bloodied rows waiting to be treated by the doctors who had set up temporary surgeries inside the ramshackle buildings rose to their feet to salute their commander.

'They honour you, sire,' said Marshal Berthier, guiding his horse up alongside the Corsican.

'They are the ones who deserve the praise, Berthier,' said Napoleon. 'They have won the day yet again.'

'They have won it because of your genius, sire,' added General Caulaincourt. 'You have overseen the destruction of the entire Prussian army today. It is a blow they will not recover from.'

'What is the extent of our victory?' Napoleon wanted to know.

'Initial reports indicate more than ten thousand Prussian dead and wounded,' Berthier said. 'Fifteen thousand prisoners taken. Thirty-four colours and one hundred and twenty cannon captured.'

'At what cost?'

'Our own casualties are in the region of five thousand, sire,' the Chief of Staff told him.

Napoleon nodded slowly and swung himself out of his saddle as he reached his headquarters. The building was already decorated with thirty captured standards fluttering gently in the evening breeze. As the Corsican made his way towards the door he was met by the stern visage of General Savary.

'A member of Marshal Davout's staff is here to see you, sire,' said Savary. 'He carries some disquieting news.'

'Perhaps he can tell me where Davout was today,' snapped the Corsican. 'I expected to see both his and Bernadotte's corps on the battlefield at some stage.'

'The news is somewhat unexpected, sire,' Savary continued.

Napoleon frowned and made his way inside the building, accompanied by Lannes, Caulaincourt and Berthier.

The officer standing inside the building looked as if he had stepped from the depths of hell itself. Barely a portion of his uniform was not torn, stained with blood or grimed with mud and gunpowder. He drew himself to attention as the Emperor entered and saluted.

'Captain Tobriant, sire,' the officer announced. 'Aide-de-camp to Marshal Davout.'

Napoleon nodded and poured himself a glass of burgundy.

'I bring news from Marshal Davout, sire,' Tobriant continued. 'He instructs me to inform you that his corps today engaged and defeated the main Prussian army ten miles north of here at Auerstadt.'

Napoleon looked quizzically at the officer, his brow furrowing.

'The Marshal estimates that he and his corps of twenty-six thousand were confronted by upwards of sixty thousand enemy troops, sire,' said Tobriant.

'Your Marshal must be seeing double,' snapped the Corsican. 'That is not possible. I, myself, have today destroyed the forces of Brunswick here at Jena. Would you have me believe that ninety-six thousand of my men have been engaged with one flank of the enemy's force while your Marshal fought and defeated the heart of that army? No.' Napoleon shook his head.

'Sire, for days prior to the battle there had been the suggestion that the Prussian army had divided,' said

Marshal Lannes. 'If this report is correct then there is every reason to believe that Davout did *indeed* face the main Prussian force.'

'Are you suggesting that one of my subordinates has won the day?' snapped the Corsican. 'Outnumbered three to one because of my own inaccurate calculations of the Prussians' true whereabouts?'

'The fault is not yours, sire,' Lannes replied. 'But that of our intelligence. You had no way of knowing the true strength of the forces that opposed us today or of where their greatest numbers lay. It has been the same for the duration of this campaign.'

Napoleon shook his head sharply.

'I cannot believe this,' he said, dismissively. 'And, indeed, if a battle took place, why was Davout forced to fight it alone? Bernadotte had orders to support him. Where was the Duke of Ponte Corvo while this struggle was taking place?'

'Marshal Davout repeatedly sent riders to Marshal Bernadotte asking for aid but none was forthcoming, sire,' Tobriant insisted.

'Why not?'

'Marshal Bernadotte gave assurances that he would support III corps but he was unconvinced that a battle was actually taking place at Auerstadt, sire,' the captain said, wearily. 'He said that your orders told him to march on Dornburg and that he would not move his corps unless instructed otherwise by you personally.'

Napoleon slammed his fist down hard on the table, his features contorted with rage.

'I instructed him, during the night, to advance with

Davout if he was at Naumburg,' he shouted, angrily. 'He chose to ignore my orders. Because of his insubordination twenty-one thousand men and fifty guns have remained idle today. Men and equipment that could have been employed gainfully in either sector.' The Emperor turned towards the maps spread out on the nearby table and swept them to the floor with one furious movement of his arm. 'This business is so hateful that if I send him before a court martial it will be the equivalent to ordering him to be shot; it is better for me not to speak to him about it, but I shall take care he shall know what I think of his behaviour. I believe he has enough honour to recognise that he has performed a disgraceful action regarding which I shall not bandy words with him.'

A heavy silence descended upon the room, finally broken by Captain Tobriant.

'If I might avail myself of a fresh horse, sire, I will carry your words back to Marshal Davout,' said the officer.

'Where is he now?' the Corsican wanted to know.

'Still camped on the field of Auerstadt, sire. The men were too exhausted to pursue the Prussians from the field.'

'What kind of losses did the III corps suffer?' Napoleon wanted to know.

'Close to seven thousand dead and wounded, sire,' Tobriant told the Emperor. 'The Prussians lost ten thousand killed and three thousand captured. One hundred and fifteen cannon were also taken.'

'Tell your Marshal he has my thanks. I will issue

orders during the night instructing him of his next manoeuvre,' Napoleon said, quietly. 'For now, he and his men deserve their rest. May it be a peaceful one.'

Tobriant saluted sharply and turned to leave.

Napoleon turned and gazed into the flames of the fire behind him.

'It seems as if the true laurels of the day belong to Davout, sire,' Lannes offered.

'He is a good man,' the Corsican replied. 'Disliked by his peers, I know, but his courage is unquestionable. Without him we could not have won such a crushing victory here today.'

'And now, sire?' Berthier asked.

'We pursue our foe,' Napoleon said, flatly. 'Chase him until he has no choice but to turn and fight or surrender. Judging by what happened today, I trust he will choose the correct option and submit.' The Corsican warmed his hands. 'Fourteen days ago, King Frederick William dared to issue me with an ultimatum. Let us see, with his armies destroyed, if he still yearns to emulate his great ancestor Frederick the First. I think not. It would be fair to say that France has been avenged, gentlemen. The battle of Jena has wiped out the affront of Rossbach. I will ensure that vengeance is exacted to the full.'

Alain Lausard moved closer to the camp fire, anxious to warm himself as the light breeze that had begun earlier in the evening now grew stronger. He sat against his saddle, peering in all directions at the dozens of similar bivouac fires that had sprung up all over the battlefield.

Most of the French troops who had remained in the vicinity of Jena and its nearby villages had done so for one simple reason: exhaustion. That coupled with severe losses had prevented certain units from participating in the merciless pursuit of the defeated Prussians now being undertaken by the remainder of the victorious *Grande Armée*. Lausard had no idea how many men of his regiment had been killed or wounded in the fighting. His own squadron had suffered particularly badly due to the suicidal orders of Captain Barthez but, as the sergeant chewed on a dry biscuit and glanced around at his companions, the dead officer was already fading into the recesses of his memory. A memory already replete with images, many of which he wished he could expunge but he knew they would remain like a bloodstain on clean linen.

Of his companions who had suffered wounds, most had been lucky in as much as they had been able to sustain treatment on the field itself. Even Delacor's stomach wound hadn't been as serious as it had first looked. The ball that had pierced his belly had lodged half an inch under the skin and dropped out after a little probing with a needle. Bonet and Moreau had taken care of bandaging their injured comrade's wounds. Tigana and Karim, as usual, had wandered off to inspect the state of the horses, many of whom had also sustained injuries during the battle. Lausard finished his biscuit and accepted the bottle of schnapps that was handed to him. Rocheteau grinned and raised his own bottle in salute.

'Easy pickings tonight,' said the corporal and the other

men laughed. 'Even plenty for *that* black devil to eat.' He tossed a piece of salt beef towards Erebus. The dog was lying close to Gaston, whose knee was heavily bandaged. The trumpeter stroked the animal's back as it chewed its newly acquired reward.

'A great victory *and* that bastard Barthez is dead,' said Delacor, shifting position painfully. 'We really *should* be celebrating.'

'Or thanking God,' Moreau observed.

'You thank your God,' said Giresse. 'I'll thank the Prussian who had *this* in his pack.' He held up a bottle of brandy and took a hefty swig.

'Is it over now?' Tabor wanted to know.

'Is what over?' Rostov asked.

'The war,' Tabor persisted. 'After all, the Prussians are beaten, aren't they?'

'Of course the war isn't over, you half-wit,' snapped Delacor. 'They're beaten and they're running but the war isn't over until the Emperor says so.'

'*Vive l'Empereur*,' said Sonnier, raising his bottle.

A number of the other men echoed the salute.

Lausard was in the process of pulling his green cloak more tightly around himself when several of the men turned at the sound of approaching hooves. Erebus began to growl ominously. Instinctively, several hands fell to the hilts of their swords. Sonnier eased his carbine from the boot on his saddle and thumbed back the hammer. Lausard could see three men approaching in the dull light of the camp fire. All three were dressed in blue uniforms heavily embroidered with gold lace, and one wore a bicorn that sported several large white ostrich feathers. All were staff officers but it was obvious that the one with the plumed headgear was the most senior of the three. It was this man who dismounted and wandered across the uneven ground towards the waiting dragoons.

'I am looking for Sergeant Alain Lausard of the first squadron,' said the officer, moving to one side as Erebus trotted towards him, teeth bared.

Lausard got to his feet and saluted.

'I am the man you seek, sir,' he said, flatly.

'You are to accompany me to Imperial Headquarters immediately, Sergeant,' the officer told him. 'Have you a horse?'

Erebus continued to growl and it was clear that the officer was less than comfortable with the big black dog standing so close to him.

Lausard nodded. 'On what charge, sir?' he wanted to know.

The officer chuckled. 'There are no charges, Sergeant,' he smiled. 'Why? Have you done something today that makes you expect retribution? My orders are to escort you to the Emperor himself.'

'Are you with the Emperor's staff, Captain?' Lausard wanted to know.

'Yes I am and if you have finished your interrogation I suggest you get your horse and follow me. The Emperor does not appreciate being kept waiting.' The officer swung himself back into the saddle and watched as Lausard carried his own saddle to his horse, strapped it in place on top of the green shabracque then finally mounted. The other dragoons watched in silence as the small procession moved away across the field in the direction of Jena, gradually being swallowed up by the blackness. Erebus, his teeth still bared, wandered slowly back to Gaston and settled down beside the trumpeter. He barked once or twice and then edged closer to the fire.

Lausard rode without looking to his right or left. He seemed unconcerned by the cries and groans of the wounded he passed. Untroubled by the sounds of spades and picks digging holes in the ground. One of the sappers on burial duty stopped momentarily to glance at the party of staff officers, saluting with one bloodied hand, then he returned to his task, dragging the torso of a French infantryman, cut in half by a roundshot, towards what would be his final resting place. He tumbled the body in upon hundreds of others. The small procession passed the slopes of the Landgrafenberg and followed the road into Jena itself, where a number of the houses were lit from inside by oil lamps. Again Lausard could hear groans and cries as surgeons worked at their grisly tasks, trying as best they could to repair the bodies of men who had been wounded by all manner of weapons. He saw soldiers supporting wounded comrades or sitting patiently with men who lay on makeshift stretchers awaiting their turn for the surgeon's probe, knife or saw. The horses' hooves rattled loudly on the cobbled streets of the town. Lausard drew his own mount to a halt as the leading staff officer signalled for the little group to stop outside the building festooned with so many captured enemy standards.

'Follow me, Sergeant,' said the senior officer, and Lausard marched briskly towards Imperial Headquarters.

The officer knocked on the door and was ordered inside. Lausard followed.

He saw Napoleon at once. The Emperor was still dressed in the uniform of a guard chausseur but his jacket was undone to expose the white shirt beneath. He was seated at a small table close to the open fire and Lausard could feel the heat even from where he stood. He glanced at the Corsican, feeling that same uncanny *frisson* he knew the man drew from all those who came close to him. The Emperor seemed to radiate power while simultaneously retaining an air of normality his army were so comfortable with. To Lausard, the man looked like any other tired soldier who had spent his day on the field of battle. The only difference was that his uniform was not spattered with blood as were most others. Marshal Berthier was also in the room, seated at a desk across from the Emperor, quill in his hand, ready to scribble down whatever instructions or orders his master chose to issue.

Lausard saluted and stood stiffly to attention.

Napoleon got to his feet, paused to warm himself beside the fire then looked at Lausard and smiled.

'Sergeant Alain Lausard of the first squadron, third dragoons,' said the Corsican, but it was more a statement than a question.

'Yes, sire.'

'Stand at ease, this isn't a court martial,' smiled the Corsican, running appraising eyes over the NCO. He saw the blood on Lausard's uniform, the bandage around his shoulder. 'You were wounded today, Sergeant?'

'Not badly, sire. There are many who suffered more than I.'

'Most of them Prussians, eh?' the Emperor chuckled. Lausard managed a smile.

'Your captain was killed in action today, wasn't he?' the Corsican continued.

'Yes, sire.'

'Killed while leading a charge in which he almost lost your regiment's eagle. You retrieved that eagle. I know this because my own brother-in-law saw you do it. Marshal Murat may have some faults but he has a good memory and a keen eye. He saw what you did. He mentioned your bravery in his report. It was a small matter to deduce your name once your squadron and regiment had been found.'

'I did what any man would have done in that position, sire.'

'That may be. But it does not detract from the bravery of your act. Bravery that should not go unrewarded.'

'There were others in my squadron who also put their lives at risk to recover the eagle, sire.'

'Of that I have no doubt. I know that men would happily sacrifice themselves for their comrades, for the army. For me. That is what you did when you saved your regiment's eagle, Sergeant. You proved your loyalty to France and to me. Loyalty is as deserving of praise as bravery and sometimes more difficult to find.' The Emperor looked in Berthier's direction and the Marshal rose and walked over, handing him a small wooden box. He opened it and Lausard saw what lay within.

The white enamel cross on the watered red silk ribbon. The *Légion d'Honneur*.

Napoleon took the medal from the box and swiftly attached it to the front of Lausard's jacket.

For fleeting seconds the two men held each other's gaze.

'I pride myself on a good memory, Sergeant, and your face looks familiar to me,' Napoleon mused.

'We met in Italy in '96, sire,' Lausard told him.

'Ten years ago,' the Emperor said, quietly. 'It seems like a lifetime. Much has changed since then, Sergeant.'

'You took away my rank, sire,' Lausard reminded his commander. 'I was a sergeant then, you made me a private.'

'I must have had good reason.' He tapped the chevrons on Lausard's arm. 'It seems my intervention was unnecessary.'

Lausard smiled then looked down at the medal on his breast.

Napoleon extended his right hand and Lausard shook it warmly.

'You may go, Sergeant,' said Napoleon, turning his back on Lausard. 'Return to your men. They are fortunate to have one such as you among them.'

Lausard saluted then turned and headed for the door. He closed it behind him and paused for a moment, looking down at his right hand, balling it into a fist then gazing at the open palm as if expecting to see some kind of imprint upon the flesh where the Emperor had touched it.

He crossed to his horse and mounted. The ride back

to his bivouac would take less than five minutes' brisk gallop through the darkness. He set off out of Jena, guiding his mount off the road and across the undulating plateau beyond the Landgrafenberg. He passed more of the burial parties, still working by lamplight, sweating despite the chill of the night. One of the men was sitting surrounded by corpses, smoking a pipe, sucking casually on it, unperturbed by the bodies on all sides of him. Lausard could see fires in the villages of Cospeda and Closewitz. Many of the buildings had been destroyed during the days' fighting but now those that remained intact were occupied by weary French troops, only too happy to enjoy what little shelter they could find. Lausard rode between the two villages and on past Lützeroda towards Vierzehnheiligen. He saw that there were twice as many Prussian and Saxon dead as French and these, after having been stripped of their uniforms, were being deposited rather more unceremoniously in their huge communal graves by the sweating sappers. Vast piles of muskets, pistols, swords, bayonets, boots, shoes, jackets and breeches had been assembled. Not to mention packs, headgear and empty cartridge cases. Lausard reined in his horse and walked it slowly along the road that led to the village.

'Lost?'

A voice made him turn in the saddle.

A sapper, stripped to the waist, his body slick with sweat and blood, stood with his hands on his hips gazing up at the dragoon.

'The French troops who fell on this part of the battlefield, where are they buried?' Lausard wanted to know.

'About two hundred yards back there,' the sapper answered, hooking a thumb over his shoulder in the direction of some woods. 'We have to bury them deep. Foxes and badgers sniff out the bodies. They soon dig them up. The locals will too. As soon as we move on they'll have them up, searching for any valuables.'

Lausard prepared to turn his horse.

'Who are you looking for?' the sapper continued. 'A friend? A brother?'

'An acquaintance,' Lausard told him, guiding his horse off the road.

'Whoever it is, he'll be worm food by morning,' the sapper called after him.

Lausard had little difficulty finding the grave. It was on the perimeter of the woods that lay between Lützeroda and Vierzehnheiligen. He dismounted, patting his horse's neck to calm it, then walked to the edge of the pit. The bodies, most still in uniform, were stacked like bricks within it. The stench rising from the hole was almost intolerable but Lausard stood there, eyes scanning the blank faces, some contorted into expressions of shock, pain and surprise. Frozen forever in that final grimace that had been etched upon them at the point of death.

'Alain.'

He turned as he heard his name.

A solitary horseman rode across to him and he could see that it was Rocheteau.

'What the hell are you doing here?' the corporal wanted to know. 'I saw you riding back from Jena. I followed you.'

As Lausard turned, the corporal caught sight of the *Légion d'Honneur* pinned to his companion's jacket.

'Is that what the Emperor wanted you for?' he murmured, staring fascinatedly at the medal.

'It isn't much, is it?' Lausard said, flatly. 'And yet men would risk their lives for it. Die for it.'

'Like Barthez.'

'He's in there somewhere, Rocheteau,' Lausard muttered, indicating the mass grave. 'Buried with men whose deaths he caused in the pursuit of this worthless bauble.' Lausard pulled the medal from his chest and gripped it in his fist.

'He wanted it, but *you* won it, Alain,' Rocheteau reminded him.

'Will it change who I am? Will it make me a better man? Will it cause those I have grown to know as comrades to treat me any differently? No. I have no need of it.' He tossed the medal into the grave. 'Barthez wanted it,' he said, quietly. 'Let him have it.'

Rocheteau gazed uncomprehendingly at his companion for long moments. 'I have known you for more than fifteen years, Alain. Yet still I wonder if I will ever understand you,' he mused.

Lausard swung himself into the saddle. 'Perhaps you should be thankful that you won't, my friend,' said the sergeant. 'Every man has his secrets. Some are best kept locked away. There are some things that should not be shared.' He tapped his temple with one index finger. 'What lies within most of all.'

'What would you want to hide from me of all people?' said Rocheteau, climbing onto his mount.

Lausard merely smiled.

'It is time to leave the dead,' the sergeant told his companion as he glanced over his shoulder towards the burial pit. 'For now, we belong with the living.'

Lausard snapped his reins, took one last look back at the grave then rode off.